Peaches *and* Screams

Books by G.A. McKevett

JUST DESSERTS

BITTER SWEETS

KILLER CALORIES

COOKED GOOSE

SUGAR AND SPITE

SOUR GRAPES

PEACHES AND SCREAMS

Published by Kensington Publishing Corporation

G.A. McKevett

A SAVANNAH REID MYSTERY

Peaches and Screams

KENSINGTON BOOKS
http://www.kensingtonbooks.com

KENSINGTON BOOKS are published by

Kensington Publishing Corp.
850 Third Avenue
New York, NY 10022

All Kensington titles, imprints and distributed lines are available at special quantity discounts for bulk purchases for sales promotion, premiums, fund-raising, educational or institutional use.

564 9914

Special book excerpts or customized printings can also be created to fit specific needs. For details, write or phone the office of the Kensington Special Sales Manager: Kensington Publishing Corp., 850 Third Avenue, New York, NY 10022, Attn. Special Sales Department. Phone: 1-800-221-2647.

Kensington and the K logo Reg. U.S. Pat. & TM Off.

Library of Congress Card Catalogue Number: 2001090407
ISBN: 1-57566-711-8

First Printing: January 2002
10 9 8 7 6 5 4 3 2 1

Printed in the United States of America

Chapter

1

"Lord, have mercy, Dirk . . . what *is* that horrible smell?" Savannah Reid's nose crinkled, the same way it did when she got a whiff of a ripe corpse in Dr. Jennifer Liu's autopsy suite. "Something curled up and died in this jalopy of yours," she said, her Southern accent soft and thick, despite more than ten years in the California sunshine, amid golden beaches, palm trees, and folks who sounded like television news anchors. She reached for the crank on the car door and quickly wound down the old Buick's passenger window.

Sitting next to her in the driver's seat, Detective Sergeant Dirk Coulter happily peeled a soggy paper towel from around something that might have been a sandwich in a previous life and bit off a mouthful. "Egg salad," he said between chomps. "Want half?"

She tried not to gag. "No. After smelling that, I may never eat again."

Dirk gave her a sideways grin, a piece of limp lettuce hanging from the corner of his mouth. Dirk Coulter didn't have a vain bone in his body. Savannah would gladly have arranged a transplant. She would even have volunteered as a donor. "We both know *that* ain't true," he said. "You're about as likely to skip a meal as I am."

She laughed at him and flicked the lettuce off his lip with her fingertip. "Neither of us is likely to grow faint with hunger," she admitted, glancing down at his beginnings of a middle-age beer belly and her own overly voluptuous curves. She took a better look at the sandwich and a memory bell chimed inside her head. It quickly changed to a jangling alarm. "Isn't that the egg salad on rye that I had left over from Chat-n-Chew Café last Friday night?"

"Yeah. What's your point?"

"That was a week ago."

He continued to munch. "So? I didn't see no expiration date on it nowhere."

"You're gonna die."

"Naw. I can eat anything. I've got the digestive system of a billy goat."

"And the manners to match."

She reached into her purse that was stashed on the floor beside a nearly empty liter bottle of root beer and pulled out a couple of Snickers bars. In seconds, she was chewing contentedly along with him.

Glancing down at her watch, she sighed. "This is the ninth day we've been on this stakeout and your kiddy pornographer hasn't shown his face . . . or any other part of his disgusting self. It's a waste of time."

"And your time is so friggin' valuable these days," he said with a nasty smirk that revealed a mouthful of half-chewed egg salad.

"I'll have you know I've raised my rates lately," she replied. "You're getting a very expensive freebie here."

"Oh, yeah. All those customers lined up at your door are paying you twice as much for your private detecting as they did before, right?"

"I prefer to call them 'clients.'" She didn't bother to mention that the line outside the Moonlight Magnolia Detective Agency had been short lately. Painfully short . . . as in, nonexistent.

"You two stop squabbling," said a somewhat irritated female

voice from the walkie-talkie that lay on the seat beside them. "It could be worse. You could be out here in the hot sun, doing jumping jacks with me and the teenyboppers. This is my third gym period in one morning. I'm pooped."

They looked across the open field of dried brown grass spread before them to a blacktopped area where the San Carmelita High School was conducting their girls' physical education classes. Tammy Hart, Savannah's assistant in her detective agency, was dressed in the school gym uniform of black shorts and a white T-shirt with a bright red bulldog logo, her blond ponytail bouncing as she performed calisthenics with about thirty students. From a distance, no one could tell she was at least ten years older than the girls . . . or see the tiny microphone attached to her shirt or the miniature, flesh-colored earpiece shoved into her right ear.

Savannah and Dirk were parked inside an overgrown clump of oleander bushes with a similar bunch of shrubbery about fifty feet away. That was where they expected their suspect to take his position and begin filming the girls in their less-than-ladylike poses.

This particular cinematographer's "art" had appeared several times recently on the Internet, on sites that pandered to the kiddie-porn crowd. Apparently, the director possessed a certain amount of technological know-how, because he had altered his product and added some disgusting footage that made the simple film anything but innocent. The police suspected the photographer had also cast himself in the starring role when adding the X-rated material, although the actor's face hadn't been shown— only his shortcomings.

And while he might have been a brilliant editor, he had neglected to notice that in the background of his cinematographic masterpiece was the east wall of the school's gymnasium, which bore its distinctive bulldog logo—big, bright red, and easy for law enforcement to trace.

It hadn't taken long for the cops to figure out that the tape had been filmed at the high school of San Carmelita, a sleepy, seaside resort town in southern California. They could even tell the angle of the shot and approximately where the dirty old guy had been standing with his camera.

All they had to do was stake out his hiding place—probably that second batch of oleander bushes—and wait.

When Dirk had been assigned to the case, he had talked Savannah into keeping him company and Tammy into supplying the nubile bait.

The three were eager to nail the creep. Dirk and Savannah were in their mid-forties; with any luck, he would appear before they became octogenarians.

"I'm gonna need a potty break pretty soon," Savannah said, squirming in her seat.

Dirk shrugged with typical male nonchalance. If it wasn't his bladder, he wasn't concerned. "You shouldn't have drunk all that root beer. I ain't leavin' now; as sure as we do, he'll show. If you can't hold it, do what I did."

"I'm *not* going to 'sprinkle a bush' as you so delicately put it. You're going to take me to a real service station with a real bathroom where I can—"

"Hey, hey, hey! We've got a customer . . . or a *client*, as you like to call them." Dirk pointed with the remnants of his sandwich at a late-model, dark-blue SUV that was pulling off the road and rolling slowly toward the neighboring bushes.

He and Savannah watched, their hearts thumping, as the driver cut the engine and sat there, looking around for a few tense moments. After studying the entire area, he seemed to focus on them, peering into the dense foliage that surrounded the old Skylark.

"Do you think he can see us?" Savannah asked.

"Naw. I checked good before. We can see him, but he can't see us. He can probably feel us, though. You know how those guys are; they've got a sorta sixth sense when they're being watched."

Even after years as a police officer and private investigator, Savannah was often struck by how "normal" some suspects appeared. The mousy, middle-aged guy in the van was no exception; he could have been anyone's neighbor, schoolteacher, or local restaurant owner. It wasn't fair.

"Sexual predators should have to wear a sign or something," she mumbled, "a tattoo on their forehead that says, 'Beware of Pervert.'"

Dirk grunted. "Yeah. If you brought your needle and ink, I'll hold him down."

Savannah picked up the walkie-talkie and said into it, "Heads up, Tam. Don't look now, but I think you might have an audience of one. Jog that cute little rear end of yours over this direction and turn him into an admirer."

"Don't run straight at us, though," Dirk added. "Work your way around the edge first. Don't wanna scare him off."

Ponytail still bouncing, Tammy left the group and began her jog, first away from them, then, gradually, adjusting her path to head in their direction.

"Duh," they heard Tammy say, panting, "you didn't have to tell me that, Dirko. I wasn't exactly going to race over there, drag him out of his vehicle, and dump him on the ground."

Dirk turned to Savannah, one eyebrow quirked. *"Dirko?"*

"If you think that's bad, you should hear what she calls you when you're not around."

The van's driver perked up as the attractive runner drew closer.

"He likes you, Tammy," Savannah told her. "I think he's in lo-o-o-ove."

"Yep," Dirk said, "he's getting out his camera. It's definitely lust at first sight."

Savannah watched, enraptured, as the suspect held his videocam to his eye and zeroed in on her friend's bouncing T-shirt. How infinitely satisfying . . . watching an idiot hang himself. Savannah had never gotten over the thrill.

For a moment, Savannah entertained the thought that Tammy's T-shirt didn't bounce quite as dramatically as her own would, if she were the one jogging across the field, but that was because Tammy ate far too many salads and not nearly enough desserts. Imagine, choosing spinach over pecan fudge.

Poor girl. Poor, scrawny, deprived child.

Savannah felt truly sorry for her . . . her and all those skinny runway models, and the magazine cover girls, and those stick-thin movie stars and—

"How long do you figure we should let him tape before we nab 'im?" Dirk said, interrupting her pity fest.

"That's probably enough," Savannah replied. "We don't want him to get suspicious. If he's using a zoom lens, like he did before, and Tammy gets much closer, he might realize she's not his type . . . a kid, that is."

"Let's go get 'im."

"Yeah, let's." Savannah spoke into the radio. "Don't come any closer, Tammy," she told her. "Stay where you are and give him something special to film. Make sure he's looking at you, not us. We're going now."

"How's this?" Tammy bent over from the waist, her diminutive but shapely bottom pointing their way, and began to bounce, touching her toes.

"That's great, kid," Dirk said, momentarily mesmerized by the sight. "Keep it up."

Even Savannah had to admit that salads could make you look pretty good when bending over in a pair of tight black shorts. So there were a few compensations for eating spinach and carrots . . . but not enough to give up pecan fudge and bouncing T-shirt fronts.

The suspect had the camera to his eye and was vigorously twisting dials, adjusting the lens for a better shot. The time couldn't be better to move on him.

Savannah nodded. "Let's go, big boy."

"Quiet and easy does it."

Quickly, but silently, they opened their doors and slipped out of the car. Leaving the doors ajar, they pulled their weapons, Dirk his Smith & Wesson revolver and Savannah her Beretta. Dirk waved her ahead, and Savannah skirted the edge of the bushes, working her way to the rear of the van. From the other direction, Dirk ran, half squatted, to the driver's side.

Tammy continued to reach for her toes, doing an excellent job of distracting their quarry. He was clueless until Dirk yanked his door open and pointed the revolver at his head.

At the same moment, Savannah entered the passenger door and plopped onto the seat next to his. She heard his gasp of surprise, immediately followed by a deep, soulful groan of dismay, and the sound tickled her to her toes. Double-dipped chocolate cheesecake and candlelit bubble baths were good, but this . . . this was the best. Life just didn't get any better.

"Gotcha," Dirk said, pressing the barrel against his left ear. "I'm an SCPD detective, and you, sir, are screwed. Hand the camera to the lady—nice and slow. That's it; lay it in her lap . . . and then place your hands on the steering wheel."

When the suspect turned to surrender his camera to Savannah, she got her first good look at his face: the fine, aquiline features, the sandy blond hair with its businessman's cut, the wide-set green eyes, the scar across his cheek . . . the one she had put there five years before.

"Well, well, well, if it isn't our old friend, Byron Swift. How are you doing, Byron?" she asked. "More importantly, what are you doing out of jail? I thought we had you locked up nice and tight."

Mr. Swift, formerly arrested and successfully prosecuted for peeking at little girls going pee-pee in the restroom at the YWCA a few years ago, had nothing to say. He simply sat there, opening and closing his mouth like a Charlie McCarthy puppet without a ventriloquist.

"Naw," Dirk said, "old Byron here is a banker with lots of bucks. He hired a big-time L.A. attorney and got himself an early parole. In fact, Savannah, I think he's been up on charges a couple of times since then, and his lawyer got him off each time."

Byron Swift found his voice, although it proved unnaturally high and squeaky, due to the stress of the moment. "I remember you, too," he said to Savannah. "You're the bitch who gave me this—"

He pointed to the now-faded white scar that stretched from the outer corner of his left eye to his mouth.

Savannah's blue eyes went cold, all traces of humor disappearing from her face. "We already settled that in court, Mr. Swift, and you lost the case. You shouldn't have swung on me. I don't like perverts who prey on children, but I take a really dim view of those who slug me in the face when I'm placing them under arrest."

"You pistol-whipped me," he whined. His bottom lip trembled, and he looked as if he was about to cry.

"I smacked you upside the head," she replied, ice in her voice. "I just happened to have a gun in my hand at the time. That's the risk you take when you resist arrest, numskull. And, by the way, my eye was black for two weeks, so stop your bellyaching."

Dirk chuckled and nudged him. "Yeah, man . . . you're lucky she didn't bust you when she had a case of low blood sugar. She probably would've shot you with that pistol instead of just whacking you with it."

Reaching for Swift's wrist, Dirk clamped a handcuff on it. "Turn around, buddy, and give me your other hand. Here, behind your back. You're under arrest, my man. Anything you say can and most certainly will be held against you in a court of law. You have . . ."

Savannah motioned for Tammy, who was already running toward the van, her former fatigue forgotten in the adrenaline rush of the moment. "Come on, kiddo," Savannah shouted through the half-open door. "You're not going to believe this. He's an old collar of ours."

"Really?" Tammy slid the rear side door of the van open and jumped into the back seat behind Savannah. "Too cool." Under her golden California suntan, the rosy blush of victory glowed.

"Yeah, too cool." Savannah looked down at the video camera in her lap, then smiled broadly at Dirk. "You're gonna owe us girls big time for this one."

Dirk's own smile evaporated, a worried look taking its place . . . the expression he usually wore any time the subject of spending money—his money—was discussed. "Why? What do you want? Dinner or expensive candy or perfume, or somethin'?"

"Well, I think we'll settle for 'something,'" Savannah said carefully.

Dirk scowled. "Something . . . like what?"

"Like . . . don't you need to go water a bush . . . for a few minutes?"

Byron Swift's head whipped back and forth as he looked from one to another. "What do you mean? You're not going to leave me alone with her, are you? I mean . . . that would be police brutality."

"She ain't a cop no more." Dirk chuckled. "She's a private citizen now."

"But look what she did to me before! I—"

"Oh, shut up," Dirk replied. "She ain't gonna hurt you . . . much." To Savannah, he said, "And this will settle it, right? If I give you a few private moments here, I don't have to buy you dinner or nothin'?"

"We'll call it even. Right, Tammy?"

Tammy nodded, eyes wide with expectation. "Sure."

"Okay, you got it. Don't leave any marks." Dirk double-checked the handcuffs, then backed out of the van, muttering something about having to "drain the dragon."

Byron Swift began to wheeze like a bulldog in a dust storm.

"Oh, chill out, will ya?" Savannah told him. "I'm not going to hurt you . . . at least, not as long as you do what I tell you to do."

A shiver swept over him, and for a second his eyes looked hopeful. But hope quickly changed to suspicion. "What? What are you going to make me do?"

Keeping her Beretta trained on Swift, Savannah reached with her left hand into her jacket pocket and pulled out a pair of surgical gloves. "Here, Tammy, put these on," she said, tossing them back to her assistant, who quickly did as she was instructed. "Then lean over here and take this camera off my lap."

Tammy enthusiastically did as she was told.

"And what do we have here?" Savannah said. "A blank video.

How nice." She snatched a tape, still in its plastic wrapper, from a pile of cassettes on the console and passed it to Tammy. "Do you know how to operate that thing?" she asked Tammy.

Tammy gave it a quick once-over. "Sure. It's pretty straight-forward. Point, focus, and shoot."

"Good. Take the tape out that's in there and be careful with it; it's Dirk's hard-earned evidence. Then put that new one in. We're going to make ourselves a little home movie of our own." She chuckled. "Yep, Tammy, darlin' . . . you point and focus . . . and if ol' Byron here says exactly what I tell him to say, word for word . . . I won't shoot him." She turned back to Swift and gave him a smile that was completely void of warmth or humor. "Now, Byron, baby . . . you're going to play the part of a sicko pervert . . . shouldn't be much of a stretch. You just take a deep breath and repeat after me."

"Hi, my name is Byron Swift. I'm the vice president of the San Carmelita Savings and Loan. I'm fifty-two years old, blond hair and green eyes, five foot, seven inches, weigh one hundred and seventy-five pounds. My hobbies are fishing, outdoor barbecu-ing, walking my dog on the beach, and filming your kids doing their exercises in gym class. I turn these home movies into porn videos, featuring myself doing nasty things with your children. I do this because I'm . . . I'm . . . I'm not going to say that, damn it . . . and you can't make me say—"

"Hey, Tam, you forgot to edit that part out." Savannah nudged Tammy, who was sitting beside her on the sofa, with her elbow.

"I'll cut it later, I—"

"Shh-h-h, I gotta hear this." Sitting on Savannah's other side, Dirk propped his sneakers on the coffee table and took a long swig from his beer bottle. Savannah promptly kicked him on the shin.

"Get your shoes off my furniture, you heathen."

Savannah's easy chairs were occupied by two other guests, Ryan Stone and John Gibson, her friends and sometimes fellow detectives. On his lap Ryan held both of Savannah's house cats,

Diamante and Cleopatra—a couple of miniature black panthers with rhinestone-studded collars. They were purring with ecstasy as he stroked them and rubbed behind their ears.

Savannah didn't blame them. Tall, dark-haired, and deliciously handsome, Ryan would have been welcome to stroke or rub her ears any time he liked.

She found John Gibson delightfully appealing, too. Though older than Ryan by around ten years, John was the quintessential British gentleman. His thick silver hair, sweeping mustache, and aristocratic English accent were irresistible.

But Savannah's fantasies had gone unfulfilled; Ryan and John were committed to each other and had been for years. She had to settle for entertaining them at least once a week, and those events constituted the red-starred days on her social calendar.

They chuckled, watching the video on her television along with everyone else, as Byron Swift continued his coerced confession.

"I do this because I'm a degenerate, who can't . . . or won't . . . help himself." The film jumped . . . another rough cut. "And I've been doing it for years, although I haven't served much time, because I have a high-priced attorney who usually gets me a sweet deal."

"Savannah, my dear," John said, "you're a most effective director. You certainly get the most from your performers."

"Why, thank you, kind sir," she replied with her best Southern-belle eyelash flutter. "Here's the good part."

"And even though I'm under arrest now . . . again . . . " Swift added, "I'll probably be out right away and filming your kids again. Be sure to look for me on the streets in a month or two. I'm . . . no . . . I don't want to . . . okay . . . I'm the twisted lech with the camera. There, are you satis—"

The film ended abruptly, followed by a round of applause.

"And you should have heard Savannah afterwards," Tammy said. "She told him she was going to send a copy of this to the local chapter of Hell's Angels—Vets on Hogs—and the Parents Against Child Molesters Vigilante Association."

"Parents Against who?" Dirk asked. "I never heard of a group called that."

Savannah took his bottle from his hand and helped herself to a long drink. "Eh," she said with a shrug, "I just made it up. I don't want him sleeping too well at night . . . or manipulating the system too hard to get out on the streets right away."

"What *do* you intend to do with this fine film of yours," Ryan asked, "submit it for Academy consideration?"

"Naw. I'm just going to stash it on a shelf somewhere and deny it exists," she said. "After all, we don't want him complaining that ol' Dirk here abused him by leaving him in a van with two vicious, vindictive females."

"Yeah," Tammy added, "I think we violated about fifteen of his civil rights there."

"At least fifteen," Dirk agreed.

"And after searching my soul . . . for at least a minute and a half . . . I can honestly say: I can live with myself." Savannah reached for the bowl of caramel popcorn on the coffee table. "How about you, Tam?"

Tammy grinned. "The guilt's a heavy burden, but I'll bear up."

Chapter
2

Several hours later, having been plied with copious amounts of double Dutch chocolate fudge, popcorn, and the potables of their choice, Savannah's guests began to take their leave.

Tammy departed first, promising to return in the wee hours of the morning to take Savannah to the airport. Although Savannah returned home as seldom as possible to the tiny rural town in Georgia where she had been born and raised, this visit was unavoidable. The oldest of nine children, Savannah had been summoned to yet another wedding.

If there was anything worse than going home, it was to a wedding not your own, without any sign of a ring on your finger, without even an escort on your arm.

Ryan and John were the next to leave, waving good-bye from their vintage Bentley as Savannah watched from her front porch. She could hardly see through the tangle of bougainvillea that was taking over the front of her Spanish-style bungalow.

"Have a safe trip to Georgia, dear," John called as they pulled out of her driveway, his silver hair glowing in the light of the streetlamp.

"Be sure to give us a ring if you need anything, okay?" Ryan added, his head stuck out the window. "In fact, give us a call whether you need us or not. We're going to miss you."

"I'll miss you, too." She blew them a kiss.

"Eh, what're you wasting that on them for," said a grouchy voice behind her. She turned to see Dirk standing there, pulling on his battered bomber jacket. "Those two aren't into *girl* kisses."

"Stop," Savannah said. "Stop right now. Behave a little better, and I might blow you . . . a kiss . . . now and then."

His eyes twinkled. "Mmm, had my hopes up for a half a second there."

She scowled. "Get real, Nacho Breath. Are you going home now, too?"

"Yeah. Some of us have to work tomorrow, while *other* people get to leave on vacation."

"Some vacation . . . watching one of my zillions of siblings get married, while I'm still . . ."

"Yes?" His eyes searched hers; she quickly glanced away.

"Never mind." Linking her arm through his, she began walking him toward his Buick, which was parked on the street in front of her house.

"Were you about to moan and groan about still being single?" he asked. "I could have sworn that was what you were going to say."

"No way. I like being single. No man's shoes to trip over . . . except your rotten old sneakers when you're here for Monday night football and the free pizza. Having the toilet seat *down*, where it belongs, all the time . . . except when you visit and leave it up."

"So, with a guy like me around, you don't need a husband. Is that what you're saying?"

"Yeah, except for vehicle maintenance, lawn care, and the occasional plumbing job, I do okay."

"But then there's the old bada-bing, bada-boom." He prodded her with his elbow.

"Eh, if I can do without having my oil changed, my tires rotated, and my pipes Roto-Rootered I can give up the old binging and booming."

His smirk faded into a look of concern. "Speaking of . . . romance . . . are you going to be seeing any of your high school buddies there in Georgia?"

For a second, memories of adolescence flashed before her mind's eye: sultry nights in pecan groves, stolen kisses behind the athletic field bleachers, daring caresses at the drive-in movie, the back seat of Tommy Stafford's '56 Chevy.

Yes, she'd had a few "high school buddies." However, only one face came to mind. Tommy's.

But did she even want to see his face again?

"No. I don't think so," she said.

"Good."

Dirk looked so relieved that she didn't bother to set the record straight, to admit she had been answering her own question, not his.

It was her turn to nudge him. "Why, Detective Coulter, I do believe you're jealous."

He jerked his arm away from hers. "I'm not neither. I just don't want you getting into trouble. You bein' so far away, I won't be able to bail you out."

Before she could protest, she recalled that he had, in fact, bailed her out—both figuratively and literally—numerous times over the years.

She looked up at his face—street-fight scars, perpetually mussed hair, and all—and felt a rush of affection for her best friend in the world. Standing on tiptoe, she gave him a kiss on the cheek.

His "stakeout shave" rasped against her lips, but she had long ago decided that Dirk's rugged masculinity was perhaps his most appealing attribute . . . along with a rabidly protective streak toward those he cared for. The rest of the world could go to Hades in a pink Easter basket, as far as Dirk Coulter was concerned, but the handful of people he loved . . . he loved fiercely.

"I'll be fine," she told him. "I'll get Marietta married off . . . for the third time . . . and I'll be right back. You won't even know I'm gone."

To her surprise, he bent down and returned her kiss, his lips

warm as they lingered just a bit longer than the usual peck on her
cheek.

"Oh, I'll know you're gone," he said, clearing his throat. For
once, he didn't add any smart aleck disclaimer to dilute the sen-
timentality of the moment. "Believe me, I'll know."

As she watched him drive away down her street, his taillights
disappearing at the corner, Savannah realized she was going to
miss him, too. A lot.

Whether she ran into Tommy Stafford or not.

"Thanks for bringing me to the airport," Savannah told
Tammy as they pulled into the short-term parking lot of the mystery maze known as Los Angeles International Airport, "and for
taking care of the kitties and the agency for me while I'm gone."

Tammy had a slight pout on her face as she swung her old, hot-
pink Volkswagen Bug into an empty spot and cut the engine.
"And all I asked in return was one little, itsy-bitsy peek at the
dress."

"You're not looking at the dress. That's it; that's all. I don't
even want to think about the damned thing, okay?"

They got out of the car, locked it, and headed for the trunk in
front. Tammy opened it and helped Savannah haul out her suitcase, carry-on, and one enormous garment bag.

"It can't be that bad," Tammy said, grabbing for the bag,
which Savannah snatched out of her hand.

"It's revolting. Let's just say, it makes me look like an enormous, upside-down tulip."

"What color?"

Savannah winced at the thought. "Fluorescent peach."

"Ouch."

"Yeah. I swear, Marietta picked that style just to make the rest
of us look ridiculous. She's not above it, you know."

Tammy grabbed the suitcase, Savannah the carry-on, and they
headed for the departure terminal. "What color is the maid of
honor wearing?"

"Mint green."

"That's not so bad . . . I guess."

"Yeah, Marietta was set on dusty rose, but we talked her out of it. Dusty rose and peach. That girl never has had a lick o' sense when it comes to colors, or dressing, or decorating . . . or men."

"This is her third time around, huh?"

They stood at the crosswalk, waiting for the constant flood of taxicabs, limos, vans, and transport buses to come to a halt. Even in the pre-dawn hours, LAX hustled and bustled. Savannah punched the signal-control button several more times, although she knew that—like the panel on an elevator—repetition did no good. It only provided the illusion of control to the puncher.

"Yeah, this is Hubby Numero Tres. And she's got two children, one from each of her exes. Impulse control isn't exactly Marietta's forte, either. She was asking everybody whether they thought it was silly for her to wear a white gown and veil. They said it was, but she's going for it anyway."

Finally, the light changed, and they started across. A nearby bus coughed out a cloud of acrid diesel smoke, and Savannah tried to breathe momentarily through her ears. Ah . . . the luxury of travel.

The electronic doors slid open, ushering them into the terminal full of harried, mostly irritated, passengers. "When Marietta asked me what she should wear," Savannah continued, as they headed for the endless queues, "I suggested that she wear a football jersey with the number 3 on the back."

Tammy laughed. "You didn't! What did she say?"

"Nothing . . . for two whole weeks. Absolutely not a word. Clammed up tighter than Dirk's wallet."

"Only two weeks?"

Savannah shrugged. "Hey, that's a record for a Reid gal. The only thing we like more than eating is talking."

"I wish I were coming with you," Tammy said as she set the suitcase on the floor at the end of the mile-long, twisting, turning, cordoned line. "All that family togetherness sounds like fun."

"It might be . . . for some other family." Savannah sighed, realizing that she didn't really mind the long, long line. It could even be longer, for all she cared. Although she hated to admit it, she was in no hurry at all to return to the bosom of her homeland. "For us," she said, "family togetherness tends to spell trouble."

"With a capital T?"

"Oh, yes. Trouble . . . in all caps, bold, underlined, italicized. We Reids don't do anything halfway."

"If that Macon doesn't shape up real quick, I'm gonna slap him naked and hide his clothes," Waycross Reid said as he drove the old Ford pickup down the pothole-ridden road. Savannah sat next to her brother and wondered, with every bounce of the shock-shot truck, if one of the exposed seat coils was going to take intimate liberties with her backside. She looked wistfully at the truck's dash, wishing there was some sign of an air-conditioner vent; she had forgotten how humid the South could be in mid-August, and she was melting inside her cotton suit.

But, while Waycross had a state-of-the-art stereo system, there was no hint of a temperature-control device. As a young man, his priorities were notably different than those of a perimenopausal female.

The saga of the Reid family "troubles" had begun the moment Waycross had picked her up at the Atlanta airport two hours before. Twenty-nine years old, the only redhead in the batch, Waycross was the oldest of her two brothers. His relationship with his younger brother, Macon, had always been rocky, at best. And Savannah usually agreed with Waycross, the more hardworking, sensible, and responsible of the two. If he said Macon was being a pain, it was probably true.

"What's he doing?" she asked.

"I don't even know what he's doing. I'm afraid to ask," Waycross replied. "But I know who he's doing it with. Since he graduated from high school he's been hanging out with those Whitney boys, and you know what trailer trash they are . . . especially that Kenny Jr. What a friggin' yahoo that one is. He's so lazy the dead lice wouldn't fall off him and stupider than a dirt clod."

"The Whitneys. Yeah, I remember their old man," Savannah said, searching her memory banks. "He drank like a skunk and practically lived in Sheriff Mahoney's rear cell. It's no wonder the kids turned sour."

As they drove through Savannah's hometown of McGill, she noted with a twang of the heartstrings some of her favorite haunts: the drugstore where she had enjoyed the occasional strawberry ice cream cone on a hot Saturday afternoon, the library where she had discovered the joy of Nancy Drew mysteries, the elementary school where she, her mother, and even her grandmother had attended. All three generations had played tag among the giant oaks and hopscotch on the hard-packed earth, where the grass had been worn away by hundreds of small, energetic feet.

But the trip down memory lane didn't take long. When Savannah was a child, McGill, Georgia, had been only three blocks long.

Now it was four.

Urban sprawl.

"Have you given Macon a talking-to?" Savannah asked him.

"I've preached whole sermons to him . . . so has Gran . . . but it just rolls off him like rain off a duck's back. You can't tell Macon Reid nothing; he knows all there is to know about everything. If you don't believe it, just ask him."

"How's everybody else doing?"

"Gran's good, full o' piss and vinegar, as always. Alma helps her out a lot."

Savannah smiled, reminding herself that there would be a few blessings to this visit. Seeing Gran and Alma were two. Savannah liked to think she loved all her siblings equally, but she had to admit a favoritism toward Alma, who had always been the one to nurse a sick kitten, rescue a baby bird, or help Gran wax a kitchen floor or even scrub a toilet when necessary.

"Alma's a sweetheart," she said. "I wish she were the one getting married, instead of Marietta. She deserves to find a good husband."

"Yeah, but I don't see that happening any time soon. She's still pretty shy with the boys."

"And Cordele?"

"Still as uptight as ever. Goes around telling everybody what they oughta and oughtn't do. She reads those psychology books and has a label for everything everybody does. I called her a busybody the other day, and she told me I'm a passive-aggressive with severe parental abandonment issues. Whatever the hell that means."

Savannah chuckled. "That sounds like Cordele. And Vidalia?"

"Going crazy with those two sets of twins, and taking Butch along with her. He works with me at the service station about eighteen hours a day. Says it's to make ends meet, but I think he's just avoiding diaper duty."

Savannah felt another surge of mixed emotions as they left the asphalt highway at the edge of town and turned left onto a dirt road. She wondered how many times she had walked this road from Gran's house to the highway to catch a school bus, to check the mailbox, or just to get away for a moment of blissful solitude, away from a house full of nine kids, perpetually runny noses, mountains of soiled laundry and dirty dishes.

With an absentee, truck-driving father, and a mother who spent more time in the local tavern than standing at a kitchen sink or in front of an ironing board, the duties of child-rearing had fallen upon Granny Reid and Savannah, the oldest of the brood. Other than producing a child every year or two and naming them after Georgia towns, Shirley Reid had contributed little to her children's welfare.

Savannah and Gran hadn't complained, though. Not even in their most private moments. Watching the babies grow into children, and the children into adults, they had figured it was time and energy well spent.

Now, looking back on it with older, more experienced eyes, Savannah wondered that she hadn't been more resentful at the time. The injustice of the situation had been lost in the chaotic hustle of caring for the babies that just kept coming. Savannah had been too busy to consider whether or not she was being used. And now, she couldn't honestly say she would have changed anything. All in all, it had been a good childhood. And what her parents hadn't, or couldn't, give to their children, Gran had more than provided.

"You did good, Savannah. Real good." Waycross gave her a sweet, loving look that went straight to her heart. It was as though he had read her thoughts. He reached over and patted her on the knee with his work-roughened, grease-stained fingers. "You had your hands full back then, and don't think we don't appreciate what you did for us."

She placed her hand over his and squeezed. "I wouldn't have missed a minute of it."

He grinned. "Not even the afternoon I brought home that snake?"

"Ah, yes . . . the snake in my lingerie drawer episode. *That* one I could have done without. The frog in the sugar bowl wasn't exactly a high point either, but all in all, it was pretty cool, raising you guys."

Waycross rounded a corner and the house came into view. As always, when she had been away for a long time, Savannah was shocked at how small and shabby it was. The simple wooden structure was commonly known as a "shotgun" house, the rooms lined up in a straight row, from the front of the house to the back—living room, dining room, kitchen, and bedrooms, one opening into the other. It was so named because, if someone stood at the front of the house and shot a gun, the bullet could exit the back door without striking a wall.

The tiny house had probably been built for a family of four, maybe five. With ten people, three bedrooms, and one bath, it had been extremely cozy, to say the least.

Desperately in need of a coat of paint, it wasn't as white as she remembered, several of the tar-paper tiles were missing from the roof, and the porch sagged on the left.

But it was home.

More importantly, it was where Gran lived. Feisty, wise Granny Reid had walked the earth for more than eighty years and generously shared her collected wisdom with Savannah and the rest of her grandchildren. Some had embraced her teachings more than others, but all had been given the benefit of her counsel ... whether they wanted it or not.

Suddenly, it was very important to Savannah to get out of the truck and into that house. As soon as the vehicle rolled to a stop, Savannah's door was open.

She was across the yard and onto the porch in a matter of seconds, replaying in her mind the memories of coming home to Gran, whose hands were always busy—peeling potatoes, folding laundry, bandaging skinned knees—but she always had time to listen, to hear how someone's day had been, to enjoy the latest bit of gossip, or to help with an arithmetic problem.

Year after year, Gran had been waiting, a smile on her face when Savannah came through the door.

But this time was different.

When Savannah barged inside, shouting, "Gran, it's me; I'm ho-o-ome!" she found her grandmother sitting in her overstuffed armchair, quietly weeping. Savannah's sister, Alma, sat on the ottoman in front of her, holding a handful of tissues. She, too, was crying.

Savannah felt her heart do a few double beats, and time slowed, as it did in those fractions of a second just before you hear something you'll never forget.

"Oh, no ..." she said, "who died?"

"Ma-ma-con," Alma replied between sobs.

Waycross had come into the house behind Savannah just in time to hear the news. "Macon's dead?" he said in a hoarse whisper.

"No, he's not dead," Gran said, wiping her eyes. Savannah was shocked to see that, for once, she actually looked her eighty-plus years. "But he might as well be. Deputy Stafford just came here and arrested him."

Savannah felt her knees go weak, from relief or fear she wasn't sure. Sinking onto the couch, she said, "What was he arrested for?"

Alma began to sob even harder, while Gran steeled herself to reply. "They say he killed Judge Patterson."

"Killed? Macon? That's ridiculous!" Savannah said. "He wouldn't—"

"Yeah, he might have," Waycross replied, shaking his head as though suddenly weary. He sat on the sofa beside Savannah.

"No! I don't believe that for a minute. Gran, do you—?"

The look of misery in her grandmother's eyes chilled Savannah nearly as much as her words. "Well, Savannah," she said, "you see, Macon's changed. He ain't the boy we used to know no more . . . been into all sorts of meanness lately." She dabbed at her eyes, then wadded the tissue into a tight ball. "I'm sorry to say that Waycross is right. Macon just might have murdered that old geezer."

Chapter

3

As Savannah hurried up to the square, two-story brick building that housed the McGill sheriff's station and city jail—
as evidenced by the bars on the upper windows—the thought occurred that she hadn't been here to bail out a relative for a long
time. About twelve years. The last time it had been her mother,
incarcerated for lawless activity. But the offense had been something simple, and customary for Shirley Reid . . . public drunken-
ness, creating a public nuisance, or, at worst, cracking a beer
bottle over an equally intoxicated companion's head.

After raiding the coffee can full of nickels, pennies, and
dimes hidden beneath the kitchen sink, Savannah and Gran
had managed to scrounge together the twenty-five dollars to
spring her.

Savannah had the sinking feeling that this problem wouldn't
be so easily solved. No pillowcase full of loose change was going
to buy her little brother's freedom.

She yanked open the rusty screen door, its holes bandaged
with crisscrosses of cellophane tape to keep the blood-hungry
Georgia mosquitoes at bay. A blast of frigid air hit her the moment she opened the wooden door and stepped inside. Apparently, City Hall had finally let go of some funds to air-condition

their deputies. And the law enforcers were taking full advantage of the luxury.

But that was the only immediately discernible difference. Otherwise, the office looked just the way she remembered it: dark, dingy, dusty, and positively reeking of intrigue. It had always been one of her favorite places. Within these walls she had first been infected with the virus—the law enforcement bug.

On the way over from Gran's, having ordered everyone else to stay at home, Savannah had a few moments of solitude to consider how she was going to handle this situation. One element of the equation was bound to be Deputy Thomas Stafford. So much for her decision to avoid him.

She wasn't sure how she would feel, seeing him again after so long. And with Macon's bacon sizzling in the frying pan, she hadn't given it a lot of thought.

So she was startled by the sensation that swept over her the moment she saw him, standing in the corner of the room beside the gun rack. He was replacing a shotgun, locking it into place, intent on what he was doing and unaware of her presence.

She had secretly hoped that the years might have robbed him of some hair, thickened his middle, etched a few lines around his eyes . . . made him a little less desirable. And he had, indeed, filled out a bit. But it was all in the form of shoulders, biceps, thighs, and calves, judging from the strategically placed bulges in his khaki uniform. He wore his blond, curly hair in a shorter style than when she had last seen him, but he didn't appear to have lost any of it.

When he turned to face her, she saw that even the crow's feet at the corners of his eyes looked good on him, giving a rugged edge to his otherwise boyish attractiveness.

He froze when he saw her, his green eyes registering first a trace of confused semi-recognition, then delight.

"Savannah! I don't believe it!" In three long-legged paces he closed the distance between them and grabbed her around the waist. "Hot damn, gal! It's good to see you."

He gave her a hug that nearly lifted her off her feet and took her breath away . . . both from its vigor and from the rush of familiar sexual heat that, surprisingly, hadn't cooled one degree over the years.

Holding her at arm's length, he looked her up and down. And just for a moment, she wished she had eaten more of Tammy's salads and less of Dirk's candy bars.

But nothing except pure admiration registered in his eyes as he took in every detail of her figure. "Shit, you look great!" he said, shaking his head. "I mean fan-friggin'-tastic!"

"And you always were a silken-tongued lad," she replied.

The lascivious grin he gave her made her knees even weaker. His hands tightened around her waist, pulling her closer. "You oughta remember," he said, dropping his voice to a throaty whisper. "We taught each other how to kiss behind the bleachers."

"Yeah, and a few other things that my granny would have skinned you alive for, if she'd found out."

At the mention of Gran, both of their moods deflated. "I guess I don't have to ask why you're here," he said, releasing her and walking over to a desk littered with wire baskets full of papers. The green, goose-necked lamp was vintage Americana, as was the leather-edged blotter. The only signs of technological advancement were a laptop computer and a fax machine.

He sat down behind the desk and waved her toward a metal folding chair beside it.

"We just picked your brother up, less than an hour ago," he said with a sigh as he aimlessly shuffled some of the papers. "You must have made record time getting here from California."

She heard the investigatory tone in his question and reminded herself that this hunk sitting before her might be an ex-boyfriend, but he was, number one, a cop. A damned good one, too, as she recalled. She felt a bit strange, being on the other side and having to watch every word she said.

"I was already on my way here," she said. "Marietta's wedding. . . ."

"Oh, yeah. I remember hearing she was going to give it another go. Some people never learn, huh?"

Her blue eyes hardened, and she didn't bother to keep the sarcasm out of her voice when she replied evenly, "And some don't have the courage to take the chance in the first place."

He stared at her for a long moment, then glanced away. "Yeah, well." He cleared his throat. "I'm sorry you've got trouble in your family, Savannah. It like to broke my heart, bringing Macon in. I've always loved your grandma, and I don't want to be causing her grief. But what are ya gonna do?"

"Find out who really did it," she suggested, reaching for the can of soda that was sitting, unopened, on his desk.

She popped the top and took a long drink, but it wasn't enough to get rid of the dryness in her mouth. Her hand shook slightly as she set the can down. She hoped he wouldn't notice.

He did.

Good cops notice everything, she reminded herself.

He reached over and covered her hand with his. For some reason, tears sprang to her eyes, and she silently cursed him for seeing them . . . for causing them. And even though she knew he wasn't personally responsible for whatever had happened to Macon, he was the readily available target.

"Savannah, I wouldn't have just snatched your brother up like that without good, solid evidence. You know me better than that. I don't arrest nobody for murder, let alone a member of *your* family, unless I'm damned sure."

From a drawer in his desk, he pulled a box of tissues and offered her one. She sniffed and shook her head. "So, what's this solid evidence you've got on him?"

Replacing the box, he said, "You're a cop yourself, Savannah. You know I can't be telling a member of the family stuff like that."

"You're behind in your news. I'm off the force. Now I'm a private investigator, so whatever you don't tell me, I'll just have to find out on my own."

He grinned at her and, in spite of herself, she had to admit he had a nice smile, friendly, laced with mischief. "Don't you go picking no locks or climbing through no windows, young lady, or you'll be in that cell with your brother."

"Speaking of . . . I want to see him."

"Sorry, can't do that either."

She stood up so abruptly that the chair nearly toppled over backward. "Don't get smart with me, Tommy Stafford! You may not be keen on telling me the ins and outs of your investigation, but you're not going to keep me from talking to my baby brother."

"Listen to me, Savannah. Macon clammed up, asked for an attorney, and the public defender's away on a fishing trip. So your baby brother's just gonna have to cool his heels there in the cell a few days till he gets back. And he *ain't* having company . . . you or nobody else."

Standing, he took a couple of steps toward her and they were nose to nose . . . or as close as possible, considering that he was about six inches taller.

Unintimidated, Savannah glared up at him, eyes blazing. "Now *you* listen to *me*, Tommy Stafford. I—"

"Tom! It's Tom now! Not Tommy!"

She shrugged. "Whatever. I'm going upstairs right this minute, and I'm going to talk to my little brother. I'm going to find out if he's all right, and ask him what this mess is all about. And you and I both know that you're not going to try to physically restrain me."

He pushed his face another inch closer to hers. "I could, you know."

"You could *try*. But we'd both wind up bruised and bloody, and in the end, I'd *still* make it up those stairs. So why don't you just be sensible and save us the grief?"

They stared at each other several seconds, the only sounds in the room those of their breathing and the hum of the air-conditioner. When he didn't reply, she spun around and stomped across the room toward the staircase that led to the cells above.

When she was halfway up the stairs, she heard him say, "You

may be lookin' good, gal, but you're just as contrary as you ever were. Maybe more."

With every step she climbed, Savannah could feel the temperature rising by degrees. At the top of the stairs, she decided it must be one hundred and ten and ninety-eight percent humidity.

Apparently, the city fathers didn't believe it necessary to provide their prisoners the luxury of air-conditioning. Their sense of thrift showed in the low-wattage bulbs hanging from bare sockets overhead.

The narrow, dim corridor that led between the two rows of cells, four on each side, gave Savannah an overwhelming case of claustrophobia. Graffiti-decorated, gray cement walls separated the cells with iron bars on the front. Rust had long ago eaten through the Army-green paint that had once been smeared on the bars and doors.

The smells of urine and unwashed bodies mingled with other odors she didn't care to identify.

McGill's jails were frequented by more drunks, sleeping off a night of overindulgence than by desperate, hard-core criminals. In the past one hundred years, these cells hadn't housed a single serial killer, jewel thief, or international spy.

The first cell on her left held an old fellow whom Savannah recognized as the town drunk. He had held that distinction as long as she could remember. The scraggly blond beard that hung to his waist had more silver hair than gold and his tanned face had a few more cracks, but otherwise he looked much the same as he had when she was a kid.

"Hey, Yukon Bill," she said, nodding as she passed.

"Did you bring me a bologna sandwich?" he called.

"Nope."

"How about a cold beer?"

"Maybe next time I'll smuggle you in a Coke."

"Eh, don't bother. Coke don't cut it."

A pair of arms poked through the bars from the cell on the far right. "Savannah? Savannah? Is that you?"

Savannah's heart jumped at the sound of the familiar, beloved voice, one she had only heard over the phone for a long time. Macon might be a pistol, sometimes a pain in the rump, but he was her baby brother.

Okay, so he's not exactly a baby anymore, she thought when she walked up to the front of his cell and looked inside. Macon had always been a tall kid, well over six feet, but now he was wide as well. Since she had seen him last, about seven years ago, he had gained about a hundred pounds. And unlike Deputy Stafford downstairs, the bulk of the weight wasn't muscle.

The smile he gave her was lukewarm, the soul light in his eyes dim, as he reached through the bars and gave her an awkward embrace.

"I wasn't figuring it would be you who'd come," he said. "But you might as well have saved yourself the effort. I'm in a hell of a mess, Sis. I mean, a *big* mess."

She stood as close as she could to the bars, wishing she could somehow cuddle this mountain of human being and take away the frightened, empty look in his eyes. "So I heard," she replied.

"They think I killed somebody."

"Heard that, too."

"Deputy Stafford says me and a buddy of mine robbed and murdered Judge Patterson. And he says he's got the evidence to prove it, too."

She glanced down at his stockinged feet. "Where are your shoes, sweetie?"

"They took 'em when they threw me in here."

He shook his head, ran his fingers through his short brush of a crewcut, and walked over to the cot that was fastened with chains to the wall. Sinking onto it, he propped his elbows on his knees and put his face in his hands.

Savannah's heart sank. The look, the posture, was a familiar one. She had seen that expression of utter defeat on many a prisoner's face, and she knew what it meant.

It was the look of guilt.

She glanced down the corridor, but saw no one, not even Yukon Bill, who had returned to his bunk.

"Macon," she whispered. "You've got to tell me . . . and I mean, the truth. Don't you dare lie to me, boy, or I swear, as soon as I lay hands on you, I'll clean your plow."

He looked up at her, but his blank expression suggested he was already bored with the subject. "Yeah?"

"Did you do it?"

He sighed. "Did I do what?"

"Don't screw around with me. This ain't the time. Did you kill Judge Patterson . . . or anybody else?"

"Nope."

She peered into his eyes with the intense scrutiny of one who had been lied to more times than she could remember. He quickly glanced away, then stared down at the cement floor.

Not a good sign, she thought. Momentarily she flashed back on the day he had come home from the local grocery store with his pockets stuffed with candy bars and bubble gum . . . far more than his twenty-five cent a week allowance would have bought.

"How was the judge killed?" she asked, clasping the cold bars with sweating fingers. The peeling paint rasped against her skin, but she was only vaguely aware of the sensation.

"Shot."

Savannah heard a sound from the other end of the corridor and turned to see Tom Stafford walking toward her, a ring of keys jangling in his hand, a disgruntled, but resigned, look on his face.

Macon jumped to his feet and stepped up to the door.

Savannah waited for Tom to say something, but he didn't. Instead he walked to the door of the cell, unlocked it, and swung it open. With a wave of his hand, he ushered her inside.

She wasn't sure if he was inviting her to join her brother inside the cell for their conversation, or placing her under arrest, too.

Her answer came a moment later as he relocked the door. "Make the most of your time," she heard him mutter under his breath. "I'll be back in about fifteen minutes."

"Thank you, Tommy," she called after him. "I mean, Tom."
He just grunted . . . and kept walking.

The moment the deputy disappeared through the far door, Savannah grabbed her brother in a rough hug, but he pulled away after only a couple of seconds.

Watching him shuffle away from her and stretch out on the cot, Savannah tried to remind herself that he had always been the distant brother. Unlike the more demonstrative Waycross, Macon had always kept his thoughts and emotions to himself. As a result, she and Gran had spent a lot of time and energy trying to figure out what was going on inside him.

But she didn't have the patience for a game of "What's Up With Macon?", considering the high stakes.

"Sit up," she said, punching him on the shoulder. "Tom said fifteen minutes and that's not long. Start talking."

Groaning, he shoved himself into a sitting position. "What's there to talk about?"

She resisted the urge to slap him silly. "How do you know the judge was shot?"

"That's what the deputy said."

"Where?"

"In his car, when he was bringing me here to jail."

"No, I mean, where was the judge shot?"

"There in that big house of his on the edge of town . . . the old mansion with the white pillar things out front and—"

"I know which one. When did it happen?"

"Last night." He gave her a quick sideways glance and added, "I guess. I mean, that sort of thing usually happens at night . . . doesn't it?"

"Did Deputy Stafford say that's when it went down?"

"I don't know. Maybe. I don't remember."

"What else did Tom say?"

"Mostly, he just told me that I didn't have to talk to him if I didn't want to and that I could have a lawyer."

"Yes. He mentioned that he'd tried to get the public defender over here, but the guy's gone for the weekend."

Macon crossed his arms over his ample belly, and Savannah saw the bruise on his forearm, just below the tattoo of a tiger that she didn't remember him having. Dark and swollen, the bruise appeared fresh.

"How did you get that?" She pointed to the bruise. "Did Tom rough you up when he brought you in?"

He looked down and seemed surprised, as though seeing it for the first time.

"What? Oh, no . . . I don't think Tom did it. The handcuffs were a little tight, me being so big and all, but . . . ."

"Handcuffs wouldn't pinch you there, darlin'," Savannah said. She could hear the fear and worry in her own voice.

"What are you gettin' at?" he replied, as irritated and guarded as she was concerned.

"Nothing, Macon . . . except that you've got a nasty bruise on your arm, the kind people get when they've been in some kind of a fight. So, if you don't remember where you got it, you'd better start figuring it out. 'Cause Tom Stafford's a good cop, and you can bet your bottom dollar he's going to ask you about it."

She reached over and laid her hand on his shoulder. She felt him flinch beneath her touch, before he pulled away.

"As soon as your attorney gets here, Tom's going to ask you a lot of questions, little brother. And he ain't gonna settle for the crap answers you've been giving me. With Tom Stafford, 'I don't know' and 'I don't remember' just ain't gonna cut it."

Chapter
4

By the time Deputy Tom Stafford returned, fifteen minutes later, to release Savannah from her brother's cell, she was about as depressed as she had ever been in her life . . . a lifetime fraught with daily blood sugar dips, monthly PMS episodes, and weekly bouts of Monday-morning, step-on-the-bathroom-scale blues.

Every brain cell in her analytical mind told her that her little brother had been a bad boy, indeed. And this time, a simple trip to the principal's office with one of Gran's apple pies wouldn't put things right.

At the top of the stairs leading to the first floor, Savannah paused. Tom, who had been walking a few steps behind, bumped into her. She grabbed him by the forearms and was only vaguely aware that he winced.

"I want to go out to the scene, Tom," she told him. "Take me out there now, okay?"

Shaking his head, he pulled away. "No way. Don't even start with that, Savannah, 'cause it won't happen. In fact, if I even catch you within spitting distance of the old Patterson place, I swear I'll haul your tail right back here and throw you in the cell with Yukon Bill."

"I won't touch anything, I swear. I won't interfere and—"

"No! No! No! I know you heard me, girl, so don't act like you didn't." He stomped past her and on down the steps. She could feel the stairs tremble with his weight. "Shit, you've always had a head as hard as bog oak, and a gift for being deaf when it suits you."

Hurrying after him, she called, "You can run, but you can't hide, Tommy Stafford. You're going to drive me out there right now, and you know it."

"No! I give you an inch, you think you're a damned ruler. That fifteen-minute visit is all you're getting outta me. Go home."

By the time he reached the bottom step, she had caught him by the back of the shirt. He spun around, his face flushed, his breathing hard. Standing on the stair above him, she could look him straight in the eyes for a pleasant change.

"You have *never*, Tommy Stafford, *never* in the history of our relationship, won an argument with me. What makes you think today's going to be any different? You just think about what's at stake here, and how determined I can be."

"Then *you'd* better think about something." He shook his finger in her face. "That little brother of yours is a punk, a no-good piece of white trash that—"

The sharp crack of her palm across his cheek surprised her nearly as much as it did him. For only a second, she regretted the slap. Then her fury flared again.

"Don't you *ever* say that about Macon or anyone else I love," she said, choking on the words. "Not ever. You hear?"

She half expected him to hit her back, and she wouldn't have blamed him if he had. One of her long-standing rules stated: If anyone, even a woman, strikes first, they deserve to get as good as they gave.

But Tom didn't hit her. In fact, the anger in his eyes faded, and when he did reach for her, it was to gently stroke her cheek with his forefinger. The simple gesture touched her heart and brought tears to her eyes.

"Savannah, I'm so sorry," he said. "I don't want to be the one to say harsh things to you. But darlin', it's true. Macon's different now. He's fallen into some bad company lately, and it's rubbed off on him."

"He's a good kid, with a good heart. I don't care who he's been hanging out with, that hasn't changed."

"It's admirable—you being loyal to your loved ones and all—but you've got to be smart about where you invest yourself. Don't spend on somebody who's not worth the cost."

"Thank you," she said coolly, "but since he's my family, I think it's up to me to set the price, don't you?"

"I reckon. But I'm your friend, and I've got a right to speak my mind on the subject."

"Okay." She drew a deep breath and added, "Once."

"I hear you."

He turned and headed toward his desk. "Now why don't you do me a big favor and get the hell outta here before Sheriff Mahoney gets back. He's out picking up Kenny Whitley, and he'll be here any minute. I don't want him to see you here and start asking whether I let you see Macon or not."

"So take me out to the Patterson place and we'll both be gone when he gets back."

"Savannah, dad-gum-it, I—"

The sudden eruption of noise on the sidewalk outside made them both forget their conversation as something sounding like an angry mob charged the front of the building.

The door opened and what appeared to be the entire citizenry of McGill poured into the station.

Then Savannah realized: It was only her family.

Gran led the pack—Waycross and Alma, as well as two more of Savannah's sisters, the bride-to-be Marietta and Vidalia, along with Vidalia's husband, Butch, and their two sets of twins. Reids filled the room, wall to wall.

Alpha female Gran was in full howl. "Where is my grandson?" she demanded of Deputy Stafford. "Savannah left almost an hour ago and said she'd be bringing him home. But since she's still here . . ." she punched a thumb in Savannah's direction, ". . . it's obvious that you're being a mule's hind end about this. I swear, I'm going to have to take this up with your granddaddy. Him and me go way back, you know."

Tom held up both hands, as though fending off a disgruntled mob. "Now, Mrs. Reid, I know you're riled up, and I understand you want to have Macon home with your family just as soon as possible. But it ain't gonna happen, not any time soon. I'm sorry, but when you get that straight, you'll feel a whole heap better."

"Don't you dare condescend to me, young man. I was an old lady when you were still in diapers. It's not your place to tell me what I should think."

"You're right, and I apologize, ma'am. I meant no disrespect." He shook his head, and Savannah couldn't help feeling a bit sorry for him. She had been in the same situation with families before. Relatives often held the idea that their loved one couldn't possibly do anything wrong, and therefore, law enforcement had to be the enemy.

Butch stepped forward, his T-shirt grease-stained from a hard day's work at the garage. He held his unruly seven-year-old son, Jack, by one hand and with the other he corralled Jack's twin, Jillian.

He gave Savannah a brief nod. "Hi, Van."

"Hey yourself," she replied. She had last seen him and her sister Vidalia a couple of years ago, when Vidalia had left him after a matrimonial spat and shown up on Savannah's doorstep. She'd had Jack and Jillian in tow and an enormously pregnant tummy. Savannah could see that the youngest set of twins were filling up and out in typical Reid style. Vidalia held one chubby cherub in each arm. She, too, gave Savannah a warm smile of welcome. But Savannah could see she had been crying.

They were all worried sick about Macon.

More worried than he seems to be about himself, Savannah thought, wishing she could give him a swift kick in the pants.

Butch turned to Deputy Stafford. "Is it a matter of bail?" he asked. "If it is, I'll haul the banker outta bed and get him to give me a loan on the garage. We don't want Macon sittin' in a cell. It just ain't right, when he didn't do nothin' wrong."

"Yeah," said Marietta, elbowing her way through the crowd until she stood front and center. "He's going to be head usher in my wedding, and he's got to go to the rehearsal and stuff like that. He doesn't have time to be arrested right now."

Dear Marietta, Savannah thought. *Always practical. Always thinking of others.*

"Marietta, don't be a fool if you can help it," Gran said, pushing her aside. "Deputy Stafford doesn't give a rat's rear end about your wedding. A man's been killed, for heaven's sake."

"That's right," Tom Stafford interjected. "A judge has been murdered, and your Macon is our prime suspect. We can't just let him—"

"Why?" Gran wanted to know. "Why do you think it's him? What evidence do you have that makes you believe he did it?"

Savannah saw her opening and dove in, headfirst. "As a matter of fact, Gran," she said, "Tom was just about to take me out to the scene of the crime. We were headed there when y'all came charging in here like General Sherman's army."

She gave Tom a quick, sideways grin. His eyes narrowed; his lips pulled tight and thin.

On a roll, she continued, "I told you, if everybody would just stay home and tend to business there, I'd take care of things down here."

Gran's sharp eyes peered at Savannah, and Savannah realized her grandmother wasn't fooled a bit by this charade. But the old lady was keen enough to see that a game was afoot and to play along.

"Oh," she said, "well, that's different. If you've got everything under control here . . ."

"Like I said," Savannah added, "Tom was just getting ready to drive me to the Patterson place to check things out. Weren't you, Tom?"

She turned to him, smiling brightly.

From the scowl on his face, she half expected him to growl and snap at her like an irritated Rottweiler. Instead, with a stony calm in his voice, he said, "Sorry, Savannah, but like I told you before, I can't just walk out and lock the door behind me when I've got prisoners upstairs."

She thought for a moment, then made her next move on the mental chessboard. "Isn't that old fella . . . the pharmacist next door . . . let's see, what was his name . . . Mr. Jeter . . . isn't he a sworn, part-time, volunteer deputy? He could come over and watch things till Sheriff Mahoney gets back, right?"

Before Tom could reply, Butch piped up, "I'll get him. Here, Marietta, hold on to these kids, and I'll fetch him straightaway."

Butch disappeared before Tom could utter a word, and only seconds later, a delighted, if rather frail and decrepit Mr. Jeter materialized. Excitement glittered in his eyes that were topped with bushy silver eyebrows. A neatly trimmed goatee sprouted from his chin, and in his white pharmacist's smock, he looked like a mad scientist from a silent movie.

"Yes, sir," he said, practically snapping to attention in front of Tom Stafford. "Butch says you need me to take charge for a few minutes?"

Tom looked down at the pharmacist, at Gran, whose stern expression dared him to do otherwise, then at Savannah. She gave him her best beguiling puppy-dog look and received a drop-dead one in return.

"You don't exactly have to be in charge of nothin'," he said, sounding like a defeated soldier at the end of a bloody battle. "Just watch the desk till the sheriff gets back."

Savannah felt her heart leap with hope. Not a giant leap, but a definite, happy little skip in the right direction.

"Sure thing." Mr. Jeter dug a badge out of his smock pocket and pinned it proudly on his lapel. "I'll keep everything under control. Sure will."

"Let's go," Savannah said, waving her family toward the door. "You guys get along home, and I'll fill you in when I get back."

"How long do you figure you'll be?" Gran asked. "Should we expect you for supper?"

"Oh, I don't know." Savannah gave Tom another look. Yes, thunderclouds had definitely gathered on his brow. She predicted the storm would break the moment he had her alone in his car. "If I'm not home once it's on the table, go ahead and eat without me. Tom here said he'd show me everything at the scene, and that's bound to take a while."

As she watched her temporarily mollified family filing out the door, Savannah heard Tom say to Mr. Jeter, "By the way, Fred . . . when Sheriff Mahoney does get back, just tell him I had to run a couple of errands. And you don't need to say nothing about . . . you know . . . all of these folks coming around. Mahoney would just get all riled up and we don't need that, now do we?"

"No!" Fred Jeter shook his head vigorously. "We sure don't need none of that."

"Come along, Savannah." Tom took her by the arm and propelled her toward the door.

Yes . . . judging by the way his fingers were digging into her biceps, she wasn't at all eager to be alone with him. Those thunderbolts would be flying right and left, and she'd have to be quick on her feet to avoid getting struck.

"Let's get one thing straight right from the get-go," Tom said as he peeled out of the parking lot and headed his patrol car down Main Street. "I'm not doing this because you finagled me into it, though Lord knows, you tried hard enough. I'm taking you out here to make your grandma happy, 'cause she's a fine person, and I think a lot of her."

Savannah dug her fingers into the car seat as he rounded a few more corners at breakneck speed. She was happy to be wearing her seat belt as she entertained fantasies of being hurled headfirst through the windshield.

So much for dodging verbal lightning bolts. The Grim Reaper would more likely appear in the form of a fatal accident at the hands of a passive-aggressive male—one who expressed his anger by applying more pressure to the pedal.

"So," she ventured, "does that mean you're not too sweet on Gran's offspring at the moment?"

"Let's just say, I've been sweeter . . . like when her offspring wasn't twistin' my arm outta its damned socket."

At the crossroads on the edge of town, they turned north onto a narrow, but smooth-surfaced asphalt road. Waves of shimmering heat rose from the black surface, and Savannah reached down to direct the air-conditioning vent onto her face.

On either side of the road, cotton fields stretched almost as far as the eye could see. Exploding from their dark husks, the white tufts looked like tiny snowballs that were somehow immune to the heat of the afternoon sun.

"How's Mary Beth?" she said, cutting him a sideways look.

"My baby sister is just fine, thanks for asking," he replied. "But then, she hasn't killed nobody lately, so I don't have to go around manipulating people into doing things that goes against their conscience."

"Against your . . . wait a second. Hold on just a damned minute!" She grabbed his arm. "Stop the car. Right here, right now!"

He did as she said, slamming on the brakes and bringing the cruiser to an abrupt halt. The stench of burned rubber filled the car.

"Are you telling me, Tom Stafford," she said, "that taking me out to the old Patterson place is violating some code of honor that you hold near and dear? 'Cause if it is, I'll get out of this car right here and walk back to Gran's. Lord knows, I don't want an old friend to endanger his immortal soul by doing me any favors."

They sat for what seemed to her a long, torturous couple of hours and glared at each other. Though it was probably no more than five seconds.

"You're a civilian," he said. "You've got no business at the scene. It's wrong to take you there."

"I'm a damned good investigator with a heck of a lot of experience under my belt, who might—imagine this, if you can—see something at that scene that you missed. Ever think about that?"

From the deepening glower on his face, she realized she had taken the wrong tack.

"Oh, I get it," she said, too angry to censor herself. "You *have* thought of that. In fact, that just might be part of the reason why you don't want to—"

"That's enough, Savannah. You may be the best investigator that ever lived, the reincarnation of friggin' Sherlock Holmes himself, but you're a family member and you've got a vested interest that keeps you from being impartial."

"Oh, come on, Tom. In a town this small, everybody knows everybody and is related to most bodies. There won't be one person involved in this case who's not biased one way or the other. Who do you figure will be prosecuting Macon if he's brought to trial?"

Tom turned away and stared at a crow on a fence post a few moments before answering, "Mack Goodwin. He's our P.A. now."

"Judge Patterson's son-in-law. Now, how's that for impartiality?"

He punched the gas, and the cruiser shot forward. "You made your point. Let's just say, I'm taking you there in an official capacity, as an investigator."

"Thank you, Tommy," she said, using her softest, too-sweet voice.

He grunted. "Just try to act like a professional, not Macon's big sister . . . if you can help yourself."

"Okay."

"And stop calling me Tommy."

"As you wish, Deputy Thomas Gilbert Stafford . . . sir."

He just shook his head, sighed, and kept driving.

Chapter
5

Long ago, Savannah had come to the realization that few things appeared as grand, when seen through adult eyes, as they had when viewed as a child. But the old Patterson estate had been built in 1855 with the intention of impressing visitors . . . an opulent display of Southern affluence. And even with jaded, experienced eyes, she had to admit the old plantation manor was, very simply, magnificent.

Fields that still yielded some of the richest harvests of cotton in the state, hillsides lined with neat rows of pecan and peach trees, and the magnificent, Greek Revival mansion declared the wealth of the Patterson family. Theirs was a rare fortune that had survived the ravages of the Civil War; or, as the post-war generations of Pattersons had preferred to call it, "The Great War of the Northern Oppression."

After passing through enormous wrought-iron gates, visitors traveled a long driveway, lined with centuries-old live oaks that formed a graceful arch, shading the passersby. Like delicate, gray-green lace, Spanish moss hung from the oaks' limbs, adding a feminine elegance that personified the "Old South."

Savannah had only ridden this road once before, when her elementary school had been treated to a Halloween field trip to the plantation to receive a complimentary pumpkin for the class jack-o-lantern.

On that occasion, while bouncing along in the back seat of the school bus, the young Savannah had allowed herself a fanciful journey back to a time when ladies in hoop skirts and yards of crinoline rolled along in carriages, spinning lacy parasols. In her fertile imagination, gentlemen in hunting jackets rode great roans and bays, as a pack of hounds bayed at their heels.

Such a grand image . . . until you completed the scene by picturing the slaves working in the nearby fields.

Like many poor Southern kids growing up in the fifties and sixties, Savannah had spent her late summers picking cotton for money to buy school clothes. And since those days, no work she had ever done compared to that back-breaking, miserable labor.

All too well, she knew the heat, the humidity, the dry, thorny husks of the cotton bolls that scratched and jabbed your hands until they bled. Stooping for hours, dragging a bag of cotton behind you that held your bounty, which was worth . . . if you were lucky . . . three cents per pound. The agony of the first hour of the day, when stiff, aching muscles and swollen fingers cried for rest and healing. But rest wasn't an option.

A talented picker who picked fast and hard from sunrise to sunset could harvest that magic number—one hundred pounds in a single day. And earn three dollars.

But only if you were white and free. The slaves had received only the minimal sustenance to ensure that they would be able to return to the field the next day. Screaming muscles, bleeding fingers and all.

No, Savannah didn't envy the people, black or white, who had worked those fields. Thankfully, mechanized harvesting had rendered that particular form of torture basically obsolete.

She had wondered, then as now, if any of the Patterson family had been troubled by the way their wealth was accumulated. And now, as then, she decided it probably hadn't bothered them one iota.

The few memories she had of the judge and his wife were of

an aloof, conceited pair, who may have opened their home every Halloween for the fifth graders of McGill Elementary, but they expected the fortunate little beggars to be oh-so-grateful for their paper cup of orangeade and the free pumpkin. And they reminded the children as they left to be sure to tell their parents to remember the kindnesses of Judge Patterson in any upcoming election.

"With Judge Patterson gone, is that the end of the Patterson clan?" Savannah asked, deciding not to add an editorial about how she figured that wouldn't be an unbearable loss.

"The Patterson name, yeah," Tom replied as he guided the cruiser into the circle at the end of the drive and parked in front of the mansion. "Patterson only had the one daughter . . . officially, that is. He's littered the county with unofficial offspring that polite folks don't talk about."

"Except behind his back."

"Of course, that's why they're considered polite. His daughter, Katherine, married Mack and—"

"The county prosecutor?"

"Yeah, and they had one little girl. Katherine died last year. It was a real shame, her not even being thirty yet."

Savannah's investigator's ears perked up. "Natural causes?"

"Don't get all excited. Talk around town said it was a pregnancy gone wrong or one of those female ailments."

"Female ailments aren't usually fatal in your twenties. What was it exactly?"

"Well, this one was fatal. And I don't rightly know what it was. That's another thing polite guys don't do—go around asking for particulars about ladies' problems."

He swung open his door. "Do you want to see this crime scene, or do you want to talk about embarrassing topics like female ailments?"

When Savannah opened her own door, the heat enveloped her with suffocating humidity. A chestful of dry, eighty-degree air in Southern California seemed to contain a lot more oxygen, she decided, than the same deep breath of Georgia atmosphere.

Looking up at the imposing mansion, with its gleaming white Corinthian pillars—eight, not the standard antebellum six—she experienced a momentary surge of insecurity. For a few seconds, she was eleven years old again and painfully aware that this house, this world, was a million miles away from the humble shotgun house on the other side of town where Gran had raised her and her siblings.

But at the thought of Granny Reid, Savannah's backbone straightened, along with her resolve. She might have been raised on the opposite side of town, far away from the local aristocrats, but she was of noble blood, nevertheless.

Chin up, she headed for the wide steps that led to the verandah and the massive front door with its beveled glass. The Pattersons might have once been proud and powerful. But the judge himself had been murdered right here in his mansion, and the patriarch who had meted out justice as a lifelong career was in need of some old-fashioned justice himself.

Whoever had killed him, Savannah was sure—pretty sure—it wasn't her brother. And that meant the real murderer was still running around as free as a crow.

Yes, the mighty Judge Patterson needed this little girl, all grown up now, from the other side of town, whether he knew it or not. Even if he was past caring, he needed a good investigator.

"A bit intimidating, ain't it," Tom said as he fell into step beside her. "Remember when we were kids and the school brought us out here at Halloween?"

"Hmmm, I was just thinking about that. The place gave me the creeps even then. Remember the skeleton they had hanging from a noose from that big oak tree?"

He looked over at the giant, gnarled oak that shaded a white lattice gazebo and laughed. "Yeah, I remember being freaked by that thing, too. Pretty tacky, now that I think of it. Very tacky, in fact, considering the brutal history of this place. Legend has it that more than one lynching victim still haunts that tree. People say they've seen them hanging there at night sometimes, when there's a full moon. But I don't reckon you need to hear about that now."

As they started up the steps, he slipped his arm through hers. It was a simple gesture, but one that went straight to her heart. Tom had always been attuned to her feelings; that had been a large part of his appeal. And, of course, the fact that he actually enjoyed kissing, for long, long sessions in peach-scented groves on a summer evening, didn't hurt.

The bright yellow police tape stretched across the door jerked her back to the present. Putting old memories, bitter and sweet, aside, she switched into professional mode.

"Has the house been sealed since it happened?"

"Sure." He gave her a sideways glance and a half smile. "What do you think, we're a bunch of country bumpkins down here? We watch *Court TV.* We know how to process a crime scene as good as the next guy."

Reaching into his pants pocket, he pulled out two pairs of surgical gloves. "Put these on," he said, handing a pair to her. "I don't want no California bimbo contaminating my scene."

After donning his own, he took a set of keys from his pocket and unlocked the heavy oak door with its beveled glass oval. "This door wasn't the original one, you know," he said as he ushered her into a dimly lit, black-and-white tiled foyer. "The Yankees knocked down the first one when they set up their temporary hospital here."

"Oh, yes, I remember our teacher telling us about that." Savannah felt a slight shiver, despite the sultry heat of the day, as she walked across the entry and heard her footsteps echo through the heavy stillness of the house.

To her left, an arched doorway led to an old-fashioned parlor with Victorian-style furniture: diamond-tufted sofa, leather wing-back chairs, Tiffany lamps sitting on marble-topped tables with clawfoot legs, and a graceful fireplace with an intricately carved mantel.

A matching door on the right opened into a formal dining room with a Waterford crystal chandelier hanging from the center of the ornate plasterwork ceiling. Mahogany wainscoting covered the lower half of the walls, dusky-rose moiré silk the upper. Heavy silver service gleamed on spotless linen that covered the table, where twelve guests could be comfortably seated.

"Oh, man, we could have used a table like that at our house," she said. "We'd have put Waycross and Macon at opposite ends and avoided a lot of food fights. More than once, Gran sent those boys to the bathroom in the middle of a meal to wash the mashed potatoes out of their hair."

"Yep, those brothers of yours always were a handful," Tom replied. "I remember when Macon got busted for selling little bags of grass at school."

Savannah smiled. "Well, at least he wasn't misrepresenting his product. He said it was grass, and it was . . . lawn clippings, not pot. So what if some of the kids tried to smoke it and got a little nauseous?"

"Did you know that I busted him myself that time when your gran came out to California to visit you for a few weeks?"

"No way!"

"Yessiree. He was making moonshine there in her bathtub, and it sent a couple of guys from the pool hall to the hospital."

"He never was much of a cook." Savannah bit her lower lip thoughtfully. "Ah . . . I do recall Gran saying something about how the finish was eaten away on the tub when she got back. Macon said he'd scrubbed it a bit too hard, trying to impress her."

"Like I said, he's a pistol."

She gave him a hard, penetrating look. "Yeah, but he ain't a killer."

"So says you."

"So says me, and I know him a lot better than you."

"You love him, too. You remember him with mashed potatoes in his hair. That sort of thing fuzzes up a body's powers of perception."

"Show me where the murder happened, Deputy Tom, and we'll see then how sharp or fuzzy my perception is."

He led her down a long hallway that bisected the lower floor of the house and into a room on the left that seemed darker, more sinister than the others, even before she walked through the doorway.

Many times before, Savannah had sensed the scene of a homicide as she approached it, the residual horror almost palpable in the walls, the furniture, the wood, the fabrics as she entered the room. Sometimes, she also experienced the accompanying sensation of an uneasy presence in the very air.

A room with no one in it should feel empty, she had often thought as a trickle of apprehension skittered down her back like a long drop of cold sweat. And having been raised with tales galore about "haunts," Savannah had to exercise a certain degree of self-control simply to remain at the scene and do her job.

Like the Southern gentleman he was, Tom ushered her in before him, although she wouldn't have minded forgoing the courtesy this once. As unseen presences went, the old judge scored pretty darned high on the old ghost Richter scale.

Behind her, Tom flipped on a light switch. Instantly, the room appeared more inviting, bathed in the golden glow from brass sconces on the mahogany-paneled walls between bookshelves that held everything from leather-bound classics to modern paperbacks. Comfortable reading chairs with giant tufted ottomans were drawn close to the fireplace, beside floor lamps with beaded fringe shades.

On another occasion, Savannah might have considered the room cozy, if it weren't for the reek of murder in the air and the taped outline in the shape of a body on the oriental carpet beside the baby grand piano.

A dark, ugly stain marked where the corpse's head had lain. Savannah could just imagine the effect the grisly scene photographs would have on a local jury. Even if the judge hadn't been well loved by his community, his neighbors would have a deep, emotional response to pictures of their neighbor lying on his own carpet, his head in a pool of blood.

"So," she said, "Colonel Mustard did it in the library with a revolver . . . or an automatic? What do you figure?"

"The coroner found the bullet inside the skull. It was a .22 . . . rattled around inside his brain a while before it came to a stop," Tom replied.

Savannah grimaced. "Nice." She walked over to the taped carpet and knelt beside the outline, studying the rug and the surrounding polished wood floor. "What time does the coroner figure he got it?"

"A little after midnight last night."

"Last night?" She stood up abruptly. "This murder happened just last night, and you've already got my brother in jail for it? That's pretty fast, Tom . . . even by big-city standards. I figured it was at least a couple of days ago."

Tom's jaw tightened, but he didn't answer her thinly veiled accusation.

"I assume you've got something you consider solid," she continued, "or you wouldn't have—"

"*Several* somethings," he interjected. "One of them being an eyewitness."

"To the murder itself?"

"To the getaway." He shrugged. "Close enough."

"Not close enough for me! Not even *nearly* close enough for my little brother to be cooling his heels in your flea-infested jail."

Tom sighed. "Like I said before: You're not exactly unbiased . . . and my cells don't have fleas, unless the prisoners bring 'em in themselves."

In the interest of cooperative investigating, Savannah decided to let that one slide.

She glanced around the room, noting the signs of forensic processing. "I see you dusted for prints," she said, pointing to a fine layer of black residue on the tabletops, some of the wall trim, and the window sills.

"Yep."

"Get anything?"

"Yep."

Savannah waited a few seconds. "You want to elaborate?"

"Nope."

She sighed. "Tom, we're not going to get very far if you give me nothing but monosyllabic answers."

"Look, you twisted my arm outta joint to get me to bring you here. I did; you're here. I never said I was going to show you my cards."

"You know what that tells me?" Her eyes narrowed as she looked him up and down. "If you've got to hold your cards that close, you're not too sure of your hand, big boy."

He winced, just slightly, but enough for her to know that her dart had found its mark.

"Did you lift any prints or not?" she asked again.

"Yeah. Several of them," he replied. "Two nice clear ones . . . your brother's. And a pretty good one that looks like Kenny Whitley's."

Savannah felt as if her heart was in a plane that had just hit an air pocket. "Where were they?"

He nodded toward the window. "Over there, on the bottom sill. They were pointing toward the room, like they would be if somebody was climbing into the house through the window."

"The window was open when you all got here?"

He hesitated and glanced away. "No. Actually, it was closed. Why?"

"Just wondering. Were there any identifiable prints on the top of the window . . . where you'd put your hands if you were closing it?"

"Yes. They look like the judge's."

Walking around the taped shape on the carpet, she went over to the window and looked outside. On tiptoe, she could see the ground below, a flower bed planted with azaleas. The ground around the bushes was bare and muddy from previous rains. A few stakes and more yellow tape marked off the area.

"What did you find out there?" she asked.

"A milk crate. And tennis-shoe prints. Two different sets."

"Did you make plaster casts?"

"Yep."

She was almost afraid to ask, "Any matches?"

"Don't know yet, but one set looks like the shoes we took off Macon when we brought him in. The size is about the same and so's the tread. We're having a lab in Atlanta look at everything, just to make sure."

For a moment, the hard, guarded look slid off his face, and she saw a dim light of sympathy in his eyes. "We really aren't trying to railroad anybody, Savannah," he said, "let alone your little brother."

"I never thought you were," she replied. "I know you better than that, Tom. Mahoney on the other hand, I never did like him very much."

"Ah, Mahoney's all right."

"Yeah? Well, I heard my mom tell a friend of hers that he paid her five dollars to vote for him, back in the late seventies."

Tom shrugged. "Don't make me no nevermind how he got the office. Mahoney does a good job. This is the first murder we've had here in ages. Mack Goodwin's a good prosecutor, too. If we do bring him a good case, he makes sure it goes to court and the guy gets put away. We don't handle our criminals with kid gloves the way y'all do in California . . . bunch o' pansy liberals."

Savannah thought of Dirk and laughed. "Don't go judging us so harshly, Deputy Tom. We've got our share of dyed-in-the-wool rednecks in the West, too, you know."

Savannah left the window and strolled around the room, her eyes scanning every surface. On the wall behind the piano hung a large, gilt-edged frame. The protective front glass had been shattered; shards of glass lay on the carpet below it. Inside, she saw half a dozen small metal objects displayed on a maroon-velvet lining. Upon closer inspection she realized they were military awards, medals from the War Between the States. Confederate, of course.

From blanks in the display, she could tell that some were missing.

"Is this what my brother and Kenny Jr. were supposed to be after?" she asked.

"Mahoney thinks so. Those things are worth a fortune if you sell 'em to the right people."

She sent him a doubtful sideways look. "Do you figure either Macon or Kenny have the connections to fence something like those medals? Or even the sense to realize they're worth anything?"

"Seems they did, huh?"

"Have you found the medals?"

"Not yet. But, like you said, it was just last night. So we're doing pretty good so far."

As she left the frame and continued around the room, she passed a glass-enclosed gun case. Inside, an impressive array of antique and modern guns were displayed against more maroon velvet, everything from pearl-handled dueling pistols to a high-powered hunting rifle.

"Why do you figure a couple of young guys would go after those medals when they could have broken into this gun cabinet instead?" she asked. "Those Whitley boys always had a yen for firepower."

"Yeah, I know. And so did your brother." Tom pointed to a small circle on the floor near the window that had been marked with yellow chalk. "That's where we found it."

"Found what?"

"The .22 Ruger that your little brother bought from the local Sports Mart last July first. I checked the records there myself this morning."

He paused and took a deep breath. "Of course, we've sent the gun and the bullet from inside the judge's head off to Atlanta. Despite its meandering around inside that hard skull of his, it was still in pretty decent shape."

Feeling her poker face sliding off into the vicinity of her chest,

Savannah turned away from him and pretended to study the guns with renewed interest. She gulped, swallowing nothing but air; her mouth was completely dry of spit.

"We won't know for sure till they get done with their tests," he added, stating the obvious that she had no desire to hear. "But we figure that your brother's Ruger . . . the one layin' over there by the window . . . with his fingerprints on the sill . . . was the murder weapon."

Chapter

6

As soon as Savannah stepped out of the truck, she smelled the heavenly aroma of fried chicken coming from Gran's house, and the savory scent nearly brought tears to her eyes. Again.

She suddenly realized that since she had set foot on Georgia soil, less than eight hours ago, she had cried at least five times, but hadn't eaten once.

Quickening her step, she headed for the back door . . . the fastest way to the kitchen and the source of that amazing smell.

Where most people might have had a backyard, maybe a lawn rimmed with flower beds, a picnic table, a swing set . . . Gran had her garden. It was a far more practical use for a patch of land than perfectly manicured grass.

You couldn't feed a starving hoard long on lawn clippings. And, a survivor of the Great Depression, Granny Reid was practical, if anything.

Part of the reason why Savannah's mouth was watering lay in the fact that, along with the fried chicken, mashed potatoes, and cream gravy, there would be a platter of ripe beefsteak tomatoes, fresh corn on the cob, and maybe some cucumber slices soaking in a bowl of brine and vinegar with slices of onion and a sprig of dill. All grown in neat, well-tended rows behind the little shot-gun house.

And tomorrow morning's breakfast would feature the world's best eggs, freshly plucked from the nests in the henhouse on the other side of the two-acre property.

To make sure everyone got off to a carbohydrate-energy packed day, there would also be a bread basket filled with hot-from-the-oven buttermilk biscuits and a pint of homemade peach preserves on the table. And if the sugar jolt wasn't enough to get your blood flowing, the hot coffee spiked with chicory would do the trick.

Having once been a confirmed "morning person," Savannah could actually remember the childhood joy of waking up to the promise of such a country feast. And she could mark the moment she had become an avowed night owl: the day she had moved to California, away from Georgia and her grandmother's breakfasts.

As she hopped up onto the back porch, she nearly tripped over the ancient bloodhound who lay stretched out beside the washing machine, his belly resting against the cool metal.

She noted the differences the years had made: the washer was now an automatic, not the old-fashioned wringer that Gran had sworn by, and Colonel Beauregard's muzzle had grown white with age. Also, he had grown, if possible, even less energetic than he had been eight years before.

"Beau Bear," she said, bending down to stroke the long silky ears, "been chasing any coons or squirrels lately?"

His lazy grunt made her laugh. He didn't even bother to open both eyes, but peered up at her from beneath one drooping lid.

"All you ever chased was your dinner bowl," she said, tickling the floppy jowls and bristly whiskers. "You're as worthless as those cats I feed and house back in California, and not half as good-looking."

Her appetite tweaked by the sounds of conversation and the rattle of cutlery against pottery, Savannah left the old hound to his day-long nap and entered the screen door. Again, she had the impression that half the county must be crammed into a tiny room, but as in the sheriff's office, a quick scan of the occupants

identified them all as her kinsmen . . . and kinswomen . . . and kinskids.

"Pull up a chair, Savannah," Gran said as she carried a bowl full of green beans from the stove to the table. "Marietta, set your sister a plate, and Vidalia, mind your young'uns before they tear up house and home."

With the beans in one hand, Gran used the other to swoop one of Vidalia's twins off the counter, where he teetered on one foot, trying to reach a cookie jar in the cupboard.

"Dang it, Jack," Butch said, leaving the table and grabbing his son by the collar, "If I have to talk to you one more time, I'm gonna slap you buck-necked and hide your clothes."

"I don't like standing at the counter to eat," Jack's twin, Jillian, complained, poking at the mound of mashed potatoes before her. "How come we have to stand up when we eat at Gran's house?"

Sitting at the far end of the table, Waycross shoved half a cornbread muffin into his mouth. " 'Cause there's not enough room at the table," he told her. "Don't bellyache. Standin' up makes you grow taller. How do you think I got this big?"

"Why can't we eat in the living room and watch TV, like we do at home?" Jillian continued. "We're missing my favorite show."

" 'Cause we're not heathens. . . ." Gran patted her on the back as she passed her and tucked a wayward curl behind her ear. "Eatin' off our laps in front of the idiot box like a gang o' Philistines."

"How come the grownups get to sit down?" Jack whined.

"Because they worked hard all day," Gran replied. "And some of us haven't had a chance to sit down yet. When you get grown up and put in a hard day's work, you'll get to sit down at the table instead of standing there at the counter. Do you need more lemonade? Is that iced tea sweet enough for you?"

Savannah glanced over at Marietta and Vidalia, wondering if either of them would offer their seat to their grandmother, or maybe, in a fit of generosity, even volunteer to help her serve.

Then Savannah sighed, realizing that nothing had changed.

As before, it was Alma who jumped to her feet. "Here, Gran, you sit down now and eat your supper before everything gets cold. I'll refill the gravy boat." She nudged Waycross as she hurried past him and said, "Get one of them fold-up patio chairs off the back porch for Savannah, and y'all schooch over to make some room for her. I swear, you've got the manners of wolves, the bunch o' ya."

After a minute or so of rearranging furniture on worn linoleum and shuffling mismatched china around the Formica-topped table, Savannah found herself seated beside her grandmother, a rapidly filling plate in front of her.

"Did anybody bother to say grace before y'all dived in here?" Gran asked.

The table's occupants looked at each other sheepishly, then bowed their heads.

"Lord, have mercy on this motley crew," Gran said, as she folded her hands and closed her eyes. "And we thank you from the bottom of our hearts for each and every one of them. They are, indeed, precious in thy sight. Thank you for bringing Savannah home to us, safe and sound, and we ask you to restore Macon to us, just as quick as you can. Be with him in his hour of darkness and incarceration and bless this food. Amen."

For one blissful moment, there was silence. The only sounds Savannah could hear were Beauregard snoring on the back porch and the ticking of the cat clock on the wall.

When Savannah was ten years old, she had saved her nickels and dimes for months to buy that clock for Gran on Mother's Day. It had big green "diamond" eyes that shifted back and forth as its tail swung to and fro.

At ten, she had considered the "cat clock," as they called it, the height of glamor, class, and sophistication. And thirty years later, she still loved it, because the clock was Gran's. And anything even remotely connected to her grandmother was sacred to Savannah.

She reached over and patted the soft, work-worn hand and gave Gran a smile that was readily returned.

Then, the three-second silence broke.

"You pray too-o-o-o long, Gran," Jillian said. "I almost went to sleep in my food."

Jack chimed in, "Daddy, if *I* go to sleep in *my* food, do I still have to eat it?"

Butch growled, a chicken wing sticking out of the side of his mouth. "Eat it or wear it."

Yes, Savannah thought, *there's no place like home.*

And that just might be a good thing.

Savannah and Alma stood at the kitchen sink, Savannah washing, Alma drying. At the table, Marietta and Vidalia were sitting, still nursing tall glasses of iced tea, discussing wedding details ad nauseum. Butch and Waycross had taken the kids—Vidalia's four and Marietta's two—into the empty lot next door to play a game of softball. Even Beauregard had stirred from his long summer's nap to join the fun. He darted among the children and tall grass as enthusiastically as if he were hunting grizzlies.

Glancing over her shoulder at her two sisters, Savannah thought of how Gran had once, kindly, described them. "Not exactly work-brickle, if you know what I mean."

But Gran was sitting in the living room in her gold leatherette recliner, reading her Bible by the light of an avocado-green pole lamp, circa 1968. As long as Savannah could remember, her grandmother had retired to that recliner after dinner to read her daily Psalm. Those few minutes were the only ones she had faithfully taken for herself every day. And the troops had been told, years ago, that she was only to be disturbed under two circumstances: the tourniquet wouldn't stop the bleeding, or the fire extinguisher wouldn't put out the blaze.

"Gran looked tired tonight," Savannah said to Alma as she passed a platter under the stream of rinse water and then handed it across to her. "I'm worried about her."

"Yeah, this thing with Macon is really takin' a toll on her," Alma replied, drying it with a dishtowel with a chain of daisies and the word "Thursday" embroidered along the border. Another

object that was sacred to Savannah; Gran had done the needle-
work. "She just can't stand it when one of us is in trouble. Once
she gets over being mad at us for whatever we done, she starts
feeling bad, thinking she did something wrong when she raised
us."

Savannah glanced over her shoulder at Vidalia and Marietta.

"I'm just worried sick about this divorce thing of Lester's,"
Marietta was saying. "If his wife won't sign the papers before the
wedding day, I just don't know what I'm gonna do! That dad-
gummed Lucille is just holdin' things up to be spiteful, you
know. She don't want him, but she don't want me to have him.
We never did get along, not even back in high school. She was
jealous when I was chosen homecoming princess instead of her,
and she never got over it. Now she's just . . ."

"And then Atlanta beat her little sister in the Miss McGill
pageant. She didn't like that either."

"Oh, I don't even want to hear about Atlanta," Marietta said,
waving a hand in front of her face as though shooing away flies.
"My own sister won't even come to my wedding. It's not like
Nashville is that far away."

"But she's got a lot going on there with her big singin' career.
She actually got a job doing backup for somebody who used to
play with somebody famous," Vidalia said, an ugly smirk on her
face that looked a lot like jealousy to Savannah.

"Yeah, now that she's a hotshot country singer, she doesn't
have time to come home and help her sister arrange a nice wedding. I tell you, I'm just plumb wore out with it all."

Savannah turned back to her dishes and ignored the rest. She
had to; it was either tune her out or beat Marietta soundly about
the head and ears with a frying pan.

"You know," Savannah said, elbowing Alma, "there are two
kinds of people in this world . . ."

"Yeah?"

She nodded toward the two at the table. "There are those who
are willing to work . . . and those who are perfectly willing to let
them."

Alma snickered, then shrugged. "I don't care, if it gives me a chance to be with you. I miss you really bad, Van."

"I miss you, too, honey bunny. You should come to visit me sometime in California, stay for a few weeks and see the sights."

"I'd love to, but I need to be here, you know, for Gran."

"I know. Maybe you both can come out together. We'll take her to Disneyland and she can raise hell with Mickey."

Alma chuckled, then lowered her voice. "Yeah, but somebody around here would have to learn how to cook and clean, or we'd come back to a starved bunch and a filthy house."

"I was wondering," Savannah whispered, "if they're here all the time. I mean, I thought Vi and Butch lived over the garage and Marietta had a place in back of her hair salon."

"They do. They just hang out here for food and baby-sitting."

As Savannah applied steel wool and elbow grease to the crusted skillet, she made a silent vow to give her sisters a stern talking-to.

Granny Reid might have more than her share of life wisdom and old-fashioned horse sense, but, like most truly kind and loving people, Gran had a blind spot when it came to those closest to her heart. And that weakness left her vulnerable to being taken advantage of.

Such behavior wasn't to be tolerated, and Savannah was prepared to do anything, short of shedding massive amounts of familial blood, to put an end to it.

The screen door opened and slammed closed. Savannah turned to see yet another of her sisters, Cordele. Dressed in a white shirt, buttoned tightly under her chin, a shapeless navy skirt, and black loafers, Cordele looked twenty-seven, going on seventy-seven. Her dark curls were slicked back with copious amounts of gel and held snugly with a black barrette—her only adornment.

"You missed supper," Marietta told her with a smirk that conveyed little, if any, sympathy.

"I grabbed an apple and some yogurt at school." Cordele set a mountain of textbooks on the table. "That's enough . . . for me."

Since she was easily twenty pounds lighter than any of her sisters in the kitchen, the dig couldn't even be considered "thinly veiled."

Cordele didn't bother with such subtleties as tact. She was, very simply, a superior human being—at least in her own opinion—so what was the point in trying to hide the fact?

When she saw Savannah standing at the sink, her eyes lit up momentarily with recognition and affection. But as she hurried over to embrace her older sister, her eyes flicked lightly over Savannah's ample figure, and a slightly sad expression replaced her smile.

"Savannah," she said, putting her arms around her waist and giving her a limp hug, "Gran said you'd probably be here when I got home. You look good. You know . . ." Another quick glance up and down Savannah's full figure. ". . . Considering . . ."

"Yeah, right. Considering," Savannah replied, giving her a hearty embrace, slapping her on the back, and not bothering to dry her wet, sudsy hands first. "I'd say a lot's happened since you left for school . . . when was it, this morning?"

"Eight o'clock. It isn't easy, you know, having to drive all the way to Macon to attend classes, getting your degree, especially in a science field like psychology."

"Eh, big deal," Vidalia said with a snort. "Psychology's just a bunch of stupid stuff about wanting to have sex with your parents, dreaming about trains and tunnels, looking at nasty pictures called inkblots, and other dirty crap like that."

Cordele's chin lifted a couple of notches. "Oh, please, Vi. Just because you have inferiority issues about not even getting your high school diploma, you don't need to insult the noble art of psychology."

"Why don't you sit down," Alma said, shoving a glass into Cordele's hand, "and have some tea?"

"No, I have to hit the books and—"

"Take the tea, Cordele," Savannah said giving her a gentle shove toward an empty chair. "And park yourself right there. We gotta fill you in on the latest family news, and you're gonna want to be sitting down when you hear this."

Fifteen minutes later, when Savannah left the kitchen, Alma was comforting an almost hysterical Cordele, while Vidalia and Marietta laughed at her.

As Savannah walked into the living room, Gran set her Bible and her glasses on the end table and rubbed her eyes wearily. "That Cordele bawling in there?"

Savannah sank onto the sofa next to Gran's chair. "Yeah, I don't think she gives a hoot about Macon, but she's convinced we'll all be ostracized by McGill high society over this."

"No more tea and crumpets with the mayor's wife?" Gran sighed and smiled. "No more thousand-dollar-a-plate fund-raisers for the chamber orchestra? Whatever will I do with all my spare time?"

"Sit in that chair with your toes pointed toward the ceiling. That's what you should be doing a whole lot more of. Let this lazy bunch do for themselves, Gran. You've spoiled them all rotten."

"Ah, old habits are hard to change, Savannah. You know that. I noticed that, even though you're officially the guest tonight, you were the one in there doing dishes. You and Alma always were my hard workers, Lord bless you. And Waycross, too. He mows the front yard for me and weeds the garden without me even asking him to."

"And how about Macon? Does he help out?"

Gran glanced away quickly and cleared her throat. "He does in his own way. Once in a while."

"When's the last time he offered to do something around here?"

Tears filled the old woman's eyes, and she reached for a half-embroidered pillowcase from the basket on the floor beside her chair. "Just last week," she said. "He, well, he brought me a pretty chandelier thing to hang over the kitchen table. It had crystal things hangin' down and all. I told him it was a little outta place in a country kitchen, but thanks anyway."

Savannah was silent for a moment, reading between the lines. Her grandmother would never turn down a gift from a loved one if it was offered in good faith. For years, she had wallpapered the kitchen with their drawings, 100% correct spelling tests, and any school paper that was a "C" or above. Whether the offering was a macaroni-encrusted picture frame sprayed with gold paint, or a piece of clay with a small handprint and an "I Love You, Happy Mother's Day" scrawled in it, any gift was precious.

"Where do you figure Macon got an expensive chandelier like that?" Savannah asked.

"Well, he didn't earn it stocking groceries at Gillespie's grocery store. I reckon he might o' got it at the same place he got that bright-red carpet that he put down in his room out there in the shed."

"What room?"

"He hauled everything outta the toolshed last summer—rigged up a lean-to to store the mower and stuff—and turned the shed into a sort of an apartment for himself. He comes in here to use the restroom and shower and the like, but he sleeps out there."

Savannah didn't want to ask, but she had to. "Did anybody around here . . . ah . . . mention that anything was missing from their house about that time?"

"Two weeks before, a new house that was being built up on the hill outside o' town got busted into."

"Were they missing a chandelier and some red carpet?"

"I didn't hear the particulars."

Gran sniffed and pulled a lace-trimmed handkerchief from the pocket of her housedress. "I guess I shoulda asked for the particulars, huh? If I'd done the right thing and made him tell me the truth . . . if I'd called the law on him . . . maybe he wouldn't be in the trouble he's in now."

Savannah moved onto the ottoman in front of her grandmother's chair and took her hands in hers. "I understand, Gran. It would've been the right thing, to make him 'fess up and all that, but it's not like the time you sent him back to Gillespie's with stolen candy and made him apologize."

"I know." She dabbed at her eyes with the handkerchief. "He's been in trouble before, you know, with him getting caught stealing the hubcaps off Judge Patterson's Cadillac last winter and—"

"He what? Oh, Lord, I didn't know about that."

"Yes, and you heard about the moonshine in the bathtub."

"Yeah, that was bad enough, but Judge Patter—"

"I know, I know. That's why I didn't say nothing. And now I wish I had of. If he'd paid for what he done then, maybe it would've stopped him in this career of crime."

Savannah had to stifle a smile; Gran had a flair for the dramatic, even under normal circumstances. And having a family member incarcerated for homicide was hardly ordinary.

"Don't beat up on yourself, Gran. There's no way to know what would have happened, one way or the other. You've taught that boy—you've taught *all of us*—right from wrong. If he wants to be a donkey's rear end and do what's wrong, he's a grown man and that's on his head, not yours."

Gran blew her nose and nodded. Her tears ceased . . . at least for the moment. "I'm glad you're here, Savannah. I don't know what I'd do without you right now."

"Don't worry about it. You don't have to do without me. I'm right here, and I'll stay till this thing is settled."

Gran's fingers tightened around hers, and for the first time in her life, Savannah felt that she was the stronger of the two women. The sudden reversal of roles startled her. "Are you going to be all right, Gran?"

"Sure I am. I got the good Lord in heaven and my family here on earth. What more do I need . . . except maybe to find out that my grandson didn't do anything worse than steal some carpet and a light fixture."

"If you're all right, I'm going to go poke around in his 'apartment' out there in the shed, see what I can find that might help."

Gran nodded. "That's a good idea. I figure the sheriff will be along any time now with a search warrant, wantin' to do the same."

"That's just what I was thinking. And I'd like to have a look-see first."

Savannah stood and headed for the door leading through the back of the house, then decided to go out the front and avoid her sisters.

"By the way," Gran said, as she reached for the screen-door handle. "I forgot to tell you, your friend, Tammy, called earlier, before dinner. She was just wanting to know that you got here safe and sound."

"Oh, that's right. I promised to give her a call, and I forgot all about it."

"I explained everything to her . . . well, at least some of it . . . and she said if you need her help with anything, you just give her a call, you hear?"

"I'm sure she meant it, too. She's family . . . know what I mean?"

Gran smiled. "I sure do. Some family you're born with, and some you choose to adopt along the way. But they're all family, just the same."

Savannah looked into those blue eyes, so like her own. They were faded, perhaps, but still alight with love and wisdom. Savannah thought, *Who would imagine that eighty-plus years could be so beautiful?*

"If you hadn't been born into my family, Savannah," Gran said, "I would've snapped you up, adoption-style, in a heartbeat and considered myself lucky."

"Same here, Gran. Same here."

The toolshed near the back edge of the property that Macon had turned into his private apartment was little more than a shack, ten feet square. As she walked the foot-worn path through the garden to the shed, Savannah saw the heavy cord he had strung from the house, along the fence, to the peach tree and then to the roof of the tiny structure, to provide electricity.

Macon had always been handy...when he chose to be. Though, unlike the hardworking Waycross, he seldom elected to make his talents useful to others.

Beauregard trotted along at her heels, ears flapping, content to have company for the moment. But as they neared the shed, he stopped in the middle of the path, sat back on his haunches, and howled.

Savannah reached down to pat his head. "You know Macon's gone, don't you. We miss him, too."

The dog whimpered once and rolled his eyes. Then he looked back at the shed and growled.

"You don't have to come with me if you don't want to," she told him. "Run along back to the house. There's supper scraps in your dish, you know."

As though relieved to be dismissed, he took off, heading back to the porch and his dinner bowl.

She laughed and continued on down the path toward the shed.

Nearby, in the poultry pen, she could hear the chickens clucking contentedly, settling into the henhouse for the night. She smelled the cozy, dusty scent of their feathers and recalled the pleasant task of collecting the eggs. Stealing an egg from under a warm, setting chicken beat the heck out of taking a Styrofoam container from the cold refrigerator in a grocery store.

But the shed itself provoked less comforting memories. Miscellaneous greasy car parts littered the ground around the door, and Savannah recalled half a dozen "redneck" and "trailer park trash" jokes about automobile engines dangling from tree limbs in the yard. Twenty—even ten—years ago, Gran wouldn't have allowed such a thing on her property. But with age, her standards and her control on her grandchildren had slipped a bit.

Savannah vowed that if she could get Macon out of that jail and the trouble he was in, she would tell him to get this mess cleaned up, pronto.

She intended to tell him to clean up a lot of things. And if threats of bloodshed were required to light a fire under his rear end, that was fine, too.

When she opened the door, it stuck, swollen from the humidity, tight in its frame. The smell of stale food and dirty laundry
greeted her as she stepped into the gloomy interior . . . and another odor that was unmistakable and all too familiar to her as a
former law enforcement officer.

"Pot," she said to herself. "Yeah, you little turkey-butt, Macon
W. Reid. We're going to have a *lot* to talk about one of these days
soon."

At least, I hope *we have the opportunity to talk about such things,*
she thought. Last week, she would have been worried to hear
that her brother was smoking dope. Now, it seemed the least of
his many problems . . . and hers.

After a few moments of feeling around in the semi-darkness,
she found the extension cord and a plug, tacked side-by-side on
the wall. When she shoved the plug into the socket, the room
was instantly bathed in light . . . glimmering, glittering light.

Gran wasn't kidding about the chandelier that Macon had
brought home. Savannah knew quality Irish crystal when she saw
it, and she also knew this fixture cost more than Macon could
have made in six months at the grocery store.

The brilliant red carpet on the floor felt at least two inches
thick beneath her feet, and that depth of color could only be produced with the highest quality wool.

But the luxury ended there.

A twin bed with some threadbare blankets and dingy sheets
was shoved into one corner. The room's only other furnishings
consisted of a plastic crate that functioned as a table. Upon the
crate sat a boombox, assorted CD's, fast-food remnants, and
empty soda bottles.

Dirty laundry lay in piles on the carpet, and the smell of stale
sweat wafted from a pair of battered sneakers that were sticking
out from under the bed.

Savannah didn't take long to examine the room. There wasn't
much to see. Not much to define a young man's life. The only
signs of productivity a couple of expensive items stolen from
some innocent person's home.

Savannah felt sick at heart, a combination of sad, ashamed, and angry. What did her brother think he was on this planet for . . . to take up space and breathe free air?

He was smart, healthy, and he had been raised to know the value of hard work, the virtue of self-sacrifice, and the difference between right and wrong.

Macon Reid had no excuse for this mess.

She shifted through the stacks of laundry, finding nothing but soiled clothes.

The CD's and boombox represented her brother's only diversions. She thought of Gran's saying about idle hands being the devil's playthings, and understood part of Macon's problems. He didn't have enough to do.

Another vow: If and when she got him out of this current predicament, she'd make sure he had more responsibilities . . . like helping his aged grandmother make ends meet, instead of being a drain on her.

But when Savannah knelt on the floor beside the unmade bed and looked under it, she discovered that her brother had at least one other pastime besides listening to rock and roll, eating junk food, and collecting unwashed laundry.

Strewn under the bed was an impressive—or depressing—collection of pornography. Having seen more than her share of the stuff, Savannah recognized the subject matter as more hard core than the usual newsstand fare.

Little brother Macon had exotic sexual tastes.

"Gr-r-rr," she said as she shuffled the junk around, trying not to see what she was seeing, "I so-o-oo didn't need to know this."

But her uneasiness about the pornography evaporated as her hand closed around something small . . . round . . . cool.

Like a coin.

A coin with a strip of cloth attached to it.

"No," she whispered. "Please, God, no. . . ."

Her fingers curled around it, and she pulled her arm out from under the bed. Slowly, with a sinking feeling of inevitability, she opened her hand and looked.

In her palm lay an old bit of tarnished metal with a multi-colored ribbon. A medal. A Civil War medal . . . similar to the ones that remained in the murdered judge's display.

"Macon," she said, closing her hand around the medal and squeezing it, as though she could somehow make it disappear. "Oh, Macon, no. . . ."

Her throat tightened until she felt she couldn't breathe. She sat down hard on the floor, leaned forward, and hid her face against the side of the mattress.

The last time she had experienced something like that, she had been sparring at her local karate dojo and had taken an unexpected roundhouse kick to her solar plexus.

As soon as she could draw air in and out of her chest again, she steeled her emotions and slid her other hand under the bed. She knew she would find another. She knew there would be at least five more beneath those magazines . . . because there were that many missing from the display. He might have divided them with Kenny Jr., but . . .

No, there were six.

Six. All of them under her brother's bed.

One by one, she found them and laid them on the carpet. They glowed in the chandelier's golden light, like jewels displayed on velvet in a window display.

Somehow, it seemed important to her to line them up in two rows. Two perfectly straight rows, side by side.

A faint voice whispered to her as though speaking from the far end of a long, dark tunnel. It said, "Evidence, Van. You're handling it with your bare hands. Homicide. First-degree homicide."

But the distant warning was barely perceptible because of other sounds, deafening in their clarity, and vivid images that flashed across the screen of her imagination: Macon sitting in a courtroom, the jury foreman reading the verdict, "Guilty, as charged"; Macon being held down by burly prison guards and strapped to a table, arms outstretched, Gran sitting behind the glass, watching, weeping quietly into a lace-edged handkerchief, her lips moving in prayer.

Savannah shook her head, trying to clear the screen. In one fast movement, she swept the medals up off the carpet. She held them so tightly, she thought she could feel the pictures, the words imprinting themselves on her flesh. The metal was no longer cold, but felt as though it were burning a brand into her skin.

Rising to her knees, she shoved the medals into her slacks pocket and knelt there, shaking. For a moment, she tasted a bitterness welling up in her throat and she thought she might be sick, there on her brother's stolen scarlet rug.

"Damn you, Macon," she whispered. "Damn you, damn you!"

With all the self-control she could muster, she finally stood . . . and wondered briefly if her knees would hold her.

That was when she looked out the tiny, dirty window of the shed and saw the car pulling up in front of the house. The sun had set, but in the dim light that remained she could see it was Tom Stafford's cruiser.

The driver's door opened, and Tom stepped out.

When the passenger's door swung open, as well, and Savannah saw Sheriff Mahoney haul himself out of the car, she felt the bile rise again. She choked it down.

The two men made their way to the front door of the house.

Savannah knew she had one minute, two at the most to . . . what? What the hell could she do?

Macon in the death chamber.

Gran crying.

Alma beside her, trying to comfort her, but . . .

The other image even clearer. The taped outline of Judge Patterson there in his library. His home. His bloodstains on the floor.

Cold blood. Murdered in cold blood in his own home.

"I hate you, Macon," she whispered. "God help me, at this moment I really do hate you."

She turned away from the window back toward the room. She reached into her pocket, pulled out the evidence. Homicide evidence that she had touched. With her bare hands.

Once again, she dropped to her knees beside the bed.

Feverishly she wiped the medals, one by one, with her shirt-tail and replaced them under the magazines.

Then she rose and stumbled out of the shed, slamming the door behind her.

The light.

She had forgotten to turn off that damned chandelier. The expensive one that her brother could never have bought on his own.

But it didn't matter.

No longer able to choke it down, Savannah ran to the edge of the yard, leaned against the cement-block fence, and retched.

Suddenly, Tom was there, his arm around her waist, supporting her.

"Hey, sugar, it's all right," he was saying, his voice soft and reassuring. He patted her hair and pulled her against him until her face was against his broad shoulder. "You're okay, Savannah. You're fine now."

She was only vaguely aware of Sheriff Mahoney standing nearby, watching, listening. No warmth or compassion radiated from his direction.

"I'm going to help her into the house," she heard Tom say. "You . . . go on ahead."

"Yeah, okay," was the sullen reply. "But don't take all night about it, hear?"

The strong, muscular arms around her tightened. "Come on, honey. We'll get you inside and fetch you a cold drink. Then you'll feel better."

But Savannah knew, even as she gratefully allowed him to lead her along, that she wasn't going to feel better about this right away. Maybe never.

Chapter

7

Savannah could have used a hot toddy before bedtime, but Gran didn't allow such "tools of the Devil" as alcoholic beverages in her house. The list of banned items also included playing cards, dice, cigarettes, and television shows where the characters used four letter words or "the Lord's name in vain."

And although Savannah had never questioned those limitations before—it was, after all, Gran's own home—a stiff toddy might have helped her get to sleep a bit faster. At least, before the crack of dawn.

Lying next to Gran on the fluffy feather bed, beneath the handmade quilt, Savannah had mentally removed and replaced those damned medals a dozen times before midnight... and that many more before the rays of the sun filtered through the lace curtains that covered the window beside the bed.

When she heard the crowing of the rooster, waking his hen harem and everyone else within cock-a-doodle-doo distance, she knew she was screwed. With basically no sleep, not to mention jet lag and the aftershock of severe familial trauma, this was destined to be a no-fun day.

She felt her grandmother stir beside her—not for the first time since they had retired. If her tossing and turning were any indication, Gran hadn't gotten much sleep either.

"You still awake, darlin'?" Gran whispered.

Savannah turned onto her side to face her. "Yeah. Still."

"Me, too."

They kept their voices low, so as not to wake Alma, who had graciously offered to give Savannah her place next to Gran and was asleep on the sofa in the living room. Savannah could hear Cordele snoring in the adjoining back bedroom.

"Was that Jesup who came in late?" Savannah whispered.

"Yes. It was one-forty-six," Gran replied. "I'll have to have a talk with her about that carousin' till all hours of the morning. She's going through one of them rebellious teenager stages, I think. Gets something new pierced every week. I swear, she looks like she got caught in a barbed-wire fence."

"Teenager? Gran, Jesup is twenty-three."

"Yes, but she's still an adolescent. Takes some longer to grow up than it does others. Jesup's what you'd call a late bloomer in the maturity department."

Savannah sighed. "You know, before this visit, I thought I knew my siblings better than I do. I had no idea how much crap you've had to put up with lately. Why don't you toss them all out on their ears? Sink or swim, but either way, they'd be out of your hair."

"Easy advice to give, but when it comes to the doin' . . ."

Savannah thought of the medals. "That's true. It's not easy to leave them there in the deep end. Even when you know it's the right thing to do." A knot caught in her throat. "It's so hard to know . . . if you're doing the right thing or not."

Gran reached over and laid her hand on Savannah's arm. Savannah felt the softness of her grandmother's flannel gown against her skin. Since she could remember, summer or winter, Gran had worn those long-sleeved, ankle-length nightgowns, made of flannel and spangled with tiny pastel flowers. This one had pink rosebuds and lace around the sleeve and neck edges.

And Gran always smelled nice. For years, when she had tucked Savannah into bed, leaned over and kissed her, and heard her bedtime prayers, Savannah could always smell the clean, fresh scent of her bath soap and hand lotion.

Lying here beside her grandmother, in her bed, the same fragrances took Savannah back to a time when this had been the safest place in the world. Gran's bed was the ultimate sanctuary from thunder and lightning, scary monsters, creepy ghosties, and even the Boogey Man himself. Nothing evil, nothing even remotely bad could touch you . . . if you were lying next to Gran.

"It *is* hard to know what's the best thing to do sometimes," Gran said, patting her forearm. "But you don't need to worry. I think you did right."

Savannah looked across the pillows into the older woman's eyes and saw a quiet peace that she only wished she could feel herself.

"Thanks, Gran. But you don't know. I—"

"I know."

The hand on Savannah's arm tightened, and Gran nodded.

"You . . . you do?"

"I saw Sheriff Mahoney leaving with that little brown paper bag with the red tape sealing it up. I figure I know what was in it. I figure you do, too."

"But how? How would you know?"

Gran sighed, rolled over onto her back, and stared up at the ceiling. "You ain't the only one in this family with a nosy streak, you know. Where do you think you got that need to know everything about everybody that's served you so well in the business you're in?"

That was true, Savannah decided. Gran had always known everything about everybody, often before they even knew it themselves. It could be quite aggravating at times.

But was she trying to tell her that she had seen the . . . ?

"I saw them medals."

Savannah nearly gasped. "*You?* You knew they were there? But how did you . . . ? When did you . . . ?"

"After we came back from the jail this afternoon, while you

were at the Patterson place with Tommy Stafford. I went out
back and searched his room. And from the look of things, I
should've done it a long time ago. All that mess under his bed,
those filthy magazines, and the place looks like a pig's sty. It
smells funny, too, and I don't think it's just from the dirty laundry."

"But you saw those Civil War medals?"

Gran nodded.

"Did you know what they were? Did you know where he got
them?"

"Of course I did. Everybody in the county knows about Judge
Patterson's collection of War Between the States memorabilia.
There's only one place those could've come from, and only one
reason they'd be under Macon's bed."

"But you left them there. Knowing." It was a statement of
amazement, not a question.

"Yes, I did." She drew a deep, tired breath. "And so did you."

Savannah lay there, unable to speak for what seemed like a
very long time. Her amazement subsided, turning to relief.

"Then you think we did the right thing?"

"A man was murdered, Savannah. Killed in cold blood."

She swallowed hard. "I know."

"And justice . . . justice is underestimated these days. It's a
holy thing. You can only interfere with it so far. Even for love of
kin."

Savannah allowed the words to touch, to soothe, to heal her
troubled spirit.

"And we've gotta remember that," Gran continued, "no matter what comes of it all. Like I've told you before, you can't judge
the rightness or the wrongness of an act by its outcome. A lot of
good decisions have caused a heap of misery in the world, but
that don't mean those decisions weren't right. We're gonna hold
on to that. You hear me, Savannah girl?"

Savannah nodded as a warm tear trickled from the corner of
her eye down into her ear. "I hear you, Gran."

*   *   *

The biscuits, the peach preserves, and the grits were even better than Savannah remembered. Sitting at her grandmother's table, shoveling in the goodies, she promised herself to get rid of the store-bought pastries in her own cupboard and celebrate her Southern heritage more often when she returned home.

So what if you lived in California with the beautiful, skinny people? They just didn't know what they were missing at the breakfast table.

Whole-grain granola and yogurt indeed.

But the food proved better than the family politics.

The meal began peacefully, as only Savannah, Gran, and Cordele were at the table. For some reason, the rest of the gang had decided to provide for themselves and were blissfully absent.

But problems started when sister Jesup dragged herself to the table and plopped herself onto the chair across from Savannah's.

"Hi, Van, good to see ya," she mumbled, burying her face in her coffee cup and draining more than half of it before coming up for air. She didn't look particularly ecstatic, Savannah thought. "When did you get in?"

Savannah had seen heroin addicts with rosier complexions. And Gran had been right about the piercings. Six studs in each ear, one in her left nostril, another through her lower lip, and when she spoke, Savannah was sure she had seen the glimmer of silver on her tongue.

And the tattoo, a Celtic chain, like a choker around her neck.

In Jesup's black pajamas, Savannah thought she looked dressed to attend some sort of ritual—like burying a dead cat at the crossroads by the light of a full moon.

"I got into town yesterday afternoon," Savannah replied. "Right after . . . you know . . . Macon was arrested."

Cordele, wearing an almost identical white shirt and dark skirt as the night before, sat primly beside Jesup. Giving her a contemptuous, sideways glance, she said, "I would have found out about Macon earlier, but *I* was at school. Where were *you*, Jes?"

"Hanging out with my friends. Where do you suppose I was? I

didn't hear about it until we all stopped at the Burger Igloo for supper."

"And what time was that?" Cordele wanted to know.

"About eight. What's your point?"

Gran cleared her throat. "That's enough, girls. No snapping at each other at the breakfast table. You can save it for when you're washing dishes later." She turned to Jesup. "But you should have come home, Jes, when you first heard there was trouble in the family. We needed you."

Jesup blushed under the gentle criticism. Savannah was relieved to see she wasn't such a hard-bitten case that she couldn't still take Gran's admonitions to heart.

With a little shrug, Jesup said, "Why would you need me for?"

"When a family's in trouble, it needs everybody. We need your strength, Jessie, girl. We need your ideas, your opinions. You're a precious part of this family, and I think you might have forgotten that for a moment last night."

"I'm sorry, Gran. Next time I'll . . ."

Her apology was interrupted by a seldom-heard cacophony of barking, growling, and baying, all coming from Beauregard as he bounded off the back porch and sailed around the side of the house, ears and jowls flapping.

"We got company," Gran said, slowly rising from the table, "and they must be strangers. Sounds like Beau's gonna eat 'em, if we don't put a stop to it." She shook her head. "I don't know what's gotten into that animal lately. He's been so high-strung and nervous, with all that's goin' on. And now we got company. Who do you reckon it is, callin' at this time o' the morning?"

"Tammy! Dirk! Oh, mercy! I don't believe it!" Savannah practically flew off the porch and straight into a threesome hug with her old friends, who met her with open arms.

Gran and Jesup grabbed Beauregard by his leather collar as he lunged at the new arrivals and sang at the top of his hound lungs.

Once Tammy and Dirk realized they were actually embracing each other, the tri-hug ended abruptly.

"When did you . . . ?" Savannah blabbered, "How did you . . . ? Oh, I don't care. I'm so happy to see you!"

If Savannah hadn't realized before that moment how much those two meant to her, how much strength she derived from their friendship, she did then. And she would never forget it.

"How do you figure we got here?" Dirk growled. "We took the midnight train to Georgia." He looked oh-so-imposed upon . . . and loving every minute of it.

"More like a red-eye flight," Tammy added. "And Dirko here snored the whole way, kept the whole plane awake."

"It wasn't *me* who kept things in an uproar. It was those black flea-bags you brought with us."

Black flea-bags? Savannah's mind searched for a cross-reference. And found one.

Along with the reason Beauregard was still going bonkers, struggling against Gran and Cordele, hurling himself toward the small compact car they had undoubtedly rented at the airport.

Tammy grinned and shrugged. "They didn't exactly like the travel cages," she told Savannah. "And I wouldn't let the airline people put them in the luggage compartment. They were under our seats, meowing all the way."

Savannah hurried over to the car and opened the back door. Sure enough. Two tiny plastic cages on the rear seat held two of the unhappiest felines she had seen in a long time. Four green eyes glared out at her, basically saying, "How could you? This is all your fault, Mom, and we'll never forgive you."

But their anger evaporated, turning to terror as Beauregard broke free from Gran and Cordele and raced to the car. A second later, the dog shoved Savannah aside as he wriggled past her and jumped into the rear floorboard of the car.

Savannah found herself in a whirlwind of hissing, barking, snarling, furry fury.

"Oh, Lord help us!" Gran cried. "He'll eat those cats whole, he will! The Colonel hates cats somethin' fierce!"

"Damn it, Beau! Get outta here!" Savannah snatched at handfuls of saggy, baggy hound hide, but couldn't get a hold.

Just when she thought the battle was lost, the dog yelped. Something changed.

Inch by inch, Colonel Beauregard was retreating.

Well, not exactly leaving under his own steam, Savannah realized when she saw Dirk's big hands locked around the dog's lower legs. Dirk was hauling the hound, kicking and yelping, out of the car, butt first.

"I got him!" Dirk shouted. "I got him! I—owww! Shit!"

"Oh, dear," Gran said, looking on sadly, shaking her head. "I was afraid of that."

Five minutes later, the weary combatants were settled in Gran's kitchen. Savannah sat at the table with Dirk, applying hydrogen peroxide to his wounded hand.

Sitting on the floor, Jesup held Beauregard's head on her lap and dabbed the long scratch on his muzzle with a cotton ball. "Did Savannah's mean old cat hurt you?" she said. The dog whined, his eyes rolling.

"Savannah's cat was fighting for her life," Savannah reminded her as she applied antibiotic cream to the small punctures in Dirk's palm.

"Those cats were in cages," Jesup argued. "They weren't in any real danger. It's not like he could actually bite them. They didn't have to reach through the bars and—"

"Oh, please! They could've died of heart failure!" Savannah snapped. "How would you like to travel for hours on a plane and then have the hound from hell—?"

"That's enough!" Gran roared. "No harm's done . . . except to you, Mr. Coulter, that is. I'm real sorry about that."

Dirk grumbled under his breath. Savannah heard something about "better not . . . rabies . . ."

She wound a strip of gauze around his hand, then gave the un-injured one a squeeze. "That was a good save, big boy," she said, "yanking him outta there like that. I owe ya."

"You bet you do, and I'll collect. I'm talking a chicken-fried-steak dinner, mashed potatoes, corn on the cob, the works."

"But don't worry about that yet," Tammy said as she sat on the chair next to Dirk's. "We're here to help you." She looked around the kitchen at each concerned Reid face. "We're here to help all of you any way we can. What can we do?"

Chapter

8

"There's no way in hell that Tommy's going to let you talk to Macon," Savannah told Dirk. "I had to twist his arm plumb out of its socket to get in myself. And that was before they found those medals under his bed."

She had filled them in on all the sordid details on the way into town from Gran's house. Now they sat in the front seat of the rented car, Tammy in the back, watching the front of the McGill sheriff's station half a block away.

Tom's cruiser was parked in front of the building. They had seen Sheriff Mahoney drive away ten minutes before in a new Ford pickup.

"*Tommy*, is it?" Dirk's ears perked. He propped his forearms on the steering wheel. Savannah half expected him to flex his biceps. "Is this *Tommy* an old buddy of yours?"

"This is a one-horse town, Dirk," Savannah replied, as evenly as possible. "Everybody here is either a friend or an enemy. And, being Southerners, we're basically friendly. Somebody's gotta actually do us wrong . . . or hurt someone we care about . . . to become a full-fledged enemy."

She cleared her throat and turned away to look out the window. "So, yes . . . I guess you could say he's a buddy of mine. But he's still not going to let you in to talk to Macon."

"Yeah, well, we'll see about that. I can outsmart a hick deputy all day long and twice on Sunday. What's the name of the local hangout?"

"What?"

"The bar where the lowlife spends most of its time and money."

"Whiskey Joe's. It's a couple of miles out of town."

Savannah didn't bother to add the fact that her mother, Shirley Reid, was one of Joe's most faithful patrons, and when she was particularly hard-up she sometimes tended bar there.

"Do you figure that phone booth over there works?" he asked, nodding toward a dilapidated cubicle leaning against a nearby service station.

"It worked last time I used it," Savannah told him.

"How long ago was that?"

"Let's just say I put in one thin dime, and my call went through."

"Oh," Tammy said from the back seat, "back in the Jurassic era."

"Exactly."

"Gimme a quarter." Dirk held out his bandaged hand.

What a cheapskate, Savannah thought. Then she reminded herself that he had taken a fang for her. *What a guy.*

She fished some coins out of her purse and dropped them into his hand. "By the way," she told him, "they don't have 911 around here. You'll have to call information to get the station's number."

"He's going to call the station?" Tammy asked, leaning over the back of the seat as she watched Dirk walk to the phone.

"Oh, yeah. This is one of his favorites . . . reporting a major row in the local dive. He throws in a few gory details about broken beer bottles and somebody's ear nearly sliced off, hanging by an itsy-bitsy flap of skin. By the time he's done spinning his yarn, ninety percent of the area's law enforcement is hightailin' it out there."

"Hm-m-m . . . " Tammy mused. "Is that a misdemeanor or a felony?"

"Depends on whether or not they catch you. Of course, Dirk's going to have to work up a Dixie drawl if he's gonna pull it off this time. Southerners can spot a Yankee a mile off."

"But Dirk's from California."

"Anybody who ain't from south of the Mason-Dixon line is a Yankee."

"How about somebody from another country?"

"They're a foreigner."

"I see . . . I think."

Savannah turned around and looked Tammy up and down. She was wearing a simple shirt blouse and a denim skirt. "Can you pull your shirttail out and tie it in a knot at your midriff?"

"Ah . . . yeah, I guess so. Why?"

"And could you roll that skirt up at the waistband and make it about four inches shorter?"

"Well, yes. Like this?"

"Yeah, and take that scrunchy out of your hair and shake it loose."

Tammy did as she was told, a smirk on her face. "Let me guess, I'm the slut bait."

"Now, now, you're in Georgia. Ladies here don't have potty mouths. I was thinking more like 'truck-stop cutie.' "

"You think it'll work on your buddy Tommy?"

Savannah flashed back on Tom's former appreciation of her own voluptuous curves.

No. Tammy's size-zero bod wouldn't do it for Deputy Stafford. "Dirk's taking care of Tom with the call," she said. "You'll have to work your wicked female wiles on someone else. And with any luck, you'll be just his type."

Four minutes later, Dirk's plan had unfolded and each of the players had changed their positions on the chessboard. Even those who weren't aware—at least, not yet—that they were playing. Tom Stafford was in his cruiser, racing off to quell the mayhem at Whiskey Joe's. The pharmacist, Fred Jeter, was leaning into the open hood of the rental car with Tammy beside him, explaining her theory of the "awful, knocking sound" her engine had been making just before the car stalled down the block from the station. Enthralled by the lengthy expanse of her lean legs, Fred had remained clueless as his jail had been invaded. And Dirk and Savannah had slipped in the front door unobserved, scooted up the stairs, and were standing in front of Macon's cell.

"Get over here. We've gotta talk fast," Dirk said, looking over his shoulder, "or our butts are going to be as crispy fried as yours."

"Who are you?" a sullen Macon wanted to know.

"Do what he said," Savannah snapped at him. "It's only a matter of time till either Jeter or Tom gets back, and we've gotta know some things."

Macon hauled his hulk off the cot and shuffled on stockinged feet over to the bars. "What? I done told you everything, Savannah. Why don't you just let it be?"

Dirk reached through the bars and grabbed a handful of Macon's T-shirt. " 'Cause you're probably gonna get tried, convicted, and maybe executed for murder, smart guy. And your sister is gonna feel lower than dog shit if she doesn't do everything she can to get you off. So, help her out, okay?"

A light of fear flickered in Macon's eyes, and for a moment Savannah envied Dirk. It had been a long time since she had instilled a drop of fear in one of her siblings. Too long. She'd have to sharpen up her intimidation and manipulation skills.

"They know you were in the Patterson mansion," she told her brother. "They've got your prints on the window sill. Your Ruger was on the floor, and they're pretty sure it was the murder weapon."

Macon stared, sullen, at the floor. "So?"

"So, you're screwed, my friend," Dirk said, releasing his hold on him. "What happened? You and your friend break in, figuring to rob the old guy?"

Macon shrugged. "We didn't know he was home. His big ol' black car was gone. We thought he was at that golf club, like he usually was late in the afternoon."

Savannah felt her stomach tighten. Of course, she had known from the evidence that her brother had been there, but there was nothing like hearing a confession with your own ears to make you sick.

"You broke in through the window, and then what?" Dirk said.

"The old man came at us, roarin' like some kind of a lion." Macon shuddered. Apparently, the memory was still rich. "He was swingin' that cane around like a crazy person. He hit me hard, right here." He pointed to the bruised area on his forearm. "And he whacked Kenny Jr. across the back, too. Hit him so hard, he knocked him right on the floor."

"And so you shot him," Dirk added.

"No! I did not!"

"Did Kenny Jr.?" Savannah asked.

"No! That's when Kenny dropped the gun . . . my gun. He was the one carryin' it. We didn't hurt the judge. Hell, we didn't get a chance to." Macon's ruddy face flushed several shades brighter. "We just hightailed it outta there. Both of us. After he got whalloped, Junior was yellin' like a scalded pig. I'm telling ya, we were scared shitless. That wasn't what we had in mind at all. We were just gonna go in there, get a few of those fancy pistols of his outta the gun cabinet, and leave. But he started screamin' and beatin' and she-e-ez! It was awful!"

"Are you telling me," Savannah said, slowly, as though he were three years old again, "that the judge was alive when you . . . hightailed it outta there?"

"Damn right, he was alive. Alive and kickin', and screechin', and swingin' that cane. Lordy, he was mad!"

Savannah glanced at Dirk and saw a look on his face that surprised her. Dirk was buying it. She only wished *she* could.

"What about the medals?" she said.

The look her brother gave her was as blank as a freshly washed chalkboard.

"What medals? What are you talking about?"

"The Civil War medals that were hanging on the wall in a frame. The frame you broke," Dirk added.

Macon shook his head and ran his fingers through his short hair, causing it to stand on end. "I don't know what you're talking about. Medals? What's that got to do with anything?"

"The medals you stole from the judge's house and stashed under your bed." Savannah watched his face for any sign of recognition, but saw only confusion.

"I didn't take no medals," he said. "I told you, we went there for some of his guns. And we didn't even get the chance to grab any of those. I swear, me and Kenny Jr. didn't take *nothin'* outta there but a couple of nasty bruises."

Savannah glanced around into the other cells which, other than the one occupied by Yukon Bill, were empty. "Where is Kenny Jr.? I thought they picked him up, too."

"They did," Macon replied. "But I heard them downstairs saying something about stashing him in the jail over in Brownsville. They didn't want us talking to each other up here and getting our stories straight."

"Don't you be talking to anybody about anything, not till you get a lawyer," Dirk said, shaking his forefinger a few inches from Macon's nose.

"I know. I know. Savannah done told me that."

"Well, you listen to her, boy. She knows what's best. And we're going to do all we can for you, okay? So you just sit tight and don't sweat it. Everything's gonna work out."

Savannah watched as Macon's eyes searched Dirk's and seemed to find something comforting in the older man. Silently, she blessed her friend. Again.

"Okay." Macon nodded and looked as though his burden had been lightened by at least a couple of ounces. "Thanks, man."

"Don't thank me. Thank *her*. She's a lot better to both of us than we deserve."

A few moments later, as they walked away from Macon's cell, heading back downstairs, Savannah nudged Dirk with her elbow. "Better than you deserve, huh, buddy?"

"Eh, don't let it go to your head. I was just bull-shittin' the kid."

"Yeah, right. I heard you the first time and . . . Uh, oh. Trouble down below."

They both heard it at the same time, and they halted there on the third step from the top.

A two-way conversation in the office at the bottom of the stairs. Somebody was getting an earful.

"When you are left in charge of this place, Deputy Jeter, you are to remain on your post, come hell or high water, or good-lookin' women with car trouble. Do you hear me, boy?"

"I do, Sheriff. I'm sorry, but she said she was afraid it was about to catch fire, and I thought—"

"That's where you went wrong . . . that 'thinking' crap. We don't pay you to think around here. We pay you to do what I say."

"Y'all don't pay me," was the soft, half-hearted reply.

"What?"

"I said, y'all don't exactly pay me. I'm a volunteer, and—"

"Does that mean you can shirk your duty, deputy? Does that mean you can go traipsin' around and leave this facility unattended?"

"No, sir."

Savannah leaned against Dirk and whispered in his ear. "We're dead. We can't stay up here all day, and when we go down, we're compost."

"No, Deputy Jeter's dead." He grinned his wry little sadistic smirk, the one he wore when he was actually savoring the prospect of conflict. "You and me . . . we're just gonna get our butts roasted."

Chapter
9

Sheriff Mahoney stood by the water cooler, his thick arms crossed over the bulge of his belly, his stout legs spread, firm and planted. Nearby, the poor little pharmacist was quaking inside his white smock, wringing his hands and looking as though he would gladly walk out of that office and into a den of rabid hyenas.

Savannah had never liked Mahoney, not even when she was a kid and he was a deputy. She didn't trust him then, and she had met too many cops like him in the intervening years who had only deepened that prejudice.

Most law enforcement officers were good people, she truly believed, who did a difficult job well, out of concern for their fellow humans.

Then there were the bullies, the tough guys who used their badges, guns, and nightsticks to bolster their already overinflated egos at the expense of those unfortunate enough to cross their paths.

Long ago, she had decided that Mahoney belonged in the second category. And she had no use for his type.

But as she and Dirk slowly descended the stairs, waiting for the sheriff to glance their way, she reminded herself that they were on Mahoney's turf, and he might very well hold the key to her brother's future.

It wouldn't be a good idea to piss him off.

Too late.

The instant he saw them, his hand lowered to the butt of the enormous revolver strapped, Western-style, to his hip.

For half a second, she thought he was going to shoot them both dead on the stairs without asking a single question.

She felt Dirk tense beside her and knew that he, too, was mentally willing himself not to reach for his own weapon.

"Whoa, and who the hell are you?" Mahoney shouted, taking a couple of quick steps in their direction.

They froze. Savannah made her hands, open and empty, fully visible to him. Dirk did the same.

"I'm Savannah Reid, Sheriff," she said quickly. "I was born and raised here in McGill. You remember me, don't you?"

He studied her, his eyes dark and suspicious under the large, yellow uni-brow that stretched from one side of his face to the other.

She noticed he had developed a bright-red boozer's nose and a patchwork of red and purple veins across his cheeks since she had seen him last. In McGill, rumors had always abounded that Mahoney liked a bit of vodka with his morning orange juice . . . and his afternoon cola, and his supper coffee, and his evening beer.

His once blond hair held more white than gold now, but it was still wavy and thick for a guy in his late fifties or early sixties. Like Tom, he had filled out considerably. But, unlike his deputy, the added bulk wasn't muscle.

He looked her up and down for a couple of moments, then a light of recognition shone in his eyes. "You Shirley Reid's oldest kid?"

"Yes, I am."

Surprising, she thought, how she still hated to admit that. It was one thing to be Granny Reid's granddaughter. But Shirley's . . . That was a pedigree she could do without.

"Then that means you been up there with your little brother, my murder suspect, doing God-knows-what!"

He walked on over to them, practically bristling under his two-sizes-too-small uniform. The khaki didn't flatter him half as much as it did Tom.

They walked down the remainder of the steps and met him halfway in the middle of the room.

"*Talking* to him," Dirk said. "That's all we were doing . . . talking."

"And who are *you*?"

Savannah cringed as Mahoney shoved a forefinger in Dirk's face. Dirk wasn't the sort to rein in his temper under circumstances like these. He, too, had a weak spot for bully cops. He liked to have them for breakfast with bacon and eggs, sunny-side up.

Dirk reached into his shirt pocket and produced his badge. He flipped it open. "I'm Detective Seargent Dirk Coulter."

He pushed it under Mahoney's nose. "And that's gold," he added, looking smugly at the tin star on Mahoney's chest.

"I don't give a rat's ass if it's studded with diamonds and rubies," Mahoney snapped. "What the hell do you think you're doing, running around free as a jaybird in my jail?"

He turned back to Jeter. "Get your lazy, no-good hind end up those stairs and check that prisoner. Search him good. And his cell too."

Jeter ran full-tilt for the staircase, flying past them.

"Do you think you can handle that, Deputy?" he yelled after the little man as he pounded up the steps.

"Yes, sir! I can . . . I mean . . . I will, sir."

"I oughta lock you both up right now," Mahoney said, running his eyes up and down each of them in turn. The fact that they were both a head taller than him didn't seem to impress him at all.

Savannah could tell he was seriously considering it. The vision of herself and Dirk locked up with Macon, and Tammy running the investigation alone on the outside, gave her a chill that had nothing to do with the air-conditioning in the office.

"On what charge?" Dirk said.

"Breaking into my jail, for starters."

"We didn't break in, Sheriff." Savannah donned her sweetest, buttery voice. "We just walked in. We would have asked for permission to talk to Macon, but nobody was here, so we just figured it would be okay if we—"

"Bullshit. I reckon you don't know nothing about that blonde out there with the broken-down car . . . that probably ain't broken-down no more." He turned to Dirk. "And you weren't the one who made the call that sent my deputy on a wild-goose chase out to Whiskey Joe's."

Dirk shrugged and gave him a half smirk. "What blonde? Whiskey who?"

"Get outta here, both of y'all, before I slap cuffs on you and throw you in the pokey."

Savannah didn't exactly break into a run, like Jeter, but she didn't allow any moss to grow on her before she headed for the door, with Dirk right behind her.

"And don't you two come back here, either, you hear?"

Savannah opened the door, shoved Dirk outside, then said over her shoulder, "Well, if for some reason we have to, I'll be sure to have Dirk call Deputy Stafford first."

She slammed the door behind them, and they hot-stepped to the rented car, which—as Mahoney had predicted—was now sitting at the curb, running just fine, with a grinning Tammy at the wheel.

"What happened?" Tammy asked breathlessly as they piled in, Savannah in the front, Dirk in the back.

"Drive!" Dirk said. "Now."

"Whee-e-e, howdy." Savannah felt her knees go to jelly. She reached over and slapped Tammy on the back as Tammy put the car in gear and peeled out. "We just escaped the iron jaws o' the law, my friend. And the seat of my britches is tattered and my arse is aflappin' bare in the breeze." She sighed deeply. "Yep, that there was a close one."

When Tammy pulled into the dirt parking lot of Whiskey Joe's, Savannah felt a wave of nausea that was the strongest she'd felt since changing birth control pills last summer. Instantly, she recognized the faded orange Karman Ghia parked closest to the store. Her mom had bought that car, used, in 1975 and had been driving it ever since. The last time Savannah had taken a ride in it, about twelve years ago, she had watched the road whipping along beneath them through at least three sizable holes in the floorboard. Her mom had warned her to leave her shoes on or risk losing them.

Driving over a mud puddle had been a particularly invigorating experience.

Savannah was surprised to see the car still running. Not only because of the sheer mileage, but because Shirley Reid was infamous for driving under the influence. Way under the influence. Savannah considered it a miracle that neither she nor the car had suffered a permanent crackup. As Gran would say: *They're both running on borrowed time.*

"You don't have to go in there, Van," Dirk said. "You can just drop me and the kid here off for a while and drop around later to pick us up. We can ask any questions that need asking."

In a gesture that touched her heart, he leaned forward from the back seat and laid a big, warm hand on her shoulder. She laid her cheek against it for a second.

"Thanks. But, like you, now that we've talked to Macon, I'm thinking maybe he didn't do it after all. And if he didn't, somebody's setting him up by sticking those medals under his bed."

She flashed back on the moment she had decided to leave those incriminating bits of evidence where they lay. Yes, she definitely had to do everything she could for her little brother. "I'm not exactly hankering to see my mom, but it might as well be now as later. Get it over with, you know?"

"I guess." Dirk didn't sound convinced. He held the firm conviction that conflict—at least the personal kind—was to be avoided at all cost.

Tammy shot her a sympathetic, but slightly confused look, and Savannah knew how difficult it was for the younger woman to comprehend what she was feeling. Although Tammy's family lived three thousand miles away from her on the north shore of Long Island in New York, she called them several times a week and visited frequently.

They were close.

And members of close families might try to understand. But they couldn't. Not really.

"I can't come home and not see my mom," Savannah said. "I mean . . . I could. But I can't. So, let's do it."

The three of them got out of the car and strolled up to the bar's front door.

Whiskey Joe's hadn't always been a dive; it hadn't always been Whiskey Joe's. In McGill's better days, the bar had been a restaurant, Julia's Place, frequented by the county's wealthy landowners. Stained-glass windows, etched mirrors, solid brass hardware on hardwood doors had set the scene for leisurely candlelit dinners. But few remnants of its former grandeur remained.

The oak door bore numerous scars from careless boot kicks and a deep crack down the middle from the front tire of J.P. Murphy's Harley-Davidson, when he had decided to crash the place one hot Fourth of July.

The floor-to-ceiling stained-glass window to the right of the door was bowed outward, roughly in the shape of a human body, from the night J.P. had been evicted . . . and missed the doorway.

Savannah could think of a lot of places on earth to pleasantly while away the hours of her life, but, unlike her mom, Whiskey Joe's wasn't one of them.

Each to his own . . . or her *own,* she told herself as she walked through the door. *Don't judge. Nobody knows enough about anyone else to judge.*

But a man is judged by his actions. Or lack thereof. A woman, too, came the quick mental response.

She sighed to herself. *So much for not judging.*

The smell of booze and stale cigarette smoke hit her, along with the familiar pinging and bells of the pinball machine and the clicking of pool balls being knocked around three full-sized tables, and the whine of a country ballad from the jukebox in the corner.

"Pretty busy for early afternoon," Dirk said, glancing around the main room, at the bar, booths, and tables that were at least one-third full.

"You oughta see it on a Saturday night," Savannah replied, her own eyes searching the room. But she wasn't counting the crowd.

She felt Tammy's hand close around her arm. "Isn't that her, over there at the end of the bar?"

Savannah wondered at Tammy's powers of detection, until she recalled that in her spare time, Tammy had scanned and catalogued all of Savannah's old family pictures into the office computer.

Following Tammy's line of vision, she saw her mother, sitting where she had been the last time Savannah saw her . . . on the second stool from the end, beneath a picture of Elvis.

Now, as then, she was holding a beer in her right hand, while smoke curled upward from the tip of a cigarette in her left.

But that was where the similarity between yesteryear and the present ended.

"I wouldn't have known her if I'd run into her on Main Street," Savannah said under her breath. "I don't think I would have recognized my own mother."

Shirley Reid had aged twenty years in eight. Once a pretty woman, who had spent an inordinate amount of time and care on her personal appearance, Shirley looked as if she hadn't brushed her hair or changed her clothing in a week. She had always been slender, but now she was painfully gaunt, her cheeks sunken and deeply lined.

Alone at the bar, with only her beer and cigarette for company, she looked frail, fragile, and terribly lost.

Savannah had been afraid of the anger she would feel when she saw her mother again, the resentment, the disappointment. But the only emotion she felt, standing in the back of Whiskey Joe's staring into her mother's lonely world, was sadness.

She turned to Dirk and Tammy, who were watching her with the depth of compassion and concern that only the dearest friends could demonstrate. "You two go on, mingle, shoot some pool, whatever, and ask your questions. Talk to you later."

They nodded and headed for the other side of the room, where a bald and burly bartender was giving a pile of glasses their requisite swish in the sink and loading them onto a draining tray.

Savannah took a deep breath and strolled over to the bar stool . . . the one directly beneath the picture of "The King."

Shirley didn't notice her, didn't even move, until she was standing right behind her. Savannah reached out and lightly tapped her on the shoulder.

"Hey, Shirl," she said. "What's shakin'?"

Long ago, Shirley had established the cardinal rule: Don't call me "Mom" in here. Not ever.

Shirley wasn't big on being called "Mom" anywhere. Especially a setting where members of the opposite sex might overhear.

As though roused out of a thick mental fog, Shirley shook her head, turned, and stared blankly at Savannah.

Slowly recognition dawned on her face. "Van? Oh, hi, baby." She waved her cigarette vaguely at the nearest stool. "Sit down. Let me buy you a drink."

Somewhat relieved that the moment for the awkward, obligatory embrace had come and gone, Savannah sat down beside her mother and laid her purse on the bar in front of her.

"It's a bit early for me," she said. "How's the coffee in here?"

"Fresh." Shirley mashed the stub of her cigarette into the ashtray and, in one continuous motion, reached for the pack on the bar, shook out another, and lit up. "Fresh . . . every Saturday morning, that is."

"Well, since it's Wednesday afternoon, I guess I'll pass," Savannah said. "How have you been?"

Shirley shrugged and looked as though she were swimming inside her clothes. The denim shirt she wore was at least two sizes too large for her, and the front was stained with something that looked like spaghetti sauce.

But she was wearing her jewelry. All of it. Shirley never left the house without her silver and turquoise rings, bracelets, necklaces, and earrings. The bigger, the heavier, the better.

Savannah had once told her that she'd better never go swimming or she'd sink straight to the bottom with all that metal.

Her mom hadn't been amused. Her jewelry was no laughing matter. Shirley had never owned much in the material world. And what little she'd had, she'd lost. Except her jewelry. Those bits and pieces of turquoise and silver were about all Shirley Reid had to show for sixty-one years of living.

"I heard you'd come home," Shirley said. "I guess you're here for Marietta's wedding next Saturday."

Savannah flashed back on the giant peach-tulip dress and gulped. "Yeah. What are you going to wear? Do you know yet?"

Shirley took a long drag on her cigarette and held it deep before releasing it through her nose. "Haven't been invited. I thought my daughter might ask me to sing at her wedding . . . I used to sing in church all the time, you know . . . but no. She didn't even invite me to come."

"Oh." Savannah could practically taste the rubber sole of her shoe. "Sorry. Maybe the invitation got lost in the mail or—"

"Or maybe Marietta decided not to invite her own mother because she's ashamed of her."

"I don't think that's why."

"That's why. I know. I called her and asked her point-blank."

"And Marietta said she was ashamed of you? She actually told you that?"

Shirley's hand shook as she knocked her ashes into the tray. "In so many words. She's afraid I'll show up drunk and embarrass her in front of her new in-laws."

Suddenly, Savannah felt as though she were treading on quicksand. It was a feeling she often had when she tried to have a conversation with her mother. "Would you be willing to . . . you know . . . not drink that day? To show up completely sober?"

"Yeah, I could probably show up sober," Shirley replied, her voice tight, her tone sarcastic. " 'Course, we all know I wouldn't stay that way at the reception."

"So, get yourself a pretty suit and show up at the church. Skip the party."

"No, thank you. I don't want to be anywhere I'm not welcome. And that witch, your grandmother, she hates me. She won't want me around."

"Gran doesn't hate you. She's never said a bad thing about you, ever. She—"

"Yeah, yeah, she's a friggin' saint. I know. I should get down on my knees and kiss her damned feet. That's what the family court judge told me when he took you kids away from me and gave you to her."

Savannah felt the rage welling up again, the fury that she had to bury, over and over and over again, year after year. She choked it down and wondered briefly if it would turn into an ulcer or some sort of cancer someday.

"I'm *not* going to discuss Gran with you, Shirl," she said. "Actually, I came by to talk to you about Macon."

Shirley downed about half her glass of beer before answering. "Yeah, Macon. Goes to show you what a fine job the old witch did of raising you guys. He's going to go away for murder! So much for the stable home life she—"

"Stop! I told you, I'm not going to listen to that crap. I want you to tell me anything you know about Macon, or Kenny Jr., or Judge Patterson."

"Macon's a pain in the ass, steals stuff around town with that no-good Kenny. And Judge Patterson . . . he had more enemies than you could shake a stick at. A zillion people in this county wanted to see him dead, and I don't know anybody who's crying about the fact that he's passed on to his eternal reward. Most everybody I've talked to figures he's roasting his hind quarters in hell right now. And in their opinions, he more than deserves it."

"Really?"

Family politics instantly took a back seat in Savannah's detective mind. This visit might be worth the heartache after all.

She leaned closer to her mother and lowered her voice, "Do tell," she said, "and don't spare any of the juicy details."

Chapter
10

"The Burger Igloo . . . what sort of a stupid name is that?" Dirk wanted to know as he, Savannah, and Tammy slid into the bright-red, leatherette-and-chrome booth. Ladies to the right, gent to the left. Like a petulant little sister, Tammy refused to sit next to "Fart-Face Dirko," as she fondly called him during adolescent moments.

To Savannah's dismay, there were many such moments in their relationship.

The jukebox boomed "Love Me Tender" while vintage posters of fifties movies decorated the wall and set the rock-and-roll theme. Other than the fact that the posters had yellowed and curled at the edges and that cracks crisscrossed the red seats, little had changed at the Burger Igloo in the past thirty years. And that was the way the citizens of McGill, Georgia, liked it.

As far as they were concerned, change was overrated.

"They serve ice cream here, too," Savannah told him, glancing over the twenty-flavor list of shakes and sundaes that hung on the wall, between the *Rebel Without a Cause* and *Giant* posters. "I think the 'igloo' part refers to that side of the menu, not the burgers or fries."

"I hope so. I hate cold fries. You know how picky I am about my food."

"Yeah, right." Tammy sniffed. "It has to be free—or at least cheap—and in front of your face. Those are your two basic requirements."

Dirk scowled at her across the table. "You could be fired, bimbo-brain."

"Not by *you*, pee-pee head. I work for—"

"Stop it, both of you!" Savannah shoved menus at them. "Or I'll whack your heads together and send you to bed without your supper. And if you don't think I'll do it, you just try me. I've had a hard last twenty-four hours, and I'd love to take a chunk out of somebody."

"Sorry, Savannah," Tammy mumbled, opening the plastic menu and peering disapprovingly at the selections. "I don't see any salads on here."

"Get real. The closest thing to a salad that you're gonna find on there is some extra lettuce on your burger."

Savannah fanned herself with the menu. Ironically, the Igloo had never had air-conditioning, for as long as she could remember, but she didn't recall it being so miserably stuffy before.

Funny, she thought, how summer heat was "sultry" when you were a teenager and "sticky" in your forties. So much for growing older and lowering testosterone levels.

She had deliberately avoided sitting in the booth in the corner, where she had received her first real, tongue-enhanced, makeout kiss from Tommy Stafford. Now another young couple occupied the booth, taking full advantage of the semi-privacy it afforded.

She decided not to glance in that direction a second time.

Some memories were better unstirred. Especially with "Eagle Eye Dirk" sitting across from her. He wasn't a detective with a gold shield for nothing.

"I suppose it's too much to hope that they might have veggie burgers in a place like this," Tammy said.

Savannah sighed. "Look, do you want a hamburger, a cheeseburger, or a double chili-cheese burger? That's it."

"Are you buying?" Dirk wanted to know.

"I guess."

"Then make mine a double chili cheese . . . with extra fries."
Tammy gave him a sad, somewhat self-righteous shake of her
head. "You're going to die."

"Yes . . . with a full belly and a smile on my face, God willing,"
he replied.

A waitress in a pink-and-white striped uniform that looked
like a Candy Striper cast-off strolled over to them, order pad in
hand.

Savannah recognized her instantly. "Jeannie? Jean Marie
Thompson, how are you, hon?"

She almost added, "Are you still working in this dump?" but
decided to be kind.

Jeannie had once been the prettiest girl in school, but as some
would say, the years hadn't been kind to her. The last Savannah
had heard, Jeannie had divorced her abusive, SOB husband and
was supporting a bunch of kids on a waitress's salary. Or at least
trying to.

"Savannah?" She leaned over and gave her a brief hug. "You
look great, darlin'. I heard you were coming to town, that you're
gonna stand up with Marietta at her wedding."

"Seems so."

Jeannie leaned closer. "I think her boyfriend's a nice guy.
He'll make a good husband . . . if he can just get that divorce in
time. The wedding's supposed to be this coming Saturday, ain't
it?"

"That's what we're figuring on," Savannah replied. "But now
with the trouble with Macon and all . . ."

Jeannie clucked her tongue and shook her head. "That's so
sad. I liked to have cried when I heard. Not the judge getting
killed, the old crab, but that Macon and Kenny Jr. did it . . . I
mean, got arrested for it."

"We don't think he did it, Jeannie," Savannah said. "And I'd
appreciate it if you'd spread the word that it isn't exactly a done
deal. We're checking into it, you know. Investigating the homicide."

Jeannie nodded, her look somber, appropriately impressed.

Savannah introduced her to Tammy and Dirk. "They've come out here from California to help me find out who really killed the judge and get Macon back home with his family where he belongs. My poor gran is beside herself."

"Oh, I'll bet she is. I know how she's always doted on you kids."

Jeannie quickly scribbled down their orders, then patted Savannah on the shoulder. "Don't you worry, Savannah. I see most everybody in town through here in a week's time. I'm gonna talk it up for you, I promise. And I'll keep my ears open too. Those truckers that sit at the counter . . . they got a lot to say about everything and everybody."

"Thank you, Jeannie. I appreciate it. We all do."

Ten minutes later, Savannah and Dirk had their faces buried in chili cheeseburgers. Tammy was sipping a milkshake and complaining that she could practically feel her arteries hardening, just watching them.

"We've gotta check out the judge's most recent wife," Savannah said. "She just moved out last March. My mom says that rumor has it, she caught him with one of his many mistresses and decided to divorce him and take him for all he was worth. The divorce was going to be final in another month or so."

"How many wives did he have?" Tammy slurped an extra-thick chunk of strawberry through the straw.

"Four."

Dirk practically choked on his chili. "Four! Good grief. You'd think he'd have figured he was 'out' after three."

"The first two died years ago. The third one lives in England now, and the last one was forty-five years his junior," Savannah said. "She works over at the country club now, in the sports shop."

"Okay," Dirk said. "We'll put her at the top of our list."

Savannah nudged Dirk with her shoe under the table. "What did you guys get while you were playing pool?"

"Ten bucks," Tammy replied.

"What?" Savannah raised one eyebrow.

"She's a hustler," Dirk said. "Played those yokels like a fiddle and squeezed ten dollars out of them before I could put a stop to it."

"Why would you want to stop her?"

"She wouldn't cut me in."

"Oh, right," Savannah said. "Besides the big bucks, what did you get?"

"That a lot of people around here hated the judge's guts," Dirk said. "He was famous for loaning people money when they really needed it and then foreclosing on their land when they didn't pay right up. That's how he wound up owning so much of the county . . . other than the half he inherited, that is. He got his jollies by repossessing cars and furniture and stuff, evicting folks who were behind on their rent, junk like that."

"And then there are the half-a-dozen bastard kids he's got," Tammy added. "The guys around the pool table say he had a little problem keeping his zipper closed. And some of those grownup kids aren't happy about the fact that they haven't been officially acknowledged as his offspring."

"Officially acknowledged . . . or financially acknowledged?" Savannah mused.

"I'm sure that's partly why they're disgruntled." Dirk dragged several fries through a puddle of ketchup and popped them into his mouth. "We gotta talk to them, too."

"So, where do we start?" Tammy asked.

"Once we've fueled up here . . ." Savannah drained her pineapple malt and waved to the waitress for a second. ". . . We'll go over to the country club and see if anybody knows why the judge wasn't there last night."

"What do you mean?" Tammy said.

Dirk reached for the mustard and squirted a generous amount inside his second cheeseburger. "Macon told us that he and Kenny Jr. were expecting the judge to be gone when they broke into the house. He was supposed to be at the country club, like he always was."

"But he wasn't," Savannah added. "And it might help to find out why . . . if anybody there knows. Also, it'll give me a chance to talk to Mrs. Patterson Number Four. With any luck, she'll have some dirt to dish on the old fella."

Tammy glanced around the room at the line of truckers sitting at the counter, the locals hanging around the jukebox, the teenagers making out in the corner.

"You know," she said, "I'll bet there's a lot of gossip dished in this place along with those greasy burgers. Maybe I should ask your girlfriend, Jeannie, if she needs some extra help."

"You, bimbo-head, waiting on tables?" Dirk laughed. "Believe it or not, you gotta have a lot on the ball to be a waitress. It ain't as easy as it looks."

Tammy's eyes narrowed. "I'll have you know, smart aleck, that I waited tables for three summers in a row when I was in college. And I happen to know how hard it is. I also know that you can find out a lot from just keeping your ears open while you're slingin' hash."

Savannah thought it over, but not for long. "I think it's a great idea." She slapped Tammy on the knee. "I'll talk to Jeannie, and we'll see if we can make a truck-stop cutie out of you, New York girl."

Having left Tammy behind to coax whatever gossip she could from the Burger Igloo's clientele, Savannah and Dirk headed for the McGill Hollow Country Club.

"Wow, this is nice," Dirk commented as they drove past the meticulously groomed golf course, tennis courts, and an Olympic-sized pool. "To see this place, you'd think the South won the war."

"Not everybody in this part of the world is poor by a long shot," Savannah replied, directing him to the main complex and the sports shop. "There's still plenty of old money in the South, as well as the *nouveau riche*. Just because folks say 'ain't' and 'cain't' doesn't mean they're hicks, you know. There's a lot of sophistication and culture around here, if you travel in the right circles."

"Spend a lot of time here when you were growing up?" Dirk pulled the car into an empty spot in the lot and cut the key.

"Oh, yeah." Savannah chuckled. "For a while there I was dropping by twice a week."

"For tennis lessons or swimming?"

"To pick up the dirty linens and to drop off the clean ones. Gran and I made extra money doing the club's laundry."

When Dirk didn't reply, she turned to see him looking at her with a funny expression on his face, one she couldn't quite read.

"What?" she said.

"Things were pretty tough for you, weren't they, Van?"

She shrugged. "I didn't think so at the time. I knew people who were a lot less fortunate. They didn't have any sort of work to do and ate nothing but government rations. *Those folks* had it tough. We had food every night, each other, and Gran. We were blessed."

"Blessed . . .yeah, right." He shook his head. "Let's get busy. You go talk to Mrs. Patterson IV, and I'll see if I can find out why the judge was home instead of out here knocking around some balls."

Bonnie Patterson looked more like somebody's daughter or kid sister than a middle-aged judge's wife. When the manager of the sports shop pointed her out, Savannah immediately decided to scratch her off the suspect list. She was too scrawny to commit murder.

Barely five feet tall, weighing next to nothing, too-frosted hair, turquoise eye shadow, and puffy pink lips, tight shorts, and a midriff-cropped stretch shirt that displayed suspiciously large breasts—Bonnie had probably been the judge's idea of a trophy wife.

But now she was hawking golf balls.

Savannah wondered how the judge's untimely death would affect his almost-ex wife's personal economics. No doubt for the better. Much better than if he had died after the divorce were final.

On second thought, Savannah put her back at the top of the list. Even a big-breasted bantam chick could pull a trigger.

"Can I help you?" Bonnie asked, her accent as thick as cold sorghum. She sidled up to Savannah, a pseudo-seductive set to her hips, her shoulders back and chest out.

Savannah didn't take it personally. Gals like Bonnie practiced that pose until using it was second nature, no matter whom they were addressing. She would have stood like that if she were talking to Gran.

"Hi. Can we have a minute for a private conversation?" Savannah asked, nodding toward the manager, who had retreated to the back of the shop and buried his head in some paperwork.

"Yeah, it's time for my break anyway." She shouted back to him, "I'm outta here, Henry, for a few minutes."

"All right. But just a few. I got stuff to do here."

"Yeah, yeah, yeah."

Obviously eager to escape the drudgery of selling sportsware, Bonnie practically ran out of the shop, dragging Savannah with her. Once outside, she slowed to a casual saunter. They headed down a picturesque stone walkway toward the river. Weeping willows dipped their delicate branches into the water's edge, and a flock of ducks paddled among the reeds, quacking contentedly.

"I don't think I've seen you around town," Bonnie said. "Who are you, and what did you want to talk to me about?"

"My name's Savannah Reid. I was raised around here, but it's my first time back in quite a while."

"Reid?" A light of recognition passed across Bonnie's face, but she quickly squelched it.

In that instant, Savannah decided that Bonnie Patterson would be a pretty darned good poker player. She must have heard about the judge's murder and the subsequent arrests.

"Yes, Reid," she said evenly. "I'm Macon Reid's oldest sister."

Both women paused in the middle of the walkway, facing each other. Savannah searched Bonnie's eyes for the expected emotions: anger, resentment, maybe even fear.

Nothing.

Yep, she thought, Bonnie could play "blank" with the best of them.

"What do you have to say to me?" Bonnie said, her voice as flat as her expression.

There was no point in beating around the proverbial bush. Savannah let her have it: "I was wondering if you might have any idea who killed your husband."

"Talk to Sheriff Mahoney," Bonnie suggested, as offhandedly as if she were recommending a hair salon. "I did, this morning, and he's pretty darned sure it was your brother."

"It wasn't."

"Well, I wouldn't know about that."

They faced off for several tense seconds as Savannah listened to the ducks quack and her own pulse thudding in her ears.

"Somebody else did it, and they set up my brother," Savannah said.

"Like I said, I wouldn't know." Bonnie Patterson smiled. Hers was a dentist-perfect smile—straight, white, even teeth. But it wasn't a warm smile, and it wasn't pretty. In fact, it gave Savannah a slight chill. "For right now," she continued, "I'm assuming that the sheriff's doing his job, and the guilty parties are where they belong . . . behind bars."

No, Savannah decided, she didn't like Bonnie Patterson and her perfect, chilly smile. Not a bit.

"Pretty lucky for you, huh?" Savannah said. "I mean, him dying right before your divorce is final. Damned fortunate timing, if you ask me."

"I don't recall asking you anything, Miss Reid. And I'm finished answering your questions, too. I don't think I want to talk to the sister of the man who murdered my husband in cold blood."

Bonnie turned her back on Savannah and returned to the shop at a much faster pace than she had strolled away.

Savannah watched . . . and mentally highlighted Bonnie Patterson's name at the top of that list. If for no other reason, because she really, *really* didn't like her.

Chapter

11

Savannah found Dirk near the tennis courts, and from the look of disgust on his face, she easily determined that his interview had been about as fruitless as hers.

"Well?" she asked as she met him on the stone walkway that wound from the pool to the courts.

"Nothing, really," he said. She noticed the beads of sweat trickling down his forehead and realized that he was suffering in the humidity as much as she. Only it wasn't his brother who had been arrested, or his sister getting married for the third time.

He really was a good guy. And she reminded herself to keep that uppermost in her mind the next time he bummed a quarter off her or a free burger.

"I talked to a caddie who said that the judge had a standing tee-off time of three-thirty every afternoon. He'd play nine holes, then have a scotch and soda over at the bar. His son-in-law, Mack Goodwin, the county prosecutor, joined him a lot of the time."

"Did the caddie or anybody hear from the judge Monday night?"

"No, but the caddie said he told him on Sunday that he wouldn't be here Monday."

"So, whatever he was doing at home the night he was murdered, instead of playing golf, it was planned, not spur of the moment." Savannah mulled that one over for a second. It had interesting implications.

"Right. Wonder what it was?" Dirk said.

"Something he had to do at home, or someone he was going to meet there."

"We've gotta fill in that blank before we get much further."

Savannah glanced around and saw a young man walking along a path that crossed theirs, dressed in tennis shorts and a polo shirt, swinging a racket. His clothes were startlingly white against his dark tan; even Gran, laundry queen, would have been impressed. His hair and eyes were the same shade of brown as his skin, and his GQ good looks rang a bell in her memory banks.

"That's Goodwin," she told Dirk. "I recognize him. It's Mack Goodwin, the prosecutor son-in-law."

Dirk grunted under his breath. He made it a practice to be unimpressed with any guy who dressed better than he did. And that constituted a high percentage of the male population. "I guess he's working out his grief on the tennis court," he said. "Looks all broken up about the old man's passing."

"Ah, you never know," Savannah said, playing devil's advocate. Not because she particularly disagreed with Dirk, but just on principle. *Somebody* had to counteract his negativity and maintain the cosmic balance.

They were both surprised when Goodwin changed his direction and came their way.

When he reached them, he flashed them a broad smile that was as bright as his outfit. But the smile didn't make it to his eyes.

Goodwin shifted the racket to his left hand and held out his right to Savannah. "You're Macon Reid's sister. I heard you were in town."

She shook his hand, but released it quickly. This man would probably be the one to try her little brother in a court of law. She had no intention of becoming a pal of his. Besides, she didn't trust anyone who smiled with their mouth, but not their eyes.

Goodwin turned to Dirk. "And you're a friend of hers from California. A detective with the Los Angeles PD, I believe."

Dirk gave him a firm handshake that made him wince ever so slightly. Savannah secretly smiled to herself. Men and their games. They were so much more overt and entertaining than women's.

"I'm not from L.A.," Dirk corrected him with obvious satisfaction. "San Carmelita. It's on the coast north of L.A."

"And you came all the way out here to help your friend's brother. How *nice* of you." Goodwin's emphasis on the word "nice" and the coldness in his eyes made the pineapple malted in Savannah's stomach do a little shiver.

But Dirk gave him look for icy look and said evenly, "What can I say, I'm just a swell guy. Besides, we wanna make sure that nobody gets a murder pinned on them that they didn't do."

"We *all* want to make sure of that," Goodwin replied. "That's why I haven't charged Macon yet . . . and won't, until I have all the facts."

"And, of course," Savannah added, "you wouldn't want to do anything until he's *at least* had a chance to talk to a lawyer, huh? I mean, it's pretty awful that he's gotta sit there, cooling his heels in jail without benefit of counsel." She turned to Dirk. "I'll bet that's against the law . . . him sitting there, unrepresented . . . even here. Don't you?"

Dirk nodded enthusiastically. "Oh, yeah. If that happened where we come from, a suspect would have all kinds of grounds to—"

"We've contacted Claude Wilkins," Goodwin interjected, "and he's cutting his fishing trip in the Ozarks short. He'll be back by tomorrow morning. That's soon enough."

"Well, not really," Savannah said. "But I guess it'll do."

"And meanwhile"—Goodwin propped his racket on his shoulder and spun it around a few times—"You two had better watch where you're stepping around here, and who you're talking to. I wouldn't want the whole lot of you up on charges for interfering with an investigation."

"That's fine . . ." Savannah stepped closer to him, until they were eye to eye. ". . . As long as there's an investigation going on. I mean, I'd hate to think that y'all are sitting around on your fists, like you've got everything figured out. My brother's a young man, a good kid, and we're talking about his life here."

"Actually, I've heard that your little brother is a bit of a punk." Goodwin held his ground as Savannah took another step closer, her fists clenched. "And my father-in-law was a good person. You ought to have seen him, Ms. Reid, laying there dead on his rug. I'll never get over coming upon a scene like that. It'll haunt me till my dying day. And if your brother did it . . . and I think he did . . . I'm going to see him strapped to a table with a needle in his arm. It's the least I can do for a man who gave me everything I've got."

Savannah could feel her pulse, pounding hot and red in her face. Her vision started to blur, and for a moment she thought she might even pass out.

With an effort, she gathered her mental and emotional reserves and resisted the urge to crumple. The last thing she wanted was to faint dead away at Mack Goodwin's feet.

She felt Dirk's hand close around her upper arm. "Come on, Van," he said, giving her a slight tug. "There's no point in standing around here, talking to this guy. His mind's already made up, and we've got work to do."

Reluctantly, she allowed Dirk to lead her away. But as they left, she heard Goodwin call after them, "You two watch yourselves. I mean it. I won't tolerate the relatives of the accused obstructing justice. You hear me?"

While Dirk filled the car's tank at the service station on Main Street, Savannah used the phone booth to call Gran.

"Don't cook supper tonight, Gran. Dirk and I are going to take care of it."

"What do you mean, don't cook?" Gran sounded as though Savannah were speaking some incomprehensible foreign tongue. "I'll probably have the whole crew over here again, and they're

ugly when they're hungry. I've already laid out the hamburger to
thaw for meatloaf."

"Well, stick it in the refrigerator and use it tomorrow night, or
the next. At least for tonight, you're off duty."

"But . . . but . . ." Gran sputtered on the other end. "Whatever
will I do with myself?"

"Why don't you sit in the swing on the front porch and watch
your flowers grow? Better yet, sing to them, and they'll grow
even faster."

Gran chuckled. "Not the way I sing, sugar. You forgot; I got a
voice that can curdle buttermilk."

It was Savannah's turn to laugh. Gran did have a bit of a repu-
tation in church for singing loudly and a tad off key.

"So do I," Savannah said. "But you always told me it didn't
matter, as long as you 'make a joyful noise unto the Lord.' You
said the Almighty ain't picky about such things."

"That's true. But I just can't imagine not making supper, I
mean . . ."

"Imagine it, Gran. It's time. *High* time somebody started taking care of *you*, instead of the other way around. Go. Sit. Swing.
Sing."

An hour later, Savannah, Tammy, and Dirk arrived at the old
farmhouse, bearing nine large pizzas from the Pizza Palace in
Brownsville. Sure enough, the house looked as though Sherman's army had invaded and set up camp.

Besides their threesome and Gran, the dinner crowd included
Alma, Waycross, Cordele, Jesup, Vidalia and Butch and their two
sets of twins, and Marietta, her two boys, and her fiancé. Just
your usual dinner for eighteen, sitting around a table made for
eight . . . tops.

Once again, the children stood at the counter, but they complained less. After all, there was pizza to munch.

The level of conversational buzz was deafening. Savannah
glanced to either side of her and saw that Dirk and Tammy were
positively stunned.

Ha, wimps, she thought with an inward giggle. So-called "normal" families had no idea what true togetherness was all about. You couldn't get much more "together" than having your sibling's elbow in your face during a meal or getting your shins kicked continually under the supper table.

"Anybody hear anything new on Macon and his predicament?" Butch asked as he shoved half a slice of pepperoni and mushroom pie into his face.

"We had ourselves a busy afternoon," Savannah said, "talking to several folks, but I wouldn't say we turned up anything worthwhile. Anybody else?"

Waycross reached for a slice of the sausage and onion pizza. "Some guys were talkin' at the garage today. They said it was Mack Goodwin found the judge dead. Said he was all shook up about it, was practically cryin' when he called the sheriff and reported it."

"Well, I guess he made a pretty fast recovery," Savannah said, dabbing at her mouth with a paper napkin. "We talked to him this afternoon at the country club, and he didn't look particularly distraught when he told us to mind our own business or get locked up."

Gran offered her a refill of iced tea. "Y'all had better watch yourself. That Mack Goodwin's known around here for comin' down hard on criminals. And we don't need the three of you in jail along with Macon."

"That's right!" Marietta agreed. "Why, our wedding rehearsal is tomorrow night! If you get locked up, Savannah, we'll be short a girl on the bridesmaids' side of the line-up. It'll look lopsided."

Her fiancé, a quiet, timid little guy with curly brown hair and big hazel eyes, squirmed a bit in his chair. Savannah guessed why, but restrained herself from asking.

Cordele, on the other hand, didn't feel the need. "Is your divorce through yet, Lester? Did your old lady sign the papers?"

Lester choked on his pizza. Marietta slapped him on the back, far harder than necessary.

"Lester's working on it," Marietta snapped at her younger sister. "He's about got the battle-ax where he wants her. They're just arguing about who's gonna get the new pickup. We've got till Saturday."

"That's only three days from now," seven-year-old Jillian added, smiling a big, red pizza-sauce grin.

"We'll cross that bridge when we come to it," Gran said, giving Cordele a warning look. "Eat your supper before it's ice cold."

Marietta's two boys, Steve and Paulie, stood at the counter with the other kids, chowing down on the pizza. Both were in their early teens, the products of Marietta's former marriages, one from each ex-husband.

Savannah saw a couple of sly smirks pass between them, and she wondered what they thought of Lester. Both were taller than their prospective stepfather, and beefier. Lester was going to have his hands full, trying to assert himself as alpha male in that household. She also wondered, not for the first time, if Marietta had thought this one through. She doubted it.

Marietta was famous in McGill for her ability to create the "biggest" hairdos for proms and weddings at her salon and for the fancy designs she airbrushed on acrylic nails.

But she wasn't so well known for her common sense.

"Boy, those pizzas weren't long for this world," Dirk whispered in her ear. He had nearly fainted when he realized how much it cost to feed the crew for only one meal.

"Yeah, there's a certain wolfpack efficiency to the way food disappears around here," Savannah replied.

"I made a carrot cake this mornin'," Gran said, pushing back her chair. "Who wants a piece?"

"You sit down, Gran," Savannah said quickly. "If you made it, somebody else can serve it."

Everyone at the table . . . and the counter . . . stared at Savannah as though she had lost her mind. Apparently, the concept of self-sufficiency was foreign around here.

"I'll get it." She stood and walked over to the refrigerator, where the cake with its thick cream-cheese frosting awaited the same fate as the pizzas. Setting it in the center of the table, in front of Marietta, she said, "Mari, would you cut Gran a piece first, and then serve our company?"

"Well, I worked all day, but I reckon I could . . ."

"Everybody at this table worked today. So, yes, I reckon you could." Savannah shoved the handle of a knife into her hand, then pushed a stack of plates at her.

Savannah turned to the youngsters. "If y'all want some cake, you clear these dishes off the table and take out the trash. Take those pizza boxes out to the burning barrel."

After a stunned moment of silence, a whirlwind of activity erupted, and in no time, the mess was cleared and the cake served.

The crowd was munching cheerfully when Beauregard scrambled off the back porch and ran, baying, around to the front of the house.

"We've got company," Gran said. "Better go get him, Waycross. If it's somebody the colonel don't like, he'll bite a hunk outta 'em."

"I need to talk to you, Savannah. Alone." Tom Stafford stood at the front door, peering through the screen, his uniform hat in his hands. Behind him on the porch, Waycross wrestled with the overly protective hound.

Dirk walked up behind Savannah, who was standing in the middle of the living room, and tossed his arm over her shoulders.

"She's having dinner," he said. "And she's had a hard day. She doesn't need no more hassle from you."

Savannah hid her surprise. Since when did Dirk do the "my woman" macho thing?

Tom ignored him. Didn't even glance his way. "Please, Savannah. Can you come out here for just a few minutes, and then I'll let you get back to your supper."

"It's all right," Savannah said, stepping away from Dirk. "Y'all go ahead and finish your carrot cake," she added to the rest of the family who had crowded behind Dirk and Tammy to eavesdrop on the situation. "I'll be right back."

"Don't you give her a hard time," Dirk called as she walked out the door and onto the porch.

"I don't aim to give anybody a hard time," Tom replied. He looked tired, exhausted even, as he looked down at Waycross and the growling, bristling Beauregard, rolling around on the porch. "Come on, Savannah. We'll sit in my car. It's air-conditioned, and I don't think the hound dog from hell can get me there." He shook his head, utterly disgusted. "Lord, what did I ever do to deserve this stinkin' job? Shee-it . . . even the friggin' dogs hate me."

The giant, finely tuned cruiser purred as Savannah and Tom talked. Most importantly, it churned icy air out of its dash vents. Savannah was truly comfortable for the first time since she had arrived on home soil.

Although she would have been a bit more comfortable had Dirk not been coming to the front door every three minutes, glaring out at them, and making a jealous-male spectacle of himself.

"So, is that guy your boyfriend or what?" Tom asked.

Savannah smiled as Dirk appeared again in the doorway, his arms crossed over his chest, a look of pure misery on his face. "Oh, I'd say he's more like my 'or what.' He means well."

"You could've fooled me. He's been stirrin' up things around town, asking questions and all, causing trouble."

"For whom?"

"For me. Sheriff Mahoney's been on me to come over here and set him straight. I'll talk to him next."

"Naw, you'll just tell me what you want him to know, and I'll pass it on," she replied. "Believe me, it'd be easier that way. Much easier."

He reached for a half-empty bottle of Coke wedged into a beverage holder in the console. Holding it out to her, he said, "Want some?"

She looked at the bottle, considering the offer, but decided against sharing the drink with him. Inside the intimate confines of the car, she was all too aware of him.

Of the nice way he smelled . . . as if he had just stepped out of a shower. That was one thing she had always liked about Tom; he always smelled good.

And the way he filled out that khaki uniform.

And the way his thick blond hair curled over his collar, and . . .

Knock it off, girl, she told herself. *With Dirk standing in the doorway and your brother sitting in a jail cell, now just so-o-o ain't the time.*

"No, thanks," she said. "I'm not thirsty."

"Oh, I thought maybe you just didn't want to swap slobber with me . . . what with *him* standing there watching."

She shot him an irritated sideways look. That was something she *didn't* like about Tom Stafford . . . his ability to read her like a front page headline.

"What do you want to say to me that can't be said to the rest of the family?" she said, in an attempt to get down to business.

"Your brother's in big trouble, Savannah. He's going to go down for this. And I guarantee you, Mack Goodwin's going to push for the death penalty."

"You told me that, in so many words, yesterday," she replied.

"Yeah, but what I didn't tell you is that I've decided he might be innocent."

She forgot all about Dirk in the doorway and turned to Tom, fully attentive. "Oh? And when did you have this change of heart . . . or mind?"

"This afternoon when I talked to him."

"You're not supposed to be talking to Macon without his lawyer."

"And you're not supposed to be sneaking into my jail to see him either. Turnin' poor old Jeter's head with a long-legged blonde in a short skirt. Honestly, Savannah, I thought better of you."

She grinned. "Hey, whatever works. Of course, *you* never would have fallen for a ruse like that."

He quirked an eyebrow. "No, I tend to fall for brunettes with big chests."

She glanced quickly over at the house, just in time to see Tammy grab Dirk by the arm and pull him out of the doorway.

"Let's don't go there, Tommy," she said softly. "It's not the time. You know?".

"Yeah, I know. Maybe sometime you'll come home . . . alone . . . and none of your relatives will be in trouble with the law."

"Well, let's don't have *that* many restrictions on a visit. There are quite a few of us Reids. The chances of none of us being in trouble are pretty slim."

She decided to take a drink of his Coke after all. Suddenly, her mouth had gone dry.

"What changed your mind about Macon?" she asked.

"I'm a cop, Savannah. If I talk to twelve people, I get lied to a dozen times. I'm pretty good at spotting a liar. I think Macon's telling the truth now . . . now that he's admitted he was there at the scene."

"That's what Dirk and I thought, too."

At the mention of Dirk, Tom's upper lip curled, ever so slightly, but Savannah noticed, and it gave her a certain perverse satisfaction. After all, he was the one, all those years ago, who had decided that they were much too young to know what they wanted in life, in a mate.

Savannah had known.

He was the only one who was undecided.

"Chicken shit" was more like it.

So, if he suffered the occasional twinge of "what might have been," he had only himself to blame.

"Also," he continued, "Macon's story matched Kenny Jr.'s almost exactly. And they hadn't had the chance to compare notes. We've kept them apart since we brought them in."

"Does Kenny have a bruise across his back, something like the one on Macon's forearm?"

"Yeah. Both look like they got whacked with a cane, just like Macon said."

Savannah nodded. "And?"

"And the medals. You're right; guys that age don't give a hoot about something like that. They'd go after the guns. Both Macon and Kenny Jr. admit that's what they were after, and it makes a lot more sense."

"So, whoever planted those medals under his bed probably did the killing, or at least knows who did."

"That's right. We've got a gal checking them for fingerprints now. It'll be interesting what we get."

Savannah swallowed hard. "Uh, yeah. Interesting."

"I'm surprised you didn't find those," he said, watching her closely. "I figure you'd just been out there, poking around, when we came along."

She turned to face him squarely. "Are you surprised that I didn't find them or that I'd leave them there for you to find?"

"Either one. Both. You're his sister."

"And I'm still a cop at heart."

They were both silent for a long moment as the engine hummed and the air-conditioner blew.

"Helluva spot to be in," he said at last.

"Yeah. It sucks."

She took another sip of his Coke, but the cola did nothing to quench her thirst. In fact, the sweetness made her a bit queasy. Suddenly, she was eager to get out of the car. Maybe to take a long walk, alone, down to the main road and back.

"Then there's the window sill," she said.

"What?"

"The fingerprints on the window sill."

"I told you already—they're your brother's."

"The prints on the bottom of the sill are Macon's . . . where he pushed it up when he broke into the house."

Tom was fully attentive. "Yes, and . . . ?"

"And the only ones on the top of the sill, on the inside, were the judge's."

"So?"

"So, when you arrived on the scene, the window was down and locked. The judge closed the window. The boys opened it to get into the house, and he shut it after he chased them out the front door. He was still alive, Tom. Dead men don't go around closing windows."

Tom sat quietly, mulling it over.

"Think about it," she continued. "Why would the boys lower it, when they might need to bail out that way? And what's the first thing you'd do if you'd fought off some burglars and chased them out of your house?"

"I'd lock the door, close the window they came in through, check the other doors and windows . . . and then I'd probably call somebody."

"Did the judge have a redial feature on his phone?"

"Yeah."

"Did y'all check it?"

"Yep. He had dialed 1,2,3,4,5. We're still trying to figure out why he would've done that. Makes no sense."

"Yes, it does." Savannah drained the rest of his soda. She was starting to feel a little better. This was business . . . a business she knew well. The familiar territory settled her nerves and her stomach.

"How? How does it make sense?"

She could tell it cost him dearly to ask.

"When the judge got rid of the boys, he may have called somebody, perhaps even the killer. It could have been somebody who already wanted to murder him. If he told them about the burglary, they might have seen their opportunity and took it, figuring it would be easy to pin the killing on Macon and Kenny Jr. And they had the presence of mind to pick up the phone and punch in some nonsense, so that you wouldn't press redial and get their number."

Tom thought for a while, tapping his fingers on the steering wheel. "It won't do them any good," he said. "We can still get hold of the phone records. It might take a little while, but . . ."

"Perhaps they didn't know that. A lot of people think that if it isn't a long distance call, there's no record. Were there any fingerprints on the phone?"

"There weren't any. I mean, none, smeared or otherwise. It'd been wiped clean."

"Like the gun."

He turned to Savannah, the light of challenge and intrigue in his eyes. "Yeah, just like the gun. Sorry to say so, Savannah, but Macon and Kenny Jr. just ain't that smart."

She gave him a wry smile. "Apology accepted."

Chapter

12

"Ifeel real bad," Gran said as she and Savannah settled into the featherbed for another night's tossing and turning, "that your friends have to go off to a motel like that. They come all the way across the country to help us out, and we can't even offer 'em a decent bed to sleep in."

"It's okay, Gran, really. Visitors in other parts of the world aren't used to Southern hospitality. It never occurred to them, when they came out here, that they'd be sleeping here at the house."

Gran sniffed her disapproval as she adjusted her pillow. "Still, I hate the thought of it. They'll probably get fleas at that run-down truckers' motel on the highway."

"I'm sure it'll be fine. As tired as they are, jet lag and all, they'll be asleep when their heads hit the pillow."

Gran was still for a while, but Savannah felt a question coming. And she had a feeling what it might be.

"Dirk and Tammy . . . they don't . . . I mean, they'll be sleeping in separate rooms, won't they?"

"I'm sure they will. But even if they didn't, even if they slept in the same bed, there'd be nothing going on. They hate each other."

"Really?"

"No, not really. But they'll swear they do to their dying days. They squabble like a couple of kids and like to drive me crazy. Sometimes, I swear I'm going to put them on 'time out' just to get some peace."

"Actually, sweetie, I think Dirk's carryin' a torch for you."

"Dirk? Naw. We're just buddies. We've been friends for so long, we wouldn't know how to be anything else."

Gran gave her pillow a couple more thumps. "Nothing wrong with a man and a woman being friends. Your pa and I were best friends from the time we met when we were fifteen, till he died."

Savannah glanced over at the dresser, where a picture of her grandfather sat, barely visible in the moonlight. But she knew every line of his beloved face. A simple farmer, Pa was the gentlest, kindest man she had ever known. No wonder he and Gran had been happily married for more than fifty years.

Everyone who knew him loved him, respected him . . . and missed him terribly.

"That's the trouble with young folks these days," Gran said. "They just go straight from being strangers to being lovers. They don't take their time, get to be good friends first. Then they wonder why, when they've been married a year or two, they run out o' things to say to each other."

Savannah chuckled. "I remember, after we'd all gone to bed, I'd hear you and Pa talking about stuff here in your bed. You'd giggle like a teenage girl, and he'd laugh that deep laugh of his. Just the sound of you two talking, getting along so good, it made me feel safe."

"That was one thing your Pa gave to all of us, that safe feeling. Without him ever saying it in so many words, we knew that he'd die defending us if he had to. He'd never let anything bad happen to anyone he loved, anybody under his roof. You were just as safe as you felt back then, Savannah. We all were, thanks to him."

Savannah felt a breeze—hot and moist, but definitely a breeze—sweep the lace curtain aside and caress her cheek. She smelled the clean, fresh fragrance of the night air.

It reminded her of summer nights when she had asked for permission to sleep on the back porch. How long ago had it been when the world was innocent, and a child could sleep outside on her own porch without fear?

"Some men have that gift," she said, reaching up and brushing her fingertips over the lace that floated on the night breeze. "They exude a male strength that makes those around them feel as though they can lean on them."

"Your Dirk is like that."

Savannah turned over to face her grandmother. "He isn't exactly *my* Dirk."

"He is, if you want him to be."

"But . . . he's never—"

"And he won't. Men may exude strength, but, bless their little hearts, for all their courage, they're cowards when it comes to matters of romance. They won't chase after a woman—at least the good ones with honorable intentions don't. Most of them won't even reach out to her . . . unless she puts her hand out first."

Savannah laughed. "Why, Gran, are you saying a woman should chase after a man?"

"Of course not. That'd be unladylike. They just have to make darned sure the guy knows they're not going to run very far or very fast if he decides to mosey over in their direction."

"I'll keep that in mind, Gran, if I ever decide I want male company on a permanent basis."

Both women sighed, settled in, and nearly drifted off to sleep.

Then Gran added softly, "'Course, there's all that extra cooking and laundry . . . and when they get sick, they're so whiny and cranky. They can just wear you to a frazzle . . . men."

"I know. That's why I'm single."

When Tammy and Dirk reappeared the next morning, bearing two dozen assorted donuts and muffins from the local bakery, Gran was slightly less impressed than she had been with the pizzas—though, the quintessential Southern lady, she only mumbled under her breath rather than objecting aloud.

"A body can't run all morning on junk like that," she muttered as she arranged the pastries on her Sunday pedestal cake plate. "Gotta have something that'll stick to your ribs, like eggs and sausage."

In the end, the donuts were passed over in favor of steaming biscuits and peach preserves.

Once everyone's belly was properly distended, their bodies fortified for the rigors of the morning, Savannah, Dirk, Tammy, and Gran sat in the living room, sipping the final cup of strong coffee.

"What's on today's agenda?" Dirk asked Savannah. "Assuming that I can move from this sofa. I don't remember when I ate that much for breakfast."

"Yesterday morning, on the flight out here," Tammy volunteered. "You should have seen him, asking the flight attendants for extras. He had three before they cut him off."

"Hey, they don't charge any extra for that," he said, as though the "free" factor explained everything.

"Yes, about today," Savannah interjected. "I think I'll go see Herb Jameson, the mortician. He's supposedly got the judge on ice over there at his funeral parlor. I'll see if I can sweet-talk him into letting me have a look at the body."

"Sounds good." Dirk slurped his coffee and licked his upper lip. "I'm going out to the Patterson place and poke around. There's gotta be servants on a place that big. Maybe somebody saw something."

"Elsie Dingle is the housekeeper out there," Gran said, "has been for the past twenty-five years. She's always got her ears on the stretch for some good gossip. Talk to her and you'll hear more than you wanna know."

"Elsie Dingle, okay. . . ." Dirk pulled a small notebook out of his shirt pocket and scribbled in it. "What does she look like?"

"She's a black lady with the prettiest head o' silver hair you ever did see," Gran said. "And she's . . . a good, stout girl."

"Stout?"

"Yes. I'd say that describes Elsie pretty good, don't you, Savannah?"

Savannah smiled. "That about sums her up. I didn't see her around when Tom took me out there, but maybe you'll luck out."

Tammy sighed and stretched her long arms and legs. She was wearing a tube top and shorts . . . her idea of a truck-stop cutie's uniform. "You guys will have to drop me off at the café," she said. "I've gotta help with the lunch crowd and keep my . . . how did you put it, Mrs. Reid? . . . my ears on the stretch."

"Yep, keep 'em all out there on stems, y'all. And you'll be amazed what interesting things you'll hear. We grow gossip around here that's thicker than the cotton."

Savannah was glad that Herb Jameson, and those like him, wanted to be morticians. Like emergency room doctors, firemen, and plumbers, she was thankful that someone in society actually chose those occupations. Because if it were up to her to do the nitty-gritty work of an undertaker, a lot of dead people would still be above ground.

She couldn't imagine why, but Herb seemed to like his job. And his colonial-style funeral parlor on the north side of McGill clearly reflected that pride with its new white paint, crisp black shutters, and brightly planted flower beds.

When she pulled Waycross's pickup into the circular brick driveway, she noticed the hearse parked at the back of the building. Otherwise, there were no vehicles around.

Good, she thought. She had hoped for some moments alone with Herb . . . and if Lady Luck was friendly, a few minutes with the remains of the recently departed judge.

She parked the truck as far to the back of the lot as possible. There was no point in leaving it out front where Sheriff Mahoney or Tom might drive by and see it.

Of course, she wasn't exactly being *sneaky*. She much preferred to think of it as being *sensible*. Getting to be "sensible" for a living was one of her favorite parts of private detecting. How many people got to tell whopping fibs, hide in the back of parking lots, or pretend they were city inspectors or dog catchers, while checking out suspects' basements and garages . . . all in a day's work?

She left the truck and entered the building through a side door. From sad personal experience, she knew what lay in the front. The dark, quiet, somber entry and the stately "showing rooms" were all too familiar to a girl who had grown up in a town with one funeral parlor.

The last time she had visited this establishment, she had been saying good-bye to her beloved grandfather. To date, the most painful day of her life.

There were many places she'd rather be. But . . . anything for a brother in trouble. Even if it meant a not-so-pleasant stroll down memory row.

"You owe me, Macon," she muttered as she entered the door and looked around. "And I don't know how you're ever going to repay me, unless you come to California and re-roof my house."

Once inside, Savannah found herself in a hallway that led from the front of the establishment to the back. The dark paneling and the navy blue carpeting gave her a twinge of claustrophobia. The cloying fragrance of flowers, mixed with the underlying smell of chemicals, didn't help to alleviate the feeling that the walls were closing in on her.

"Mr. Jameson," she called. "Yoo-hoo, Mr. Jameson, are you here?"

No reply.

The term "deadly silence" floated through her head, but she pushed it aside. One ghoulish joke tended to lead to another, and she didn't need to go down that mental road right now.

"Mr. Jameson? Hey, is anybody here? Anybody at all?"

The squeaking of a door at the back end of the hall set her nerves buzzing.

"Hello?" she called.

"Yes?" He appeared out of the dark, a figure dressed in white from head to toe, a shining metal instrument in his hand. An enormous knife.

Actually, it could have been forceps or a simple flashlight. But in her over-stimulated imagination, it was a twelve-inch butcher knife.

"I'm Herb Jameson. May I help you with something, dear?" he asked.

The soft, almost effeminate voice sounded anything but sinister. Savannah cursed herself for her foolishness. In her scant memories of Herb Jameson, he had been kind, helpful, and courteous when making the arrangements for her grandfather. A silent, almost invisible presence, he had directed the funeral from behind the scenes with a high level of professionalism.

"Mr. Jameson," she said, heading down the hall toward him. As she drew closer she saw that he was holding not an implement of destruction, but an ordinary flashlight. "I don't know if you remember me, but I'm Granny Reid's oldest granddaughter—"

"Savannah! Why, of course I remember you, honey. You went to school with my middle girl, Amy. How have you been?"

"Fine, Mr. Jameson . . . until lately, that is."

The smile faded from his deeply tanned face, a complexion more like that of a farmer than an undertaker. Then she remembered that Herb Jameson, like the departed judge, enjoyed his golf.

"I know," he said. "I heard your brother was picked up for the judge's killing. That's just so sad . . . the whole miserable story. I'm working on the judge right now, getting him ready for showing tonight."

"Tonight? So soon?"

"Actually, it's not that soon. If we're going to have a nice presentation, we need to do it right away. I've waited about as long as I can . . . you know . . . sheriff's orders."

"The sheriff has delayed the burial?"

"Well, he hates to give up the body, just in case he needs to go over it one more time for some reason."

"He's been 'over it' more than once?"

Herb Jameson nodded, and Savannah noticed he had lost a lot of that wavy hair he had been so proud of. "Oh, yeah, with a fine-tooth comb. He doesn't want to miss anything. Not too many homicides in his career, I don't suppose."

"That's good, very good," Savannah said, meaning it. She was convinced that a thorough investigation was the only hope Macon had.

By re-examining the corpse, Sheriff Mahoney might be just trying to get more evidence on her brother, but he might also be questioning his own original conclusions.

Savannah walked up to Herb Jameson and laid a hand companionably on his arm. "Mr. Jameson," she said, "I'm Macon's sister, but I'm here as a professional. I used to be a police officer, and now I'm a private investigator."

She saw the guarded look come into his eyes and knew he had guessed what she was going to ask next. So she hurried on, before he had a chance to say no.

"I'm trying to help my brother, it's true," she said, "but I'm also trying to find out what really happened to the judge. I'm looking for the truth. That's all."

He shook his head and gave her the same sad, compassionate look she remembered from her grandfather's funeral. But it didn't look practiced; Herb Jameson really was an empathetic soul.

"I really shouldn't, Savannah. If the sheriff found out, he'd—"

"He won't. I give you my word, he won't. And I promise not to even touch the body. I just want to look at it."

She gently squeezed his forearm. "I have some experience in these matters. I've investigated numerous homicides in my career. I know more than I want to know about murder, Mr. Jameson. And knowing it has scarred my soul. Please, let me use what I know to help my brother. Please."

Savannah was mildly surprised to see that Herb's preparation room appeared to be state of the art. Although she hadn't spent a lot of time hanging out in the mechanical bowels of funeral homes, she was impressed with the display of stainless steel and high-tech looking equipment. In some ways the room reminded her of the autopsy suite of her friend, Dr. Jennifer Liu, the coroner back home in San Carmelita.

Well organized, glass-fronted cabinets held uniformly labeled embalming supplies. Countertops and the linoleum floor gleamed like those of an operating room. A modern autoclave and a disinfection tray on the wall held instruments to be sterilized. A small washer and dryer in one corner stood ready to clean soiled linens and clothing. One of several chemical odors she smelled was good old-fashioned bleach.

At the foot of the embalming table, a ventilation fan hummed, pulling the air out of the room and away from the practitioner. And beside the table sat a rolling utility cart, upon which was laid out an array of cosmetics and intricate tools she didn't recognize.

But whether surrounded by the trappings of modern science or not, the body on the table still looked profoundly dead.

The judge was nude, lying on his back, a bright lamp on an extendable arm shining directly on his face. The brilliant light made him look pathetically pale, vulnerable, and weak.

Not at all the way Savannah remembered him when he had been passing out paper cups of orangeade to the kiddies at Halloween.

Herb Jameson took a snowy white towel from a nearby cupboard and spread it across the judge's mid-section. The gesture touched Savannah and gave her a warm feeling toward the undertaker, who cared about a man's modesty even after the man himself was long past caring about such things.

"Go ahead," he said. "I was just starting to close up the wound in his forehead there. If you'd come along half an hour later, you wouldn't even be able to see it."

She smiled at him. "Pretty good at what you do, huh?"

"I am, if I do say so myself. When the family looks at him for the last time, they're going to carry that memory picture with them for the rest of their lives. It's my job to make him look as much like the man they knew and loved as I possibly can."

She saw a glow of pride in his eyes, and for the first time she saw why, maybe, someone might choose this line of work.

"It's not just a technical, mechanical, biological function we perform," he continued. "It's an art, an important art."

The image of her grandfather in his casket flashed across her memory. He had looked so natural, so peaceful, as though he had simply fallen into a deep sleep. Herb Jameson had done his job well then, too.

Then she thought of the people she had spoken to so far about the judge. Unlike her grandfather, he didn't seem to be particularly loved or deeply grieved.

"Who are you doing it for?" she asked. "Why don't you just have a closed casket?"

"The judge may not have made a lot of friends in his lifetime, but his little granddaughter loved him. More and more children are coming to funerals these days, and I think it's a good idea. It shows them that life's precious, that our days on earth are limited and should count for something. I want her to look into that casket and see the man who played ball with her, who took her for walks and read her stories. I want her to be able to say a proper good-bye."

He leaned over and touched the round, black-edged hole in the judge's forehead. "And I don't want her to see what your . . . what somebody did to him. She can do without that in her memory."

Savannah stepped closer to the table and peered down at the bullet wound. "It's a neat, round hole," she said, "not star-shaped."

"No," he said, "it wasn't a contact wound. And no gunpowder tattooing around the hole, either. I put that in my autopsy report."

She was impressed. Not bad for a small-town undertaker and emergency, stand-in coroner.

Jameson touched the dead man's shoulder in a sadly comforting manner. "I wonder if he saw it coming."

"Did the bullet go straight in?"

"Front to back, burned a tunnel right through the brain matter. I found it laying right against the skull, a little flattened but still intact."

"Then he probably saw it coming. But hopefully, he didn't have long to think about it."

"I'd like to think he didn't suffer, that it was quick." He fingered the bullet hole. "Now I have to close this up and make it disappear, as best I can."

"That'll take some careful stitching," she said.

He grinned. "No, we've got super glue now. You'd be surprised how much we use it to prepare a body for burial. It sure makes our life easier."

Savannah didn't reply. There were plenty of things about the undertaker's methods that, for her own peace of mind, she preferred not to know.

She studied the rest of the corpse, looking for any other signs of injury. And found some.

"His right hand is bruised, here across the palm and especially between the thumb and forefinger."

"Yes, the sheriff and I noticed that, too. Don't know what it means, though. Kind of a strange place for a defensive wound."

"But perfectly logical for an *offensive* wound."

Herb looked confused but interested. "How do you figure?"

"My brother and Kenny Jr. have confessed to trying to burglarize the judge's house the night he was killed. They say he caught them in the act and took his cane to them. Whacked them both pretty good before they escaped out the front door."

Herb nodded and glanced down at the contusion. "That would explain the discoloration there. If he hit them hard enough, he might bruise his own hand like that."

"They say they hightailed it out of there, right after he smacked them. That he was alive when they left."

"Hm-m-m . . ." He didn't appear impressed. "That'd be pretty hard to prove, considering all the evidence."

"There's not that much evidence, and none of it's conclusive."

Again, his eyes filled with compassion. "I'm afraid that may be up to a jury to decide, Savannah."

She found it hard to look into his face, honest and straight-forward, knowing that he believed her brother was a cold-blooded killer. She returned her attention to the body.

"Mr. Jameson, how long do you suppose it takes for a bruise like that to form after the initial injury?"

He thought a long time before admitting, "I don't know. A while, I suppose."

"Yes. A while. He hit my brother and Kenny Jr. hard enough to bruise them and himself, too. If they were the murderers, what do you suppose they were all three doing for that 'while' after he hit them with the cane, and they fired the shot that killed him?"

Herb shook his head. "I don't rightly know."

"I don't either. But it sounds like my brother might be telling the truth. That he and Kenny Jr. were long gone by the time the judge died . . . with that substantial bruising on his hand."

For the first time since she had arrived, Savannah saw Herb Jameson waver, just a little, to her side of the story. And for the first time since she heard her brother had been arrested for homicide, she felt just a wee bit hopeful.

Chapter

13

"I really wish you would've let us bring home a bag full of burgers for lunch," Savannah said as she and Dirk sat down to Gran's table and a meal of Great Northern beans, ham hocks, and cornbread.

Gran placed a bowl of mustard greens on the table along with an enormous pitcher of iced tea. "Hamburgers, donuts, and pizza. Lord have mercy, y'all will die young, eating garbage like that. It clogs up a body's system." She turned to Dirk, "You want a bologna sandwich with that, hon? Pa always had to have a bologna sandwich with his dinner or it wasn't a meal to him. I've got white bread and mustard for it, too."

Dirk grinned, and Savannah silently blessed him for not pointing out the inconsistencies in a line of logic that considered hamburgers garbage and bologna nourishment.

"No, thank you, Mrs. Reid. This is more than enough, really."

"You don't have to call me Mrs. Reid, child. I'm Gran to everybody in town, except at church where they call me Sister Reid."

"Okay, Gran. Thanks for making the cornbread. We love it when Savannah makes it for us back in California."

Gran beamed at Savannah. "So, you find time to do a bit of home cooking, in spite of that busy schedule of yours?"

"Oh, she spoils us rotten," Dirk answered for her. "Fried

chicken, barbecued ribs, even catfish and hushpuppies some-times."

Savannah shrugged. "Gotta make sure nobody faints dead away from hunger."

"Nobody's ever going to die of hunger in the presence of a Reid woman," Dirk said. "It just isn't allowed."

Gran eased herself into her chair at the head of the table. Savannah noticed with dismay that she was moving a bit slower these days, and she grimaced sometimes, as though her arthritis were acting up.

"Well, I'm afraid that don't apply to *all* the Reid females in this house. Alma's about the only one who's taken to cooking. The others would live off cold cereal and TV dinners if I didn't put something better before 'em."

"You've gotta stop that, Gran," Savannah said, reaching for a square of the hot cornbread. "You've spoiled those kids some-thing shameful, and they're lazy as can be. They're not children anymore. They're adults who should be fending for them-selves . . . and taking care of you in your old age."

Gran puffed up like a river toad. "Whose old age? Ain't no-body old around here."

"Okay, chronologically enhanced," Savannah offered.

"That's better . . . I think. . . ." Gran grabbed Dirk's glass and filled it with tea. "But you're right. I'm starting to see that now. Chances are, I haven't done them any favors, letting them get away with mur . . ."

Her voice trailed away, and a sadness came into her eyes that hurt Savannah deeply. Gran shouldn't have to grieve; she had suffered too much already in her long life.

Dirk cleared his throat, breaking the awkward silence. "How did it go over at the funeral home?" he asked.

"Mr. Jameson was nice. He's a good man."

"Always has been," Gran interjected.

Savannah continued, "He even let me see the judge's body . . . for all the good it did."

"Nothing helpful?" Dirk asked.

"Not really. The shot was fired from several feet away. And that doesn't tell us much. No other wounds, except a bruise on his palm. The darkest part being right here. . . ." She pointed to the area between her own thumb and forefinger.

"He probably gave himself that when he hit them with his cane," Dirk said, cramming his mouth full of beans.

"Yeah, that's what I told Mr. Jameson."

"Does any of that help or hurt our Macon?" Gran asked.

Savannah sighed. "Not really. It substantiates his version, in the sense that the bruise would have taken a little while to form. It wasn't done immediately before death."

"But that doesn't really help Macon either," Dirk said. "The sheriff or Mack Goodwin could say they hung around a while, giving the old man a hard time before they finally shot him."

"How did you do with Elsie?" Savannah asked him.

"Not even as good as you did. She hated me on sight. Said she'd already had it up to here with cops asking her questions. Practically threw me out of her kitchen."

Gran chuckled. "That sounds like Elsie. She and I've gone to the same church for years. I always did like her. She's full 'o vinegar, that one. Speaks her mind, she does."

"Yeah, well . . . she spoke it quite loudly to me today," Dirk agreed. "I think if I'd hung around another minute or two, she would've started chucking pots and pans at me."

Gran glanced over at the counter and the coconut cake she had baked that morning for the evening's supper. A grin lit her face. "Elsie's got a real sweet tooth," she said. "If you want to try *your* luck with her, Savannah, I'm sure I could butter her up with that cake. If I know Elsie, she won't be chuckin' no pots and pans with one of my homemade cakes under her nose."

"We might as well head around to the back of the house," Gran said when she and Savannah stepped out of the pickup at the Patterson mansion. "This time of day, Elsie will still be working."

"Even with the judge dead?" Savannah asked, falling into step beside her.

"With a house this big, there's always a heap of work to be done, whether anybody's living here or not. You couldn't *give* me a place like this. Too danged much bother."

Savannah smiled to herself, thinking of Aesop's fable about the fox and the sour grapes. But she thought better of mentioning the fact that it would have been a lot easier to raise a passel of kids in a sprawling mansion than in a shotgun house.

While little had changed about the front of the antebellum house since the Civil War, the back had been transformed. Instead of stables for horses and an old-fashioned courtyard, there was a modern swimming pool with a whirlpool and a swim-up bar, a tennis court, and a putting green. The barns were now multi-car garages housing half a dozen vintage classics.

In the pastures, delicate thoroughbreds grazed, instead of the sturdy draft horses that had been used to pull the grand carriages in days gone by.

They stepped onto the back porch with its white wicker tables and chairs with bright floral cushions. "This is the kitchen door," Gran said, rapping loudly. "Elsie's like me . . . spends most her life standing at the kitchen sink. I'd like to have a nickel for every potato the two of us has peeled in our time."

A second series of knocks brought Elsie Dingle to the door. Sure enough, she was holding a dish towel in one hand and had suds on the other.

Gran was right about Elsie's magnificent head of silver hair. It glowed like a halo around her dark face and softened an otherwise severe countenance that looked as though its owner had endured more than her share of suffering in life. And she was, indeed, a stout lady. She may have been deprived of certain things in her life, but apparently, food hadn't been one of them.

Elsie was scowling, as though highly irritated at the interruption . . . until she saw Gran.

"Sister Reid!" she shouted, reaching out with a soapy hand to grab Gran's sleeve. "Why, come right in, sugar! No point in standing out there in the hot sun. You'll melt."

When Gran held the coconut cake out to her, the grin on Elsie's face grew even wider.

"Oh, now, you didn't have to do that," she said, grabbing for it. "But I'm just so glad you did! I know how good your cakes are . . . the best part of any church potluck!"

She pulled them and the precious cake into the kitchen, which was large enough to contain most of Savannah's California bungalow. With great ceremony, she guided them over to a breakfast nook in one corner and set the dessert in the center of the doily on the table, twisting it first one way, then the other, until she decided it was properly displayed.

Savannah didn't recall ever being in this part of the house, and was surprised and pleased to see the blending of old world and new in this cavernous room. On one side stood the brick fireplace with its assortment of cast iron hooks, cranks, and pulleys, where enormous pots had once hung over the blazing fires. Spits, now empty, had turned massive hunks of beef and pork, whole turkeys, grown on the plantation, as well as miscellaneous game from the nearby woods and swamps.

But on the other side of the room, modern appliances made the cook's work much lighter: a chef's stove, microwave/confectioner's oven, a double refrigerator and walk-in pantry, a center island with a vegetable sink, garbage compactor, and industrial-sized dishwasher.

White tile and highly polished copper gleamed in the sunlight that streamed through leaded-glass windows with cobalt-blue and yellow accents.

"Sit yourselves down right there," Elsie said, pointing to the booth in the nook, "and I'll fetch you something cold to drink. I've got fresh limeade, and iced tea, and—"

"I think the tea would be best with the cake," Gran said.

"Then tea it is. I'll get us some glasses and some plates, and we'll be in business."

"May I help you?" Savannah asked.

"You sure can, by sitting down there and telling me everything you know about this awful business with the judge and Macon. And then I'll tell you everything I know about it."

Savannah sat and grinned across the table at Gran.

This was going to be one of her easier interviews. Unlike many subjects, Elsie Dingle certainly wouldn't require the rack or thumbscrews to tell all *she* knew. And then, there was the coconut cake. . . .

"I can't begin to tell you how good it is to have company," Elsie said as she shoveled in a mouthful of the moist cake and chewed blissfully. "This place is lonely, not to mention spooky, without anybody around. Especially considering what happened right in that other room."

"I don't know how you can stand it," Gran said, shaking her head. "I mean, this old house has haunts enough just from the war, let alone with the recent goings on."

"Boy, howdy . . . it sure does." Elsie leaned forward and lowered her voice, as though afraid some unseen presence might overhear. "I still haven't gone into that library. I don't think I ever will. The dust and the cobwebs can just pile up, for all I care. I'd rather walk on a bed of broken glass than tread those rugs."

"Well, actually," Savannah said, "you aren't supposed to go in there. It's still cordoned off with the police tape, isn't it?"

"No, the sheriff came by this morning and took all that away. Said they'd done all they needed to do, you know, with the investigation and all." Elsie glanced down into her glass of tea, as though suddenly embarrassed. "I want y'all to know . . . I don't put no store at all by what the sheriff's saying about it being Macon that done in the judge. I know that none of your grandchildren would do something so awful, Sister Reid. Everybody in town knows that's just a heap o' baloney. We were all interceding for you last night at the Wednesday night prayer meeting, asking the Lord to shine a light o' truth on what really happened."

"Thank you, Sister Dingle," Gran told her. "We sure appreciate those prayers. We can use all we can get right now."

Savannah decided the time was as good as any to jump in. "Actually, Miss Dingle, that's why we're here . . . other than to offer the cake and condolences, that is. We're trying to help the good Lord out with that 'light o' truth' business. And we were thinking that maybe you'd have some opinions on what happened to the judge."

"Oh, mercy! I have opinions. I've got more opinions than Carter's got pills, but as a rule, nobody wants to hear them."

"We do," Gran piped up. "We want to hear it all. Let 'er rip, Sister Dingle."

Elsie took a long drink of tea, a long deep breath, and said, "I think there's at least a dozen people in this town who could've done in the judge. He sure gave folks more reason to hate him than love him. But the one I'd put my money on . . . if I were a gambling woman, which I'm not . . . is that soon-to-be divorced wife of his and her man."

"Her man?" Savannah was all ears. "You mean, a man other than the judge?"

"Oh, honey, she had a dozen men on her fishing line when she hooked Judge Patterson, and she didn't exactly cut 'em loose just because she'd slipped a diamond ring on her finger."

Gran frowned, confused. "But I heard she left him, because *he* was the one who was steppin' out."

"He was. And she did. But just because she fools around doesn't mean she's not the jealous type. I think she figured an old fellow like his honor was past all that. But the judge . . ." Elsie covered her mouth with her hand and giggled. ". . . Just when he was starting to slow down a little, he discovered the wonders of that Viagra stuff. And it got him all riled up again. Why, he chased women till his dying day, he did."

"And you think that's what got him killed?" Savannah asked.

"Oh, no. I think she shot him for his money. She's got her tennis instructor, that Alvin Barnes, and he's who she wanted . . . at least, in *that* way. But she got used to having better, living here with the judge and all. Her standard o' living dropped considerably when she stomped out. And she ain't the type to be happy just living on love, if you know what I mean."

"And you think she actually shot him herself?" Savannah asked.

"Either that, or she told Alvin to do it. She wouldn't have had to twist his arm outta the socket, you know. He figured the judge had done him a great disservice by not acknowledging him as his son . . . since the whole town knows it. He's the spittin' image of the judge."

"Where were you, Elsie, when the murder happened?" Savannah said, as gently as she could.

But it wasn't gentle enough for Gran.

"What do you mean, asking Sister Dingle a fool thing like that?" Gran demanded. She turned to Elsie. "I'm sorry. You'll just have to excuse Savannah. Being a police officer just ruined her manners . . . asking a fine, church-goin' woman for an alibi for murder! I swear . . . !"

Elsie laughed good-naturedly. "Oh, I wasn't offended at all. The sheriff already grilled me like a well-done steak about that night, I don't mind saying. I was in my room, above the garage. It used to be the carriage house in the old days, and the overseer lived there. It's a real nice room, away from everything, peaceful and quiet."

Savannah had a sinking feeling. "So peaceful and quiet that you didn't hear anything?"

"Not a solitary thing. I left work early that afternoon, went to my room, and took a nap. Slept through the whole thing, I did. I was dead to the world till the sheriff and Mr. Goodwin came pounding on my door. By then, well, it was too late for the judge."

Although she didn't really want to see it, Savannah observed a definite lack of mourning on Elsie's part, considering that the judge had been her employer for more than twenty years.

"You left early?" Savannah said.

"Yeah, the judge told me to."

In spite of her embarrassment over having a "rude" grand-daughter, Gran was getting into interrogation mode herself. "Why did he do that?" she asked. "Did he usually let you go early?"

"No. He never did. The judge was a man who wanted a day's work for a day's pay. Never made any bones about that. But Monday afternoon, he told me to quit early, that I looked tired."

"Were you?" Savannah asked.

"No more than usual. I figured he wanted to get rid of me so he could have some new woman over, try out those pills again. I mean, why else would he miss his game of golf? He must have been staying home for somebody special."

"Do you have any idea who it might have been?"

"No, I wish I did. I wish I'd been nosy enough to peek out the window a couple of times. I might have seen something, and then your Macon wouldn't be sitting there, cooling his heels in jail." She sighed. "But I'm not as young as I used to be. I was tired, and when you're worn out, you're just not as curious as you oughta be."

Savannah grinned. "That's okay, Miss Dingle. You've been a lot of help. You don't happen to have any concrete reason to think Bonnie Patterson or Alvin Barnes might have killed him, do you? I mean, other than your own intuition?"

"Nothing that would hold up in a court of law." She smiled slyly. "I know what you're after, Savannah. I'm no dummy. I watch *Court TV* all the time, and I know what it takes to get a conviction. Believe me, if I had anything like that, I'd have given it to the sheriff already. I never did like that Bonnie. She's just snooty and shallow and not nearly as bright or as pretty as she thinks she is. And, even if I did like her, I don't cotton to people getting away with murder."

"Okay, then let's put it this way," Savannah continued. "Is there anything in particular that makes you think they did it? Did you see anything or hear anything that stands out in your mind?"

"Well, yes." Elsie nodded thoughtfully. "I had to throw them out of this house, Bonnie and Alvin, this past Sunday night."

"The night before the killing?" Gran asked.

"That's right. I came home from evening church service about half past seven, and I was going on back to my room, when I saw a light on here in the kitchen. Now, the judge doesn't ever come in the kitchen. I don't think he's been in here once in his whole life—a woman's place and not a man's, you know. And his car was gone, so I figured he was still at the club, having a bit of supper there."

"And Bonnie and Alvin were here in the kitchen?" Savannah asked.

"No. I figure they came in this way and left the light on, but they were upstairs in the judge's bedroom."

"I'm afraid to ask what they were doing," Gran said. But she didn't look afraid. She looked eager.

"Naw, they weren't doing *that*," Elsie replied. "Although I wouldn't put it past her. They were walking around, picking up stuff like some silver candlesticks and a crystal candy dish, and the judge's humidor. Whatever struck their fancy, I suppose. I told her to leave everything where it was or I'd call the sheriff, 'cause according to the divorce papers, she wasn't supposed to just waltz in and help herself. She'd already gotten everything out of the house that she was entitled to."

"What did she say when you told her to leave?" Savannah cut another slice of cake and laid it on Elsie's empty plate.

"Let's just say she called me things that no man should say and no lady should hear. But that was Bonnie's way. She always has had a filthy mouth on her. White trash, that's all she is, and I don't mean nothing racist by calling her that either. I just call it as I see it."

"I understand," Savannah replied. "And then?"

"Then I marched downstairs to the kitchen, and I got myself my marble rolling pin out of the cupboard, and I went back up there and told them they'd better reconsider."

"And?" Gran asked.

"And they put down the stuff, and they left. I meant business, and they knew it."

"Did you tell the judge when he came home?" Savannah said.

"I did, and I can tell you, he was fit to be tied. He called Sheriff Mahoney and told him to arrest them right away."

"Did he?"

"I don't think so. The sheriff said it wasn't exactly breaking and entering, since she used her keys on the back door and the divorce wasn't absolutely final yet. So, it's sorta still her house. But he did have the locksmith out to change the locks."

"When?"

"Sunday morning."

"The day he got killed?"

"Yeah, I reckon it was. Do you think that's got anything to do with it?"

Savannah shrugged. "I don't know, Miss Dingle. It's like trying to put together a big puzzle when you don't have all the pieces and you don't know if the pieces you have even go to this puzzle."

"And your grandma says you do this for a living." Elsie looked a bit puzzled herself, and Savannah couldn't blame her.

"It *is* a strange way to make a living," Savannah agreed. "But in this case, of course, the stakes are a lot higher." She turned to Gran. "I think we'd better get going, now that we've just about polished off this cake. I've got a few other people to talk to yet today."

"And there's Marietta's wedding rehearsal tonight," Gran reminded her.

"Oh, goody. I'd forgotten about that." At the very thought, Savannah's brief sugar fix from the cake vanished, leaving her weak with fatigue.

Elsie stood and gathered up their dirty dishes. Savannah and Gran grabbed the glasses and the tea pitcher.

"Like I said," Elsie said as she carried the plates to the sink, "I was feeling mighty lonesome and a bit spooky here in this house all by myself. Or, at least, just me and the ghosts."

"The ghosts?" Savannah placed the pitcher into the gigantic refrigerator.

"Oh, yes, we've got a whole batch of ghosts who hang out here," Elsie said, her dark face absolutely straight. "Most of them linger in the dining room, on account of that's where so many of them died . . . when the house was converted into a hospital for the soldiers. A lot of limbs were amputated and a heap of lives lost right there in that dining room. I don't go in there after dark."

Savannah wasn't sure what to say, so she just nodded as though she understood completely. She glanced at Gran, who seemed equally convinced.

"And the judge himself was poking around there in the library last night," Elsie continued. "So, now I *sure* won't go in there again. They're just going to have to hire somebody from town to clean it. This girl ain't doing it."

Savannah shut the refrigerator door. "Wait a minute. What do you mean, the *judge* was in there, poking around?"

"Well, I didn't actually see his ghost, because I wouldn't go in there, but it had to be a haunt because it wasn't anybody human in there. I would have seen them go in or out."

"Unless they came or went through the window," Savannah suggested.

Elsie seemed to consider her theory for a moment, then discard it. "I don't think so. Sounded more like a ghost to me."

Savannah opened her mouth to ask the housekeeper to explain the difference, but Gran shot her a warning look.

Savannah chose her words carefully. "Do you think it would be okay if I were to poke my head in the library now? I mean, it's broad daylight, and I think it would be all right, no matter what sort of activity there's been in there. The judge knows I mean well."

Elsie looked questioningly at Gran, who gave her a slight nod. "I think it'd be all right," she said. "Savannah does this sort of thing for a living, remember. She'll know how to go about it and not upset . . . anybody."

"Okay," Elsie said finally. "Go on, if you feel you have to. But tread lightly and respectfully. I can tell you, because I knew the judge well, and I know all about haunts: His honor is still mighty mad about what happened to him. And I don't rightly blame him."

Chapter

14

Savannah did tread lightly, not only out of respect for the recently departed judge, who—according to at least one expert—might now be a restless ghost. But also because she didn't want to disturb any new evidence that might be lying about for the finding.

"Haunt, my butt," she said, but only in the softest whisper as she walked down the hall. There was nothing to be gained by offending either Elsie or Gran, who both believed as firmly in wandering spirits as they did in the world of flesh, blood, and concrete.

Besides, for all she knew, they were right. And there was no point in stating her doubts so loudly that the judge himself could overhear . . . if he were still on the premises, as Elsie believed, rather than in the hereafter or in Herb Jameson's funeral parlor along with his earthly remains.

Little had changed about the library from when she had been there before, Savannah decided, when she pushed the heavy door open and looked inside. Sheriff Mahoney, Tom, or some assistant had wiped away most of the fingerprint dust and swept up the glass from the shattered front of the display frame. But Elsie would still be appalled if she saw the disarray and the sooty residue that remained. It was just as well that she stayed out of here for a while, or the sheriff and Tom would surely get an earful about the mess they had left behind in her otherwise spotless house.

But the crime scene processing dust wasn't the only residue. Elsie was right; there was still an uneasy presence in the room. And whether it was ghostly or strictly of this world, Savannah didn't want to spend any more time in the room than necessary.

The midday sunlight streaming through the windows lit the mahogany paneling, the soft leathers, the gleaming brass and stained glass accessories. Any other time, she might have been tempted to pull a book from the shelves and snuggle into one of the giant chairs. Except for that creepy, shivery feeling that tickled at the nape of her neck . . . and the dark stain on the oriental carpet.

Other than being cleaner and better lit, the room appeared exactly the way it had before. But someone—and she wasn't prepared to believe it was a ghostly someone—had been here. And she had a feeling that if she looked hard enough, she could find evidence of their visit.

With a practiced eye, she studied every inch of the floor, looking for a dirty footprint, an indentation in the carpet, any small object that might have been left behind, even a thread, a hair, a leaf or twig.

But she found nothing.

Likewise, the surfaces of the furniture were smooth and fingerprint free, having been freshly wiped by whoever had cleaned the room.

Nothing seemed to be out of place. The books, desk accessories, telephone, family pictures, and knickknacks appeared to be sitting where they were before.

Having pulled on some latex gloves from her handbag, Savannah walked over to the gun cabinet and checked it. Although it was unlocked, the judge's classic firearms seemed to be safe and secure.

"Okay," she said to the room's unseen previous visitor . . . a blurry, faceless figure in her mind's eye. "What did you do in here? You snuck in here to get something, or to see something, or to leave something behind. What was it, huh?"

It was on her third time around, checking every piece of furniture, every nook and cranny, that she saw them . . . several small scratches on the brass hardware that decorated the top drawer of the rolltop desk.

The lock had been forced.

Of course, the desk was probably a hundred or more years old, which meant the damage could have been done by someone wearing a hoop skirt and pantaloons, but it was worth a look.

She pulled a small, but powerful, penlight from her purse and pointed the beam on the scratches.

They were new. At least, fairly recent, because the marks glowed brightly in comparison to the somewhat tarnished metal surface.

Savannah felt her pulse quicken as she laid the penlight on the desktop and gently tried the drawer.

Oh, yes, she thought, as it slid open with the precision of a well-made piece of furniture. *Open, Sesame. And what do we have here?*

The drawer was fairly deep, the type used for storing files and papers, rather than pens and pencils, like the neighboring shallow one. And at first, all Savannah could see was green.

Forest-green file folders, suspended from a wire rack, contained all manner of paperwork relating to the judge's life, professional and personal.

She sighed, knowing how the rest of her afternoon would be spent—perusing these files, one by one, looking for something. Of course, she had no idea what she was looking for . . . until she found it.

And even as she headed for the kitchen to ask Elsie if she could borrow some sort of cardboard box to hold the drawer's contents, Savannah had a sneaking, sinking feeling that, even if she spent the next few hours learning far more than she ever wanted to know about the judge's life, she was going to come away empty-handed.

Because instinct told her that Elsie's "ghostly" visitor had come and gone . . . taking the good stuff with them and leaving her with such jewels of information as overdue utility bills, last year's stock reports, and the judge's prescription for Viagra.

"Well, that was a total waste of time," Savannah said as she fell back onto the bed in Dirk's motel room. "And boy, am I bushed."

Her arms flung outward, she looked as though she had just taken a shot, dead center, from a Wild West gunslinger. And she felt like it, too.

"I *hate* going through paperwork," she grumbled. "Have I mentioned that I'd rather get a pedicure from a guy with a weed whacker than search for clues in a stack of papers?"

"I believe you did mention that," Dirk replied as he continued to return the green folders to the cardboard box. "A couple of hours ago."

"Only then," Tammy added as she scooped another pile off the dresser and handed it to him, "it was a manicure from a dude with hedge clippers."

"And I've still got to go to that wedding rehearsal," she groaned. "The fun just never ceases!"

"Is it a dress rehearsal?" Tammy asked eagerly. "Are you going to wear the upside-down tulip dress?"

Savannah opened her eyes and shot her a poisoned look. "Don't you just wish."

"Tulip dress? What's that?" Dirk wanted to know.

"Forget about it." Savannah slapped both hands over her eyes, trying to blot out the mental picture. "It doesn't matter. I'm only going to wear that monstrosity once, for about seventeen minutes . . . or however long it takes Pastor Greene to hitch those two nitwits. And if either of you show your face at the church, I'll never speak to you again."

"What time's the wedding?" Dirk asked Tammy.

"Four o'clock."

"I'll pick you up at three-thirty. Wear something pretty."

"I will. I've got this slinky little blue slip dress that really shows off my—"

"Oh, will you two just stop?" Savannah sat up suddenly. "I mean it! Some things are off limits for teasing, and that damned dress is one of them!"

Completely ignoring her, Tammy and Dirk continued their conversation.

"I hear it's peach," Tammy said, carefully arranging another armload of files. "A really, really *bright* shade of peach. Practically glows in the dark. With poofy capped sleeves, and—"

"I'm gonna hurt you, I swear."

"And this wide sash around the waist and—"

"If I have to get off this bed, as tired as I am . . ."

"And a great big ol' bow across the butt, and—ow-w-w! Shit! Dirk! He-e-elp!"

"Will you, Marietta, take Lester to be your lawfully wedded husband?"

Standing next to her sister, watching Marietta gaze up into her fiancé's eyes, loved ones lined up across the front of the small country church, Pastor Greene, prayerbook in hand, leading them in this rehearsal of the sacred wedding vows . . . Savannah could almost feel her heartstrings twang a little.

Almost.

But not quite.

The whole scene would have been far more romantic if Savannah hadn't seen the wild-eyed redhead slip into the church a second before with a shotgun in her hand.

"Gun!" Savannah shouted, momentarily forgetting that she was in the company of civilians, not law enforcement personnel. They simply turned and stared at her, as though she had committed some major social faux pas.

"Hit the deck! Get down on the floor and stay there!" she screamed at them as she turned and hurried down the center aisle of the church toward the armed female.

Nice time to be without my Beretta, she thought, flashing back on the fateful moment when she had stashed it high on the top shelf of Gran's bedroom closet.

Who needs a gun at church? she had asked herself.

Now she had her answer: The maid of honor . . . if the present-and-hard-to-get-rid-of wife was attending the rehearsal.

She didn't have to be told that the shotgun-totin' mama was Lester's wife, the one fighting the divorce that was supposed to have been final by now.

"Now, now, you don't wanna go waving a gun around like that in the house of the Lord," she told her in her most easygoing, down-homey voice. "It just ain't right."

The disgruntled redhead raised the weapon to her shoulder and aimed it directly at Savannah's face. "You stay right there or I'll blow your fuckin' head off!" she yelled.

The practiced way she handled the gun and the wicked gleam in her eyes set off alarms for Savannah. Mrs. Lester meant business. So Savannah decided not to mention that using the "F" word in church wasn't a good idea either.

She halted about ten feet from the woman and held her hands up in surrender. "Don't shoot me," she said. "I'm a nice person. And I've got a husband and four kids and a couple of cats who love me and who'll starve to death if you kill me."

Okay, so you aren't supposed to lie in church either, she thought, *but surely the Lord'll understand, considering the circumstances.*

"I know you're mad and unhappy," she continued, "and I don't blame you, but bringing a shotgun in here is only going to make things worse."

The redhead laughed. "It's gonna make *y'all* feel worse. That's for sure! But *I'm* gonna feel a whole lot better after I pump some shot into the bitch who broke up my family!" She stood on tiptoes and stared over Savannah's shoulder. "Where are you, Marietta Reid? Come down here right now and take what's comin' to ya!"

Suddenly, Savannah realized she was no longer alone. She had reinforcements: Pastor Greene to her left and Gran to her right.

"Lucille Marie," Gran snapped, "you put that thing down before you hurt somebody."

"I *aim* to hurt somebody, but it ain't you. So stand aside, Mrs. Reid."

"I ain't goin' nowhere till you put that gun down," Gran said, stepping closer to her.

Savannah's heart caught in her throat when she saw Lucille turn the gun toward Gran.

A dozen takedown scenarios played through her head, but they were all too risky. Lucille was still a good ten feet away; the chance that she could reach her before she could pull off the shot . . .

"That's quite enough!" roared a deep, authoritative male voice.

It took Savannah a couple of seconds to realize it was coming from Pastor Greene.

"I'll not have this sort of carryin' on in my church, young lady." He simply stepped forward and snatched the gun out of her hand. "You should be ashamed of yourself, Lucy, bringing a gun into a house of worship! Why, you went to Sunday school right down there in the basement, and we taught you right from wrong. There's just no excuse for this. None at all!"

With an even more practiced hand than Lucille had demonstrated, he cracked the breech of the gun and dispensed the shells in one fluid movement.

Savannah's mouth dropped open. Apparently . . . and thankfully . . . there was more to the soft-spoken, silver-haired pastor than met the eye.

"You get yourself into my study," he told Lucille, pointing to a door in the back of the church. "You and I are gonna have a long overdue talk about the state of your eternal soul . . . not to mention your messed-up marriage and your behavior here tonight."

When Lucille didn't move fast enough to suit him, he gave her a shove from behind. "Get in there now. I mean it!"

He turned back to Savannah and Gran . . . and the rest of the marriage party, who had risen from their prone positions on the carpet and crept to the rear of the church once the rampaging Lucille had been disarmed.

"I reckon ya'll will just have to go on without me," he said. "Or better yet, let's call it a night. The rehearsal's over."

They watched, speechless, as he strode across the sanctuary, disappeared into his office, and slammed the door behind him.

"Well! If that isn't a fine how-do-you-do!" Marietta propped her hands on her hips and turned on her sheepish fiancé, who looked as though he had lost several years off the end of his life in the past five minutes. "And, boy . . . you didn't exactly hurl yourself between me and danger, now did you, Lester?"

Savannah reached for her sister. "Marietta, don't. It's not going to help anything by—"

"Oh, shut up, Savannah!" She shook her hand away. "I've got a fiancé and two mostly grown boys and do you think any of them would place themselves in harm's way to protect me? Not one of them! They just laid there, facedown on the rug like a bunch of spineless wimps!"

Standing behind her, Paulie and Steve seemed to shrink three sizes in their jeans and T-shirts. They were both white and trembling, obviously traumatized, and now horribly emasculated.

Savannah's self-restraint snapped. "No, Marietta, *you* shut up!" she told her. "Don't say another word. You made this mess and you dragged the rest of us, including your two boys, into it."

"Don't you talk to me like that, Savannah Reid!" She took a step forward and shoved her face into Savannah's. "Who do you think you are, Miss High-and-Mighty, telling me what I—"

"Marietta, stop that!" Gran said, trying to step between them.

Savannah reached out with one finger, placed it on Marietta's chest, and pushed her sister back to a comfortable distance. In a soft, but deadly tone, she said, "Go . . . home . . . now. And give this whole situation some serious thought. For once in your life, be smart, Mari. If not for yourself and your own future, for your boys."

Marietta whirled around so fast that Savannah thought she might do a complete 360-degree turn, but she caught herself and stomped out the back door of the church.

Gran walked over to her great-grandsons and placed a hand on each of their shoulders. "You boys did just fine," she told them. "Your mama's just upset and scared. She didn't mean what she said."

"Sure she did," Steve replied, his lower lip trembling. "I guess she would've been happier if we'd gotten killed, as long as we were protecting her like she deserves, right?"

"You did exactly what you should have done," Savannah told him. "Everything turned out okay in the end and that's all that matters."

"Yeah," Paulie said. "Everything's just jim-dandy."

Lester stood, head down, hands deep in his slacks pockets. "What a mess," he mumbled. "What a freakin' mess. I better go talk to Lucy. She's gotta be real upset to have done a fool thing like this."

Without another word he shuffled over to the pastor's door, knocked softly, and disappeared inside.

One by one, everybody filed out of the sanctuary, until only Savannah and Gran remained.

"I know you meant well," Gran said, lacing her arm through Savannah's, "with what you told the boys. But everything didn't turn out okay tonight."

"Yeah, I know." Savannah sighed, her knees turning to warm jelly from the adrenaline still coursing through her bloodstream. "No trigger was pulled and nobody's hide got perforated, but things aren't all right by a long shot."

Chapter

15

Savannah was still wearing her pajamas and Gran's chenille robe when Tammy and Dirk knocked on the front door. From the excited look on Tammy's face, Savannah knew, even before she let them in, that she had news.

"Okay, I heard something!" Tammy said as they entered the house, ignoring the baying Beauregard, who nipped at their heels as they passed him on the porch. "All that hash-slinging finally paid off, last night about midnight."

Balancing what was only her second cup of coffee in one hand, Savannah pushed them in the general direction of the sofa. "Sit," she said. "Do you want a cup of java?"

"No," they both said in unison.

"Well, I do ... while it's still hot." She eased herself into Gran's comfortable recliner. Her grandmother was out back, tying up tomato vines in the garden, and wouldn't be in until the heat and humidity became unbearable. "Okay," she said to Tammy, once she was settled. "Spill everything you've got."

"Bonnie Patterson and Alvin Barnes have been fooling around since—"

"I told you that yesterday afternoon at the hotel," Savannah said, blowing the steam that was rising from the lip of the cup. "I already—"

"Oh, hush," Tammy snapped. "You don't know *everything* I know, so be quiet and let me tell you something for a change." Savannah stared at her assistant, mouth open, then turned to an equally shocked Dirk. "The kid's getting feisty in her old age."

"Yeah, wonder where she's getting it?" Dirk said with a grin.

"Sorry, Tam," Savannah said, "the floor is yours."

"Thanks. Bonnie and Alvin have been a hot commodity since long before she married the judge. And according to a couple of his honor's former caretakers, who were having a Lumberjack's Deluxe Breakfast this morning at the counter, they never stopped seeing each other. Every day when the judge was off playing golf, and Elsie Dingle was taking a nap, Alvin snuck in the back door and . . . hokey-pokey."

Savannah thought of Elsie, her bright eyes and sharp curiosity. Alvin must have been a pretty good sneak to get past her on a regular basis.

Tammy continued, "These two guys were talking about how Bonnie and Alvin had set the whole thing up, from the very beginning, to take advantage of the old man. The judge had a bypass years ago, and they counted on him kicking off pretty soon."

"That was pretty dumb on their account," Savannah said. "Most people who've had a bypass can live a long, normal life if they take care of themselves."

"And the judge did." Tammy sat on the edge of the sofa, still wearing her uniform of short shorts and a tube top. Savannah was surprised those gardeners had been able to converse at all in the presence of such blatantly displayed female pulchritude. "Except for his evening scotch and soda, he did everything the doctor told him, low-fat diet, nine holes of golf every day."

"And Bonnie and Alvin got impatient," Dirk added, stealing her thunder. "They got to thinking the old fart never was gonna kick. So they helped him along."

Tammy gouged him in the ribs with her elbow. "Hey, I'm the one who served greasy eggs and bacon and toast slathered with butter, yuck, to get this. Have some respect."

Savannah cleared her throat. "These two caretaker guys, they said all this while they were downing their Lumberjack Breakfast?"

Tammy nodded. "That's the sum of bits and pieces that I overheard in the course of half an hour."

"Okay, that's all very interesting," Savannah said. "It may even be true. But the bottom line is: It's just gossip. And if we're going to get Macon out of the slammer, we're going to have to take Sheriff Mahoney more than that."

"Yeah, I told her that," Dirk said, "but she's got some more. Go on, kiddo," he told Tammy. "Tell her about the Navigator."

Wriggling like a kindergartner who needed to visit the little girls' room, Tammy said, "Alvin's put money down at the local Ford dealership for a brand-new Lincoln Navigator with all the options. The salesman was having a Spanish omelet with his wife, but hers was a Denver skillet scramble, no cheese."

Savannah lifted one eyebrow. "We've gotta get you out of there, Tam. I'm starting to worry."

"Forget about me. Don't you see the significance of him ordering a new black Navigator when, until now, he's been driving a bomb of an old Pontiac that's missing a fender?"

"As I said before," Savannah replied, "it's interesting, but hardly incriminating."

Tammy shook her head in exasperation. "Don't you see? He's profiting from the judge's death!"

"Honey, often, when people die, other folks profit. It's the way of the world. But it doesn't mean that everybody who receives an inheritance is a murderer."

"Bonnie's buying a matching Navigator, fully loaded, all in white. And the local furniture dealer was in, too . . . plain toast, hold the butter and black coffee. And she's ordered a lot of new furniture . . . a bunch of contemporary, ultra-modern stuff . . . for the mansion."

"Now *that's* a crime."

"And she's talking all over town about how she's going to send

Elsie Dingle packing when she takes over the house. Says she never did like the old lady and won't put up with her sass."

Savannah's eyes narrowed; her lips thinned. "That does it. Miss Priss Bonnie Patterson and her no-good boyfriend Alvin are going do-o-own."

For some reason, which she couldn't explain, Savannah hadn't expected someone named Alvin Barnes to look like a Greek god.

So much for expectations.

Stretched out on his back on a chaise beside the pool, his golden skin gleaming in the sunlight, Alvin B could have been Mr. July in any beefcake calendar. The red thong-style swimsuit barely did the job of containing his assets.

The spitting image of his father, the judge? Savannah thought as she approached him, trying to remember who had said that.

Thinking of the thin, wizened man on Herb Jameson's embalming table, Savannah couldn't see even a remote resemblance.

As she walked around the end of the pool and up to his chaise, Savannah smelled the strong scent of coconut oil, mixed with a musky cologne or aftershave lotion, and saw that Alvin was thoroughly greased, from his thick, dark hair to his bare toes. Reflector sunglasses hid his eyes, so she couldn't tell if he was awake or sleeping.

"Hi," he said, answering that question as she sat on a deck chair next to his chaise.

She was glad she had told Dirk to take Tammy back to the café while she did this interview. She would have freaked, being this close to so many bulging muscles. While she, on the other hand, was perfectly cool and collected. "Hi. I'm Sa—" Her voice broke like a pubescent teenager's, but she quickly recovered. "—vannah Reid."

"Yes, I recognize you." He sat up halfway, leaning on his elbows, accenting marvelous pecs. On his wrist he wore a sports watch that Savannah instantly recognized as one of Tag Heuer's nicer models. Apparently tennis instructing paid a heck of a lot more than private detecting.

"You recognize me?" Savannah asked. "Have we met?"

"No. But Bonnie described you . . ." He reached up and lowered his sunglasses just long enough to peer at her over the top of the frames. After a leisurely look up and down her figure, he replaced them. ". . . Described you to a tee."

Not being blind, Savannah couldn't help but see the disgust in his eyes. And not being deaf, she couldn't miss the nasty note of sarcasm in his voice.

Mr. Perfect Body had apparently been told by Miss Priss that Savannah was no hardbody.

Several searing obscenities raced across her mind in mile-high, flashing, red-neon letters. But, professional that she was, she swallowed the words and imagined, instead, several excruciating forms of physical torture she could easily inflict on him. And would, if given the chance.

Better yet, she'd just nail him for first-degree murder.

"Then you know why I'm here," she said. "I'm investigating the judge's murder to find out who really did it."

Even from behind the silver lenses, Savannah could see his surprise. Apparently, ol' Alvin wasn't accustomed to such candor.

"I'm trying to figure out who actually pulled the trigger," she continued, "you or Bonnie."

He bolted upright on the chaise and ripped off his glasses. She saw the anger in his eyes. And now that they were uncovered, she saw that his eyes did, indeed, look exactly like his departed father's. She also saw the fear, and she felt a thrill of success.

Bingo! Bull's eye! Gin! All in one!

"Had to do it now, huh?" she said. "I mean, if the old man wouldn't roll over and play dead, like he was supposed to from his heart trouble, you'd just have to help him along. And you couldn't wait . . . what with the divorce becoming final."

As Savannah saw the anger on his face quickly escalate to pure rage, she mentally checked the location of the Beretta in her purse. Her vivid imagination also ran through a few judo moves, flipping him headfirst into the pool.

"This club is private property," he said. "And you aren't a member. You'd better leave."

"Oh, I'm the guest of a member."

"Who?"

She said the first name that came to mind. "Mack Goodwin. He's a good friend of mine."

"Well, Mack's my friend, too. And I don't remember him having anything good to say about you or your brother. In fact, he said he was going to see the little punk strapped to a gurney, getting put down like a dog before this is all over. And he said you'd better not get in his way."

Savannah knew her own limitations. And she was just about to do serious harm to Alvin Barnes.

So she stood and turned her back on him. But before she walked away, she shot one more verbal dart over her shoulder.

"I'll be watching you. Bonnie, too," she said. "And you won't even know I'm there. Count on it, you sonofabitch."

By the time Savannah drove to the sheriff's office, she had two speeches memorized. One if Mahoney was there and a second if she were lucky enough to catch Tom alone.

When she charged through the door and saw her former boyfriend sitting at his desk, filling out a stack of papers . . . all by himself, she launched into monologue number two.

"Tom, I need your help, and please just keep an open mind, okay?"

He stared up at her blankly, and she hurried on before he could say no.

"You may think I'm nuts, but I'm telling you, Bonnie Patterson and Alvin Barnes are in cahoots somehow in the judge's homicide. And I think if you go out to the Patterson place and dust for fingerprints on the left drawer of the judge's rolltop desk, you'll find one of their fingerprints. Now if it's Bonnie's, I realize that won't prove anything, but if it's Alvin's . . ." She took a deep breath. "Well, that won't really prove anything either, but I'm telling you that they're in on this. I know it! Macon didn't do it."

"I know."

It took her a second to apply the mental brakes. "What? You know what? That Bonnie and Alvin—"

"That Macon didn't do it. That's what this is, right here." He pointed to several papers spread across his desk.

She leaned over and peered at them. "Release forms?"

"Yeah, I'm letting him out as soon as I'm done here."

"Oh, my, I . . ."

Suddenly, she found it difficult to stand, so she sank onto the folding metal chair next to his desk. Time seemed to slow as she sat there, holding on to the cold steel of the seat with her hands, listening to the air-conditioner crank away.

He smiled at her, and it occurred to her, not for the first time, that Tom Stafford really did have a gorgeous smile. No wonder she had loved him for all of her adolescence and a good part of her adulthood.

For all the good it had done her.

"You're releasing him. Oh, Tommy that's wonderful! I can't tell you how much this means to me, how much it'll mean to Gran. She's been so worried and—"

"Aren't you going to ask me why?" he said, leaning back in his chair and putting his hands behind his head.

"No. I learned a long time ago: If it's good news, just take it and run! I don't care why."

He kept grinning at her.

"Okay," she finally said. "Why? Did you figure out, too, that it was Bonnie and Alvin?"

"No. It wasn't those two. They're worthless and they're not above it, but it wasn't them."

"Then who?"

"Clifton Oprey."

"Clifton? That old guy who farms down there by the river?"

"*Did* farm. Thanks to the judge, Cliff lost his place about six months ago. His wife, Sally, took sick . . . cancer or something . . . and Cliff ran up a bunch of hospital bills. She died anyway, and after working like a dog all his life, Cliff was deep in debt. The judge took a second mortgage on his land, then worked behind the scenes to get Cliff's credit cut off, so that he couldn't plant this spring. The judge foreclosed on the farm and threw Cliff off the land that had been in his family four generations."

"How nice of his honor. No wonder people are happy he's gone. I hear he's done that sort of thing plenty of times over the years."

"Cliff hasn't been the first. That's for sure. But thanks to Cliff, he'll be the last."

"Have you picked him up yet?"

Tom pointed his thumb toward the ceiling. "He's right upstairs in the cell next to Yukon Bill."

"You must have some pretty good evidence against him, I mean . . . if you're releasing Macon and . . ."

"And considering all we've got on Macon. Is that what you mean?"

"Something like that."

"I got a confession." He reached across the desk and picked up a yellow legal pad. "Signed and dated," he added, shoving the notepad into her hands.

Savannah scanned the brief, but concise statement, written in crude, shaky penmanship and signed by Clifton Oprey.

"Well, I'll be damned." She thought of Bonnie and Alvin, and how much she had wanted to pin this killing on them. She also thought of Clifton, who had seemed old and broken to her the last time she had seen him . . . years ago.

But you didn't look a gift horse in the mouth to see if his dentures fit. Her baby brother was getting sprung.

"Do Sheriff Mahoney and Mack Goodwin know about this yet?" she asked, dreading the answer which she was fairly certain she wouldn't like.

"The sheriff knows. He's the one who brought Clifton in. He's gone out now to tell Mr. Goodwin in person."

Tom looked up from his paperwork and held her eyes for a long moment. Finally, he said, "I gotta tell you, Mack ain't gonna like it."

She nodded. "So, maybe you'd better get that paperwork done." She scooted her chair around next to his. "Need any help?"

Chapter
16

Savannah and Tom finished the release papers in record time, but it still wasn't fast enough. No sooner had Tom signed and dated the final form than the front door crashed open and Mack Goodwin rushed into the office.

The prosecutor didn't look nearly as cool and collected as he had at the country club. His sports shirt and jeans looked as though he had slept in them, and his formerly perfect hair was a tangled mess.

Sheriff Mahoney followed close behind, appearing equally upset. Savannah had never seen Mahoney looking anything but bored or cocky. If *he* was worried, things weren't going well for somebody.

Goodwin gave Savannah only a brief scowl as he swept past her and up the stairs to the jail above.

Mahoney paused at the desk and whispered, "We got trouble, Tom. Mack ain't buying it." He glanced down at the forms on the desk. "Ditch those papers. I don't want him seeing them."

When he, too, disappeared up the stairs, Tom slid the stack into a drawer and followed the two men without a word to Savannah.

Although she knew she should just quietly slip out the door, she couldn't. Even if her brother's life weren't on the line, curiosity alone would have driven her up the steps.

Before she even got to the top, she heard Mack Goodwin saying, "We're supposed to believe that you're the one who killed the judge, huh? You? How old are you anyway, Clifton, seventy? Seventy-five?"

"I'm seventy-one, which is only a couple of years older than the fella I killed," she heard Clifton Oprey reply. "Don't you think I'm up to it? It don't take a young man to pull a trigger."

She reached the uppermost step and peered down the hallway that bisected the jail. Mack Goodwin was standing to the left, gripping the bars of a cell, red-faced and glowering at its occupant, who was out of Savannah's line of vision.

"Okay, so *you* shot Judge Patterson," Mack said in a sarcastic tone. "With what? You tell me, Cliff Oprey, with what, pray tell?"

"A twenty-two caliber pistol."

That seemed to take Goodwin aback, but only for a second. "And where is the murder weapon? What did you do with it?"

"I threw it in the river, where nobody's ever gonna find it."

Goodwin grasped the bars even tighter. "Well, what if I told you that the gun that killed the judge was found, right there at the scene of the crime. Huh? What would you say to that?"

Savannah waited, breathless for the reply. It was a while coming. She could practically hear the wheels of Clifton's brain whirring, spinning out an answer.

"You ain't neither," he finally said. "You may have a gun, but it's not the one that did it. I told you, I shot him and I tossed the pistol out in the water. Way out."

"We have the bullet from my father-in-law's brain," Mack told him. "It was analyzed in a lab in Atlanta, and they say it was fired from the gun that was left in the library close to the judge's body. So, how could you have done it with another gun?"

"That's not what I heard," Clifton said. "I heard over at Whiskey Joe's that the bullet was banged up so bad from bouncing around inside that bastard's hard skull that you couldn't get a match. That's what I heard."

Savannah perked up; there was a ring of conviction to Cliff's words.

And the angry look on Goodwin's face, along with the quick glance exchanged between the sheriff and Tom, told Savannah that Cliff had heard right.

"A match," Tom had told her.

Oh, well, she thought. *He's not the first cop to lie in the course of an investigation.*

A sense of relief—no matter how small—swept over her. No ballistics match to her brother's gun.

That had to be good news, no matter what happened with Clifton Oprey.

"Don't believe everything you hear at Whiskey Joe's," Mack told the old man. "I don't. And I don't believe that you killed Judge Patterson. I think you hated him, and you would have *liked* to shoot him. But you didn't. You're just bragging, trying to impress your buddies and some women there at the bar."

"I wrote a statement—a real, official confession," Cliff argued. "And I signed it, too. You ask Deputy Tom there. He'll tell you."

Mack turned to Tom, who gave a slight nod.

"Yeah, well, I'm going to get to the bottom of this," Mack said, "and when I do, you'll still be in jail, Cliff, but it won't be for anything as sensational as killing a judge. It'll be for obstructing justice, that's all. And everybody at Whiskey Joe's will be laughing at you. Just wait and see."

Mack turned away from the cell, and Savannah decided it might be an excellent time to backtrack down the steps.

She did. Quickly. And by the time the prosecutor, the sheriff, and Tom were downstairs, she was sitting demurely in the folding chair beside Tom's desk.

"I guess we'll have to cut the Reid boy loose," she heard Tom say over his shoulder.

"No way," Mack replied. "We've got him for that stolen rug and light fixture. He's not going anywhere. Reid and Oprey both stay right where they are until we figure out what's going on."

"Yeah, that's what I think, too," the sheriff added. "Reid can cool his heels a while longer."

Suddenly, Mack Goodwin seemed aware of Savannah's presence. "What are you doing here?" he demanded.

"Never mind what you're doing," the sheriff snapped, "just get the hell outta here."

Savannah didn't wait for him to tell her twice. But as she hurried past them, she paused just long enough to whisper, "Fingerprints. Desk drawer. Check 'em," to Tom.

Then she was out the door, down the street, and in Waycross's pickup. With the door locked.

No point in hanging around where you weren't wanted.

She decided to check in at "home base" and let Gran know the latest news about Clifton. Years ago, Gran had been close friends with Cliff's wife, Sally, and Savannah figured Gran would have a definite opinion about this turn of events.

"It's bull pucky. Pure and simple." Gran stood at the kitchen counter, dragging pieces of raw chicken through a dish of buttermilk and then rolling them in another plate of flour, salt, and pepper. "Clifton's had a hard time of it since Sally died, but not so hard that he'd lose his mind entirely and murder somebody."

At the table, Alma sat, quietly putting together a jigsaw puzzle of the New York City skyline. "Mr. Oprey's real sweet," she added. "He wouldn't hurt a fly, no matter what he's said in the past about hating the judge's guts."

Gran shot her a warning look over the plate of chicken parts. "You might want to keep that sorta talk to yourself, sugar. Till this whole thing's settled, we don't need to be the ones throwing the oil of gossip onto the fire. There's plenty around who'll be more than happy to do that."

Savannah reached for a paring knife and the bowl of potatoes in the sink.

"No, you don't," Gran told her, slapping her hands away. "You've got more important work to do than peeling potatoes. Your friend, Dirk, called a while ago."

"Dirk? What did he want?"

"He's at Whiskey Joe's," Alma said, snapping one of her pieces in place with a little grin of satisfaction. "He wants you to come over there soon as you can."

Savannah silently groaned and placed the knife back in the drawer. The last thing she needed right now was another walk down family lane with Shirley Reid. She had actually hoped to leave town without bumping elbows with her mom again.

But, since Dirk was well aware of her feelings, she knew he must have a good reason for asking her to drop by.

"Maybe she won't be there," Gran said softly.

Savannah looked up to see her grandmother watching her, eyes full of sympathy.

"She'll be there," Alma added without glancing up from her puzzle. "She's always there."

"Oh, goody," Savannah muttered to herself when she saw Marietta's Chevy pull into the driveway beside Waycross's truck. "So close, but no escape."

A freshly coifed, but slightly tipsy Marietta got out of the car and headed straight for Savannah, or as straight as she could considering her inebriation.

"Hey, big sister, I want to have a word with you. Right now!"

"Well, I don't want a word with you, except to mention that you shouldn't drive when you've been drinking, Mari. You'll kill some innocent person."

"There you go again, sticking your nose in where it doesn't belong, giving advice that wasn't asked for!"

"Come on, Marietta, and I'll give you a ride home."

"I don't want to go home. I came here to see you, to give you the chance to apologize for the way you acted last night."

Savannah sighed and shook her head. "Apologize, huh? Get in the truck, and I'll drop you by your shop. We can talk on the way."

Marietta wavered, teetering on her high-heeled slides. "Since I'm here, I might as well stay for supper."

"I don't want Gran to see you drunk. Get in the truck."

"But my boys are going to show up any minute now. Them and me, we usually eat over here of an evening."

Taking her by the arm and leading her to the pickup, Savannah said, "Yeah. We're gonna talk about that, too. I'm going to give you some more advice that you don't want. Like, grow up and stop taking advantage of a kind old lady who loves you."

Whiskey Joe's happy hour customers were in fine form when Savannah arrived.

Nothing like half-priced drinks to make fools out of a roomful of local yokels, she thought as she entered the door and dodged a flying swizzle stick with a lemon twist.

The television, mounted on the wall behind the bar, was blaring the early edition of the regional news. She was just in time to hear the end of the story about Clifton Oprey's arrest with all the pathetic details of Clifton's previous losses and his public vows of vengeance.

As the weatherman took over the broadcast, the room erupted in arguments about Cliff's guilt or innocence.

Without taking an official poll, judging on pure volume and passion alone, Savannah would have to say that the "guilties" had it. That was a scary thought, she decided, considering that this was the pool from which any impartial jury might be drawn to try either Clifton Oprey or her own brother.

Glancing around the room, she quickly spotted Dirk, hovering near the pool tables with a mug of beer in hand and a bored look on his face.

Of course, there was no way to actually tell if he was bored or not, as that was Dirk's usual expression—the only exceptions being when free food was within reach or when reading a suspect his rights. Then his mood soared to the lofty heights of "mildly interested."

As she headed toward him, he saw her and met her halfway.

"Gran said you wanted me to come by," she told him, her

mouth close to his ear so she could be heard above the tumult. "You got something?"

"No. I tried to talk to your mom over there . . ." He nodded toward the perpetually occupied stool beneath the Elvis photo. "And she basically told me to shove it. Guess she doesn't like my face."

"Naw, it's not your face," she assured him. "You've got a great face, considering how many times it's been planted in the dirt and dragged on the asphalt and pummeled into a bloody pulp and—"

"Okay already!"

"She just hates cops."

He quirked one eyebrow. "Oh, yeah? She must have been thrilled when you joined the department."

Savannah studied the woman in the corner, who didn't seem to be aware of her arrival. Although she must have, Shirley didn't appear to have moved from that spot since the last time Savannah had seen her.

For a moment, Savannah entertained the question of whether someone could sleep while sitting, drinking, and smoking.

"My mom hasn't been thrilled about anything I've done since the day I was born," she said.

"Sorry, Van."

She turned back to Dirk and saw him giving her a much more sympathetic look than she would have thought him capable of.

Smiling at him, she said, "Don't be sorry, really. It's okay. Gran was wonderful to us. Most kids growing up with moms like Shirley don't have the blessing of a grandmother like mine. I wouldn't change a thing."

He offered her a drink of his beer, but she shook her head. "Thanks anyway. What were you trying to get out of Shirley when she basically told you to file it in the realms of the nether world?"

"I heard that farmer, Clifton Oprey, was talking to her right before he confessed to the judge's killing. But when I asked her about it, she bristled like one of your cats when I yank its tail."

"You yank my cats' tails?"

"It's a figure of speech, Van. Good grief!"

"It'd better be. I'd hate to have to jerk a knot in *your* tail, and you know I'd do it if I caught you tormenting my animals."

She didn't like the little smirk he gave her; she'd been hoping for abject terror . . . or at least moderate intimidation.

"I mean it."

"I know you do. Go talk to your mama, and see what she had to do with this convenient turn of events."

"All right." She sighed. "But the next time I mention that I'm coming home for a little vacation and family bonding . . . don't let me."

Chapter

17

"Why isn't Macon outta jail yet?" Shirley Reid asked as she released a double stream of smoke from her nostrils. "I mean, with Cliff confessing and all, I'd have thought you'd have him home by now. What's holdin' up the works?"

The bartender walked over to Savannah, who was sitting on the stool beside Shirley, and slid an enormous glass of iced tea across the bar to her. "Compliments of the gentleman over there," he said as he pointed to a waving, grinning Dirk on the other side of the room.

"Tell him, 'Thanks, but he's no gentleman, and he's still sleeping alone tonight,' " she said, after a long swig. She turned to her mother. "I did what I could, Mom, but it wasn't enough. They don't believe Cliff's confession."

"What's not to believe?" Shirley twisted one of the enormous turquoise rings on her forefinger. "He hated the judge, made no bones about that, ever since the judge took his farm and Sally died."

"Having somebody make a false confession isn't exactly unheard of, you know. Besides, they found some stolen stuff in Macon's room, and they can hold him for that alone."

Shirley sagged on her stool. "Well, dammit, then. That was a lot of trouble for nothin'."

"What do you mean, a lot of trouble?" When Shirley didn't respond, Savannah nudged her with her elbow. "What trouble? What did you have to do with Cliff's confession?"

"Nothing. Much."

Not for the first time, Savannah briefly entertained the wish that she had been adopted. Or maybe found on the side of the road or under that cabbage leaf someone had told her about when she had wanted to know where babies come from.

"What did you do to talk that dear old man into confessing to a homicide?" she asked, dreading the answer.

"I might have mentioned that if he *did* confess, they probably would believe him and it would give you a chance to find out who really did it."

"Oh, thanks, Mom. Nothing like a little pressure. Now I've got both him and Macon dangling over the fire I'm trying to put out."

"So try harder."

"Easy for you to say, when . . ." She swallowed the rest of her sentence—the comment about Shirley's tailbone being rooted to the barstool and all.

Instead, she said, "I'm surprised Cliff would take such a drastic step, just because you asked him."

Shirley shrugged. "I might have mentioned that it would be a really nice thing to do for that wicked witch of a grandmother of yours, after all she did for him after he lost his wife. 'Course, I didn't call her a witch when I was talking to him."

"No, of course not. What did you do, remind him of how Gran brought meals over to him and even cleaned his house a few times after the funeral?"

She nodded. "And of how she had Macon bring him home from here a few times when he'd had too many, and how she had washed him up and Macon had put him to bed."

"Honestly, Shirley . . . that was low."

Savannah was surprised when her mother slapped her. She shouldn't have been; it wasn't the first time. But she had never seen it coming and was always shocked when it happened.

She had to reach deep inside for the self-control to keep from knocking her backward off her bar stool.

She's your mother, she heard Gran's voice saying in the recesses of her conscience. *Respect the station.*

"You've bitched for years," Shirley said, "that I was a rotten mother. Well, I was trying to help my kid, okay? And if you don't like the way I was going about it, to hell with you."

"That's enough."

Savannah spun around on her stool to see Dirk standing behind her and Shirley. His face was flushed, his eyes narrowed as he glared at her mother.

His big hand closed over Shirley's shoulder, and Savannah saw her wince. "Don't you ever, *ever* do that again," he said, his voice low, but shaking. "Because if you do . . ." His hand tightened, and Shirley whimpered. ". . . I'm going to forget that you're a woman and break your jaw. Got it?"

Savannah slid off her stool and picked up her purse from the bar. "I'm done here anyway. Already heard wa-a-ay more than I wanted to."

"I'm really sorry I even asked you to talk to her," Dirk said as they walked out of the bar together and headed across the parking lot to her brother's pickup. "If I'd have known she was going to hit you, I never would have—"

"Don't worry about it, buddy." Savannah slipped her arm companionably through his. "It's really no big deal."

"I don't believe that. Your own mother slaps you across the face in a public place, and you say it's no biggy? I've seen you karate chop the crap outta guys for less than that."

"You don't understand. It's not all that important, because *Shirley* isn't that important to my life. If Gran ever slapped me, I'd be devastated."

He covered her hand with his and squeezed it. She liked how it felt, warm and comforting.

"Your grandmother really was more of a mom to you, wasn't she."

"Hell, yeah. Shirley's more like an irritating sibling."

"You've got a lot of those."

She grinned up at him. "Alma and Waycross are cool."

"Alma, Waycross, and you . . . that's three out of nine. Not that great, considering your grandmother's good upbringing."

"One good grandma can only do so much to balance the books. A lot of other factors went into the way we turned out."

She fished in her purse for the truck's key, but the one street lamp, mounted on a pole in front of the tavern, didn't do much to illuminate the area.

"Are you going back to your grandma's?" he asked.

"I reckon. She was frying up chicken when I left. There'll probably be leftovers. Wanna follow me over?"

His face lit up, nearly enough to help her find the key. But then he shrugged. "I don't know. Your poor grandmother's got enough people bummin' food off her. She doesn't need another mooch."

"So, stop by the little grocery store there on the highway and pick up a contribution."

"Like what?"

"Anything with more than fifty percent fat calories should do nicely." She found the key and was unlocking the truck's door when she heard the low, thrumming roar of a powerful automobile engine approaching and headlights swept across the parking lot as a car pulled in.

"It's Tom," she said, even before she saw the cruiser.

"Oh, goody. Let's go." He jerked the truck door open and motioned for her to get in.

She swallowed a grin. "We really should say hi. He might have something new."

He grumbled, but slammed the door closed and walked with her over to the cruiser.

Tom got out and immediately headed in their direction. "Good evening," he said, directing the greeting more toward Savannah than Dirk.

"How's it going?" Savannah replied.

Dirk radiated silence.

"You guys coming or going?" Tom tucked his shirttail into his trousers, flexing biceps and pecs.

Savannah tried not to notice. Because she was sure that, if she did, Dirk would notice her noticing.

Men . . . they certainly made life more complicated.

"Going," Dirk said, managing to spit the word out in one curt syllable.

"You off duty? Looking for a cold one?" Savannah asked, nodding toward the bar.

"Still working. I'm looking for Alvin. See him in there?"

"Save yourself the trouble," Dirk mumbled. "He ain't there."

"Why are you looking for him?" Savannah ventured. "If you don't mind me asking?"

Tom grinned at her. She could feel Dirk tense beside her.

"You can ask," he said. "Since you were right, you can ask anything you want."

"About what?" Savannah wanted to know.

"About Alvin's fingerprints being on the judge's desk drawer. How'd you know?"

It was Savannah's turn to smirk. "Just had a feeling. I also think he killed Judge Patterson. Since I'm on a roll, are you going to believe me about that, too?"

Tom chuckled. "Whoa, girl. Let me get my hands on him first. And when I do, I'll turn him upside down and give him a good shake. We'll see what rattles and rolls out."

Savannah couldn't remember when it had felt so good to lie in bed and allow the fatigue of the day to melt away from her body and into the featherbed.

At least for eight hours or so, the investigation was on hold, dinner finished, dishes done, friends and most of the family gone. And with her cats lying, one on either side of her feet, like kitty bookends, it was almost like being home.

Gran climbed into bed beside her, smelling of bath soap and talcum powder, and, for just a moment, all was right in Savannah's world.

The illusion of safety evaporated as Gran settled under the covers and said, "Did you tell Tommy Stafford to let Cliff out of that jail . . . that he wouldn't have said a blame-fool thing like that if Shirley hadn't put him up to it?"

Savannah hesitated, considering whether or not to tell the truth. But she had learned long ago that, with Gran, you might as well spill it—the whole truth, and nothing but. She could spot a lie at a hundred paces, and heaven help you if you were the one who had uttered it. In Savannah's childhood, lying was one of the only sins that could actually land you behind the toolshed with a switch, ripped from a nearby tree or bush, applied to your rear end.

That . . . and smoking cigarettes . . . or drinking beer.

"No, Gran. I didn't mention it to Tom."

"Somebody needs to." She punched her pillow, fluffing it. "Clifton's way too old to be in jail. If he has to sleep on one of those cold steel cots, his arthritis will give him miseries."

"But he volunteered . . . so to speak. And believe me, there's nothing cold about those jail cells. There's no air-conditioning up there, like there is downstairs in the offices."

Gran's silence told Savannah that she should have kept that tidbit to herself. Her grandmother was worried enough already, without her adding details to the grim picture.

Savannah rolled onto her side and looked at Gran. In the moonlight, she saw the glint of tears on her cheek, and her own heart ached for this lady who had done nothing to deserve this pain at her age.

Nothing, but to love too much.

Savannah reached out and gently brushed the tear away with her fingertips. "I can't say anything to Tom on Cliff's behalf, Gran. I'm already feeling a mountain of guilt over not getting rid of those medals when I had the chance. By doing the right thing I could have condemned my brother to a murder he didn't commit. I'm not going to do anything else virtuous to aid the side of justice."

"Of course you are." Gran pushed her hand away . . . but clasped it afterward. "I don't want to hear foolishness like that. You're going to do whatever you believe is right, and the Lord's gonna reward you for it. He'll make sure Macon is safe in the end."

"Did you think that maybe it was the answer to one of your prayers . . . Clifton confessing like that?"

"No! It never occurred to me that God would approve of a man lying through his teeth . . . or his dentures, in Cliff's case. Your mother put him up to it. We both know that."

"I still think it's a blessing that's bought us some time . . . time to investigate, to prove Macon's innocence. Aren't you the one who's always telling me that the Lord works in strange ways?"

Gran was silent for a long time. Finally, she said, "You know I don't like it when you use my own words against me. And you also know that you're not so big that I can't still give you an ol' fashioned whuppin'."

"I know." Savannah giggled. "That's why I save that particular tactic as a last resort, when I can't come up with anything else . . . and when you're too tired to chase me down."

By the time Savannah shuffled into the kitchen the next morning to get her all-important first cup of caffeine, Gran already had the assembly line going. Bacon and pork sausage were sizzling on the stove, biscuits baking in the oven, and on the back burner, a pan of grits bubbled.

Cleopatra and Diamante had followed Savannah in from the bedroom and were doing figure eights around her ankles. "I know, I know . . . you're famished," she said as she paused to pour some Kittie Kiddles into a cereal bowl and place it out of the way behind the garbage pail.

At the back door, Beauregard pressed his wet nose against the screen and whined pitifully.

"Pay him no nevermind," Gran said. "He's been fed, watered, and petted. He's just raisin' a stink 'cause he's jealous."

Savannah glanced over at the stove and its bounty. "Good heavens, are you expecting Sherman's armies to drop in this morning?" she said, taking a mug from the cupboard.

"Oh, yes, they'll all be coming by, it being Saturday and laundry day," Gran said, adding several more strips of bacon to the skillet.

"They come over on the weekend to do your laundry for you? How very considerate of them."

"That'll be the day. Marietta and Vidalia don't know the difference between washing a white T-shirt and a red wool sweater."

"You do their wash and their kids', too?"

Gran shrugged. "Well, they're busy, you know. It ain't easy, making ends meet and bringing up a family these days. If I can help out a bit, I don't mind."

Growling under her breath, Savannah took a drink of her coffee, then set the mug aside. "I'll make the gravy," she said. "And I'll finish up those eggs, too."

Gran looked completely nonplused. "But why? What would I do with myself?"

"Sit right there in that chair," Savannah said, pointing to the table, "and supervise. You're over eighty years old. It's high time you got promoted."

As predicted, the gang began to pour into the tiny house at exactly the same time as the gravy was poured into the bowl. On the back porch, pillowcases bulging with laundry began to stack up next to the washing machine.

"Are we having a wedding today or not?" Vidalia asked as she herded her two sets of twins into the kitchen and in the direction of the table. "I called Mari last night, but she . . ." Giving Savannah a loaded sideways look, she continued, ". . . she wasn't feeling like talking and said she didn't know yet."

Didn't feel like talking, huh? Savannah thought as she pulled the pan of biscuits from the oven. *Drunker than a skunk on a Friday-night bender is more like it.*

Alma rushed through, a tornado dressed in her Donut Heaven

uniform, and grabbed a couple of biscuits, wrapping them in a paper napkin. She bent over briefly to pet both cats. "If Mari wants me to stand up with her in that ugly peach dress, she's going to have to call me at work and let me know in time to come home and change."

"Yes, we're all terribly worried about not getting the opportunity to wear those dresses," Savannah said, swatting her on the rear with the oven mitt as she flew past on her way out the back door.

"I lo-o-ove that dress, and I can't wait to wear it." Vidalia sank onto a chair and looked around the table. "I'm going to wear mine again to the Sweethearts' Cotillion over in Auburndale. Where's the strawberry jam? You know I don't like peach preserves."

"Well, I don't live here," Savannah said, gently pushing Gran back down onto her chair, "but I'd bet the jam's . . . in the refrigerator. Feel free to get up and help yourself."

Jesup stumbled in from the bedroom, wearing men's black boxer shorts and a gray T-shirt. "I told Mari point-blank that I'm *not* wearing that stupid dress. I refuse to be seen in public wearing that abomination."

Gran looked her up and down. "But you don't mind being seen at the breakfast table lookin' like that. Go put some breeches on."

With a deep sigh and an exaggerated eye roll, Jesup turned around and stomped out of the kitchen.

Cordele had just appeared, neatly dressed and tightly buttoned into her white blouse and navy skirt. "Personally, I don't think any of us are going to be attending a wedding today. Marietta has serious commitment issues, stemming from her parental abandonment issues, and since Lester is a prime example of the Peter Pan Complex, it's just as well that they—"

"Cordele, shove it—a biscuit, that is—in your mouth," Savannah said, smiling sweetly. "Before they get cold, that is."

"Where's the butter?"

Vidalia smirked. "Let me guess . . . it's in the refrigerator. Help yourself."

Savannah slid a plate brimming with eggs, bacon, sausage, and grits in front of her grandmother. "There you go, Gran. Sunny side up, just the way you like them."

She turned to the rest of the table. "And the skillet's right there. Feel free to help yourselves."

"But . . . but . . ." Vidalia sputtered.

"Gran is the one who always . . ." Cordele added.

"I like Granny Reid's eggs," Vidalia's daughter, Jillian, whined, her lower lip trembling. "Mommy's have those icky ruffles around the edges, and they're hard to chew."

"But Granny Reid is busy eating her own breakfast," Savannah said, pressing down hard on her grandmother's shoulders to keep her from rising from her chair. "And if your mama's eggs aren't quite as good as Gran's, it's because Mommy hasn't had as much *practice*. The more she does it, the better she'll get."

The phone on the wall rang, and again Savannah held her grandmother down. "If you try to get up one more time before that plate's empty, I'm going to superglue your backside to your chair," she said.

Gran looked up at her, shocked for a second; then she grinned broadly. "Okay," she said.

Savannah reached for the phone. "Hello, this is Grand Central Station, but it *isn't* Granny Reid's Country Café. May I help you?"

"Savannah?"

She recognized the caller instantly. "Tom?"

"Yeah. Come over to the country club. Right now."

"What is it?"

"Maybe an accident," he said. She could hear the misgivings in his voice. "But I think it's probably another murder. Shake a leg and get over here as quick as you can. If you want to, bring that buddy of yours—Dirt, Kirk, whatever—along, too."

He hung up before she could ask the obvious: "Who's dead?"

Chapter
18

"Stafford must figure he's in way over his head, if he asked you to bring *me* along," Dirk said as he pulled the rental car into the country club lot and parked next to Tom's cruiser.

"Yeah, that's what I think, too," Savannah replied.

"Do you suppose he'll mind that I came along?" Tammy asked from the back seat.

"From the way Tom sounded on the phone, I'd bet that he'll be happy to get all the help he can," Savannah assured her. "You've got to understand, in this little town, a burglary is a catastrophe. I'll bet there hasn't been a double homicide since Lord knows when, if ever."

They got out of the car and walked across the lot. "Tom's got his hands full," Savannah continued, "and I don't know how much help Sheriff Mahoney is when it comes to investigations. He's more the simple, 'swing the nightstick and keep the peace' type."

Even from the parking lot, they could hear voices—loud and excited—coming from the direction of the pool.

"Well, that answers the question 'Where?'," Savannah said as they headed in that direction. "I guess we'll be finding out 'Who' soon enough."

When they arrived at the pool area, they saw a yellow police tape circling the chain-link fence that surrounded the pool. A dozen or so spectators stood, their fingers laced through the fence, chattering to each other as they watched the show inside.

"Good, at least he's set up a perimeter," Dirk said.

The ring of gawkers opened a space near the gate to allow them through, though several of them shouted warnings: "Hey, Deputy Stafford says you're not supposed to go in there!" "You'd better not; you'll get in big trouble!"

Three figures knelt on the side of the pool, examining a body that lay sprawled on the shiny blue and white tiles. Tom, Herb Jameson, the mortician, and the little pharmacist cum law enforcement officer, Fred Jeter, were bent over the corpse, deeply involved in a hushed conversation.

As Savannah and her cohorts approached, Tom was the first to notice. At first he looked irritated, then relieved when he recognized them.

"Who are those dopey-looking pinheads with him?" Dirk whispered to Savannah.

"A volunteer sometime-deputy and the local mortician who's now the acting coroner."

"Oh, man, we *are* in trouble."

"Be nice, Dirko," Tammy warned him.

"Shut up, bimbo-head."

"Stop, both of you! Or I won't take you out for ice cream later."

Savannah craned her neck, trying to see the body's face, but Herb Jameson's backside was blocking her view.

Visual obstructions aside, she knew even without confirmation the identity of the dead person. That long, lean, muscular body and skimpy red swimsuit were all too familiar to her.

The short life of Pretty Boy Alvin Barnes had apparently come to a tragic end.

And, while Savannah certainly hadn't been president of his fan club, she hated to see anyone taken so young.

"Thanks for coming," Tom said as he stood and motioned them over.

Once brief introductions were made, the Moonlight Magnolia gang joined the others in a ring around the deceased.

"Who found him?" Savannah asked, carefully scanning the body for anything unusual that might point to a cause of death other than the obvious—drowning.

"The caretaker," Tom said. "He came out this morning at seven to skim the pool and saw him floating facedown in the water. He called me and Dr. Fleming. Doc got here about the same time I did, and he pronounced him."

"No chance of resuscitating him?" Tammy asked.

Tom shook his head. "Rigor was already present. The doctor took the internal body temperature and said he probably died late last night. But he wasn't sure, because he didn't know how the water would affect the natural heat loss."

"Is that the doctor's incision?" Dirk pointed to a small, bloodless cut on the body's abdomen.

"Yeah," Tom replied. "He said he needed to stick the thermometer into the body like that to get an accurate reading."

"He was right. That's how they do it," Herb Jameson said with quiet authority.

Savannah looked down into the open, vacant, staring eyes and wondered, as she always did when looking at a corpse, at how empty the body appeared once the soul had departed.

Noting the Tag Heuer watch on his wrist, Savannah remembered how proud he had been of it. A lot of good the expensive jewelry did him now.

"Have you turned him over yet?" Dirk asked.

"Oh, yes," Fred Jeter said, his eyes sparkling behind his thick lenses. "We flipped him over before, and that's when we saw it."

"Saw what?" Savannah asked.

Tom reached for the body's arms and motioned Dirk to get the feet. "Let's turn him, and you can see for yourself."

Once they had rotated the dead man, the gaping split in the back of his scalp was all too obvious.

"Ouch," Tammy said. "That must have hurt."

"Actually," Tom added, "Dr. Fleming said the blow might

have knocked him right out, so he may not have felt much of anything."

Herb Jameson reached out and gingerly touched the edge of the wound. "I've been a member of the club for years," he said. "And I often swim out here. I don't know how many times I've seen Alvin do a fancy flip off the board, showing off, you know. I'm not surprised he whacked his head like that."

Dirk frowned, studying the ugly gash. "That's what you guys figure happened? He did this himself, diving off the board?"

"And hitting his head on it, yeah," Tom replied. "At least, that's what Dr. Fleming and Herb here think."

"It's a common enough accident," Herb said. "You've got to be careful with those dives. If you smack your head on the end of the board on the way down, you can be unconscious by the time you hit the water. If you're alone and nobody fishes you out, you drown."

"Was Alvin in the habit of swimming alone out here, late at night?" Savannah wanted to know.

Herb nodded. "He sure was. Sometimes he and Bonnie... well, you know, they liked each other and . . ."

"So we heard," Tammy said.

"Have you spoken to Miss Bonnie yet?" Savannah asked, trying to make the question sound like an offhanded remark.

Tom gave her a loaded look. "Nope. I haven't. I was looking for her and Alvin all night long. Well, now Alvin's accounted for, but it seems that Bonnie's still missing."

"This here's Alvin's locker. I'll get it open for you, right away." The grizzled old caretaker gave them a yellow, crooked smile as he spun the combination on locker number 27. The lock released and he deftly removed it.

"There ya go," he said proudly, as he threw the door open and stepped aside.

"Thanks, Zachariah," Tom said as he took a giant flashlight from his belt, turned it on, and shone the beam inside the locker.

"You've been a big help. You go along home and take a nap. It's been a hard day, what with you finding him and all."

"That *was* awful," Zachariah agreed, his proud smile temporarily dimmed. "It's been a long time . . . since the war in fact, that I saw a dead person. Outside o' the funeral home, I mean. I'm bound to have a few nightmares about it."

"Yeah, we're all going to have those," Fred Jeter said with a shudder. "Him staring off into space like that gives me the creeps."

Savannah ignored the conversation and stepped across the long bench that ran between the two rows of dressing-room lockers. She moved closer to Tom and Dirk, who were peering into the late tennis instructor's unit.

"What do you see?" she asked. "Anything interesting?"

Tammy wriggled her way in, too, standing on tiptoe to look over Savannah's shoulder.

"Just a white shirt and pair of shorts," Tom said, "hanging on the hook there."

He gingerly lifted the garments out and held them up for all to see.

"No blood on them," Dirk said, echoing what everyone was thinking.

"And some tennis shoes," Tom continued his inventory, "and a shaving kit."

When he unzipped the leather case, Savannah got a strong whiff of the musky fragrance that Alvin had been wearing when she'd questioned him.

"Nothing special in here that I can see." Tom handed the case off to Dirk, who looked it over and passed it along to Savannah.

She searched the contents and realized that the potent, musky smell was actually from a stick of roll-on deodorant, not a shave lotion or cologne.

"Some travel information," Tom said, lifting out a handful of vacation brochures, featuring luxury cruises to the Caribbean.

"Suppose he was daydreaming," Savannah asked, "or coming up with actual ways to spend some ill-gotten gains?"

"What do you mean?" Tom gave the literature to Herb and turned back to the locker.

"I mean . . . he had put a substantial amount down on a Lincoln Navigator, and Bonnie had done the same on a matching one. I was just suggesting that they might be lining their pockets with somebody's hard-earned money . . . not their own."

"If they had any money," Tom agreed, "it would have been from someone else's efforts. Those two never had anything that somebody else didn't give to them."

"The Tag Heuer watch?" Savannah asked. "That had to cost a pretty penny."

Tom, Herb, Fred, and Zachariah all traded smirks.

"What?" Dirk asked. "You guys got some idea who paid for that, too?"

Tom chuckled. "Let's just say . . . a lady who will remain un-named. A rich lady in town who has nothing to do with this case, but kept Alvin busy on the side."

"Are you sure she's got nothing to do with this?" Dirk said.

"I'm sure." Tom removed the sneakers from the floor of the locker, then trailed the beam of his flashlight over every inch of the now-empty interior. "She's got more money than sense, but she's no killer. The only law she's broken is the law of matri-mony."

"There's been a few of those kind of ladies here at the club," Herb said, "who've kept Alvin busy. He's kinda like Bonnie that way: Didn't mind . . . getting his hands dirty . . . for a bit of extra cash or a pretty toy."

"That's it," Tom said, sounding disappointed. "The shirt and shorts, which he probably wore today. These shoes . . ." He held them out for display. ". . . Which have his wallet and car keys in the right one and his socks in the left. The shave kit. That's all she wrote."

"Wait a minute." Herb Jameson studied the shoes thought-fully. "The socks and his wallet, but . . ."

"Yeah, so?" Dirk leaned over him, practically breathing down his neck. "Is there something you want to tell us?"

The mortician nodded. "Something's different."

"What? What's different?" Savannah asked, resisting the urge to strangle the information out of him.

"The watch."

They all looked at each other questioningly.

"What about the watch, Herb?" Tom said. "Tell us."

"It just occurred to me. His watch is still on his wrist. He wouldn't have been swimming with that expensive watch on."

"Why not?" Savannah asked. "It's a Tag Heuer. They're water-resistant, believe me."

"I know," Herb replied. "I told him that when I saw him taking it off here in the locker room . . . several times in fact. I teased him about it, that he was afraid to wear it in the water. But he was obnoxiously proud of that watch. He had a ritual; he always took it off and stuck it in the toe of his tennis shoe along with his wallet and keys."

"Well, maybe he got over his fear of drowning the thing this time," Dirk said, sounding suddenly bored with the whole conversation. "There's nothing here. Let's put it all back and go. That body's getting ripe out there in your hearse."

"Hold on," Herb said, excited. "Did you say those clothes, the shirt and the shorts, were hanging on the hook?"

"Yeah," Tom replied. "The hook on the right. Why?"

"No, no way." Herb was practically jumping up and down. "Alvin was a neatnik, really picky about the way he looked. And he always made a big deal about folding his shirt and his shorts just right and laying them down, all nice and neat, there on top of his shoes."

They gave him a look that said they thought he was much too pleased with himself for making this mundane observation.

"Really," he insisted. "I'm telling you, he had a routine, like a ritual. We all noticed it, even hassled him about it. He'd stick the wallet and the watch in one shoe, the socks in the other, then he'd make a big production out of folding his shirt and shorts and putting them right there on top."

"Okay," Tom said, "but the socks and the wallet are where they belong."

"So whoever put those clothes in there must've known part of his routine, but not all of it."

Tom shook his head and sighed. "Herb, I know you think you're on to something, but—"

"Just a second." Savannah did a quick mental inventory of the locker's contents. "Something else is missing."

"What?" Tammy asked.

"Underwear." She waited while they all looked at each other and took stock of the clothes. "I mean, Alvin might have been one of those fellows who liked to just let things flop free in the breeze, but . . ."

"Oh, he wore underwear," old Zachariah piped up. He had been standing, silent and forgotten behind them, leaning against the wall. "Yessiree, bob! Alvin was famous for his knickers!"

"That's true! He was!" Herb said. "Everybody knew that he wore underwear!"

Savannah was almost afraid to ask, but . . . "How?"

Zachariah cackled and smiled a big, snaggly, gummy grin. "He was always wearing those thin white shorts, and everything showed right through 'em. Yeah, Alvin was famous for his leopard prints, and those red and purple paisley ones, and at Christmas . . ." He practically collapsed on the floor from laughing, and Savannah started to worry that maybe it was a hysterical reaction from finding the body earlier. "And at Christmas time," Zachariah said between gasps, "he wore some that said, 'Kiss Me Under the Mistletoe.' And guess where the mistletoe was?"

"I can just imagine," Savannah said dryly, slapping Zach on the back to help him catch his breath.

Once Zachariah had recovered, she turned to Dirk. "Hand me that shirt," she said, taking the white polo shirt from him.

She turned it inside out, then sniffed the sleeves.

"Alvin never wore this shirt," she said.

"How do you know?" Tom snatched it out of her hand and looked it over.

"The same way I know if I can get another wearing out of a sweater back home. Smell the pits. Nothing but laundry soap and bleach."

She took the shaving kit from Tammy, unzipped it, and removed the deodorant stick. "When I met him before, I thought he was wearing some god-awful, strong-smelling cologne. But it's this deodorant. Man, you could deodorize a week-old dead horse with that stuff. If Alvin had worn that shirt, even for a minute or two, the pits would smell."

"Maybe he forgot to deodorize after showering," Tom said.

"A tennis instructor, no deodorant in this heat and humidity? Then it would smell like sweat. Not fabric softener."

They all stood quietly for a moment, mentally digesting.

"Did you check the edge of the diving board for traces of blood or hair?" Dirk asked Tom.

Reluctantly, Tom nodded. "Yeah, I walked out there earlier and looked."

"Nothing, right?"

"Right."

"I didn't think so," Dirk said. "Late last night, somebody hit our buddy Alvin over the back of the head and killed him . . . or at least knocked him out. There was probably blood all over the clothes he was wearing. So they put some swim trunks on him, dumped him in the pool outside, and planted these clothes here to look like he'd been diving and smacked his head."

"They knew something about his routine," Savannah said, "like his locker combination . . ."

"That's nothing," Zachariah said. "The combinations are on a list in the top drawer of the office desk, or somebody could've looked over his shoulder when he was unlocking it himself."

". . . And they knew he put his wallet and keys in his shoes," Savannah continued, "but not that he put his watch in there, too."

"And they didn't know about his folding routine," Dirk added.

Tammy grinned broadly. "And apparently they hadn't been

around when Alvin bent over or they would have known that he had a fetish for crazy underwear."

"Naw," Savannah said, "they just forgot the knickers. It's hard to remember everything in the heat of the moment... you know, like right after you've killed another human being by smashing their skull in. Yep, at a time like that, no matter how smart you think you are, you're just bound to forget something."

Chapter

19

Savannah jiggled the lock pick slightly and heard that soft tell-tale click that told her she had done it again—successfully executed a felony "break and enter."

Standing at Alvin Barnes's back door, she and Dirk cast another cautious look around to see if anyone might be watching. But the neighborhood seemed remarkably quiet for a Saturday afternoon.

"You're a bad influence on me, Van," he said. "Usually I limit myself to bending the law slightly out of shape, but I generally stop short of actually breaking it."

"It's Tom's fault," she said. "I asked him politely for the keys. By refusing, he put me in a difficult spot. If he catches us and locks us up, he'll have nobody but himself to blame."

He shook his head and chuckled. "I can't believe I actually understood that. I've been hanging out with you way too long."

Quickly, silently, they slipped inside the house.

"Good grief," she said, looking around at the white, sparkling surfaces of the kitchen, "this is the cleanest place I've ever been."

"Sure doesn't look like *my* bachelor pad."

Scenes of Dirk's trailer flashed across her mind, visions of rusty TV trays, stacked orange crates, an old school-bus seat—

and that was just the furniture. But she decided to be kind and let the moment pass without comment.

"Yep, Alvin was a neatnik, all right," she said, pointing out the spotless glass table with its basket of fake fruit neatly arranged in the center.

Dirk opened the refrigerator and a couple of cupboards. "I swear, I think he alphabetizes his cereals."

"No way."

He pointed to the shelf where, indeed, Alpha-Bits were to the far left, followed by Cheerios, Cocoa Puffs, and Wheaties.

"Oh, boy . . . I don't *ever* want to be that organized."

"Don't worry; you won't be."

The living room proved just as orderly, with magazines stacked neatly on the chrome-and-glass coffee table. Three remote controls lay side by side next to a stack of cork coasters.

"See," Savannah said. "There are men in the world who use coasters!"

"Not *real* men. He probably ate quiche and needlepointed in his spare time."

"Judging from the six-pack he was sporting on his belly, I'd say he spent a lot of time in here," Savannah said, pointing to a mini-gym set up in a small bedroom off the living room area. A stationary bike, a chin-up bar, an abs machine, and assorted free weights were arranged in meticulous, military order around the room. The walls were mirrored.

No surprise there, Savannah thought. *Why torture yourself with exotic devices and not give yourself ample opportunities to admire the results?*

Farther down a short hall she found the bedroom. Although this room was as neat and spotless as the rest of the house, the leopard bedspread and tiger-striped rug revealed a less civilized aspect of Alvin Barnes's personality. Over the bed hung a gilt-framed print of a pair of black panthers in a jungle setting.

"Overdone," Dirk said, sticking his head into the room. "Overt. A decorator's feeble attempt at primitive expression."

"Eh, you're just jealous. You'd love to entertain a member of the feminine gender in a room like this."

"Hell, I'd be happy to entertain a feminine anybody *anywhere* these days."

"Speaking of the feminine persuasion," Savannah said after opening several drawers before coming to one containing women's clothes. "A lady is . . . or was . . . living here, too."

"Bonnie?"

"Probably, although if it's her, I withdraw the 'lady' part."

Dirk slid open the closet door. "Don't think much of her, huh?"

"Not much at all."

In the adjoining bathroom, Savannah found sanitary napkins under the sink and hairspray in the medicine chest. A hot pink toothbrush with glitter in the handle rested in the holder, next to a navy-blue one.

"Alvin left abruptly," she said. "But Bonnie packed."

"Are you sure?" Dirk asked, joining her in the bathroom.

"Oh, yes. I'm sure."

"But that's gotta be her toothbrush. I mean, even a guy who's Mr. Susie Homemaker wouldn't stick a thing like that in his mouth."

"So she left the toothbrush. She probably had another. There's no makeup case. No woman with spider lashes and frosted blue lids is going to go anywhere without her 'Face in a Bag.' And there are no hair-grooming implements except that one dryer, and that's a guy's. No curling wand, steaming rollers, nothing to create that 'big hair look' that Bonnie had going. She packed."

Dirk nodded. "Okay, maybe she killed Alvin . . . and the judge, too, for that matter."

"Maybe the judge, but I don't know about Alvin. He was a lot bigger than her. That wound on the back of his head was straight across. No angle. She was so much shorter than him, that if she swung something at him, the line of the wound would probably angle upward."

"That's assuming they were both standing. What if he was bent over when she whacked him?"

Savannah said nothing for several seconds, then wrinkled her nose as though smelling something odious. "I hate it when you pop my bubbles."

"Like you're not always stickin' your fingers in mine. Besides, I agree. I don't think a short, scrawny chick like Bonnie caused that nasty gash. It's possible, but I'd put my money on a guy with some beef."

Savannah gave the bathroom and bedroom another look. "Whoever did it, they didn't do it in here. Nothing bloody happened in these rooms. Let's search the yard."

In the backyard, they checked again for potentially nosy neighbors and saw no one.

"I wish my trailer park was as quiet as Alvin's neighborhood," Dirk said as he strolled along a sidewalk that led from the back door of the house toward a garage and then the alley at the rear of the property. "There's always kids runnin' around, yelling their heads off, throwing Frisbees—"

"Drunks throwing beer bottles. . . ." Savannah added.

"Oh, shut up. That's usually only on Saturday nights when the old fart next to me and his battle-ax wife mix it up."

Savannah followed him, looking at everything, searching for anything that warranted her attention. Long ago, she had learned that when conducting an investigation, you seldom know what you're looking for . . . until you find it.

The yard was small and simple: a patch of dandelion-free grass; a couple of flower beds containing close-clipped bushes; a cement driveway that, unlike hers at home, had not one spot of oil on its surface; a garden hose coiled in perfect loops on a hook on the rear wall of the house.

As she worked her way toward the back of the lot, she noted a garbage-burning barrel where the sidewalk ended at the alley. Dirk was leaning over it, examining its contents.

"Anything good?"

"Naw, just ashes and crap."

Oh, well, she thought. *Too much to hope for a slightly singed, bloody shirt or only half-burned murder weapon. And, while you're dreaming, a full set of perfect fingerprints on said weapon.*

As she walked along the side of the garage, past a large rhododendron, she paused and did a double take. The garage wall, like the rear of the house, had a garden hose on a hook.

"Hey," she said, "check this out."

He hurried over. "Yeah, so what? It's a hose. Probably for when the fire in the barrel gets outta hand."

"It's messy."

"What do you mean, messy? It's wrapped up nice on a hook."

"Nice by your standards, and even by mine. But not Alvin Barnes's standards. Look at the one on the house. The coils are all even, lined up next to each other. This one's just sorta wound around, like the rest of the world would do it."

She looked down at the ground, the freshly raked soil around the base of the rhododendron. It was damp.

Kneeling on the sidewalk, she felt the dirt and grass on either side. They, too, were wet.

"Somebody hosed this area down," she said, "recently."

"Maybe Alvin was watering his flowers."

She checked the ground around the bush directly across the sidewalk on the other side. "The grass is wet beside the sidewalk, but the dirt under the plant is dry. Why would he water one, but not the other?"

She stood, turned back toward the house, and let her imagination go to work. "You know," she said, "this would be a good place to pop somebody. At night, it would be pretty dark back here. If he were bringing the garbage out—Alvin would be meticulous about that—you could hide right here behind the rhododendron bush and when he got about here . . ."

Dirk swung like he was knocking one into the bleachers. "Whack!"

"Yep."

She walked up to the wall and placed her cheek against it,

looking down the length of the white stucco surface. "Somebody rinsed off the wall in this section right here," she said. "There's dust . . . not a lot, but some . . . all along the wall, except for an area right there, where the ground's wet."

"Blood splatter," Dirk said. "He was washing off the evidence."

"Maybe. If that's where the killer struck him, that's about where the blood would land."

"And on the sidewalk."

"Exactly."

"And he'd wash it down really good, to make sure he'd got it all, and it would probably still be wet."

"Just like this. . . ."

"Yeah. Just like this."

Savannah looked back at the house, the driveway, the sidewalk and the alley. "Okay, let's run this down," she said. "I want to knock off Alvin Barnes. Maybe I know that he takes his garbage out every night at a certain time, maybe I don't. But either way, I wait out here behind the bush. He comes out and I let him have it on the back of the head. He goes down."

Dirk nodded thoughtfully. "Then you probably wrap up the body in something you brought along to protect your trunk, dump him in your car—"

"Which would probably be here in the alley, so that he wouldn't have seen it earlier."

"Then you go into the house . . . the door would be unlocked . . . and you get a clean set of clothes out of his closet."

"But you forget the underwear."

He shrugged. "Hey, murder's stressful. Especially the premeditated, cold-blooded kind."

"Where do you suppose he took off the bloody clothes and changed him into the swimsuit?"

"If it were me . . . I'd do it here, after he's in the trunk. More private than the club. I'd strip him off there in the car and wrap the bloody clothes around his head, soaking up the rest. I'd put the trunks, or whatever you call those pansy things, on him then."

Savannah turned toward the alley. "And I'd put the clean clothes in the car and take off."

"And after you got there?"

"Pull the car onto that strip of road right by the pool, make sure nobody was around, take him out of the trunk, and throw him in the water. Then I'd plant the clean clothes, the wallet, and the keys in his locker."

"Forgetting the watch."

"Right. Then I'd dispose of the clothes, the weapon, and whatever I'd wrapped the body in."

"Where?"

"Oh, please . . ." she said. "Who do you think I am? Madame Sophia with her crystal ball?"

"Without those things, we don't have a case."

She shrugged. "We don't need to prove a case right now. We just need a working theory about what happened."

"And you think that's what happened?"

"Yeah, don't you?"

"Close enough . . . for a working theory, as you call it."

They looked around the yard once more, and finding nothing more, they left.

As they drove away, Savannah said, "You wanna know the scary part of all this?"

"He's smart."

"That's right. And cold. And methodical."

They rounded a corner and hit the highway.

"Bonnie Patterson?" Dirk asked.

"Cold enough? Probably. But not tall enough. And definitely, definitely not smart enough. If I had to guess, I'd say that Bonnie Patterson knows who killed the judge, who killed Alvin, and she's running for her life."

Chapter

20

Dirk dropped Savannah off at Gran's house and left with the intention of tracking down Tom Stafford and sharing information with him. Savannah had warned him that Tom might not be as imaginative in his interpretation of the untidy hose and the wet sidewalk. But he said it would also give him the opportunity to find out if Tom had anything new.

Savannah figured she had to at least stick her head in the house and make an appearance, just in case a wedding really was on the family agenda.

Visions of violent peach dresses danced through her head as she hurried through the screen door and into a living room full of hysterical, crying women.

After a closer look and a more accurate assessment, she decided that, although the room was brimming with Reid sisters, only one was actually sobbing hysterically.

"Mari! What's wrong?" She rushed to take her distraught sister in her arms and got pushed away for her troubles.

"What do you *think* is wrong?" Marietta's eyes were puffy red slits in a swollen white face. Her usually perfect hairdo hung to one side of her head, a lopsided French twist. "It's off! He went back to . . . back to . . . Lucille!"

She collapsed onto the sofa, where Alma enveloped her in a

tight hug and rocked her as though she was a six-year-old whose puppy had just died.

Cordele sat next to her and primly patted her hand. "You know, it's probably just as well, Mari. Lester had unresolved issues with his ex-wife that would have contaminated any—"

"Oh, shut up, Cordele!" Marietta said, throwing her hand off. "You just shut your fat mouth before I slap you stupid! None of you've got a lick o' sense. None of you have any idea the pain I'm going through here. The soulish agony."

From the vicinity of the recliner, Waycross's voice rose in a plaintive, wailing rendition of an old spiritual. "Nobody knows de trouble I see. . . ."

"You go to hell, Waycross!" Marietta screamed. "Go straight to hell, do not pass go, do not collect two hundred dollars! You hear me, boy!"

"That's quite enough," Gran said quietly, stepping from the back of the room. Calmly, she dried her hands on a dishtowel, then stuffed it into the pocket of her apron.

She pushed Vidalia, Cordele, and Jesup aside. "Let me by," she told them. "I've got somethin' to say about this ordeal. And I want ya'll to perk up your ears, 'cause I ain't sayin' it twice."

Walking over to the couch, she took Marietta by the shoulder and gave her a gentle shake. "First of all, you suck in that cryin', Marietta Reid, and conduct yourself like the lady that I know you are. Sit up straight, fine and proud, chin up."

Marietta gave it a half effort. Alma pushed a handful of tissues at her, and she blew her nose loudly.

"That's right," Gran said. "You've suffered a heavy loss. Your heart is broken, and your pride wounded. But others have suffered a lot worse with grace and dignity, and you will, too."

"But . . . but . . ." She hiccuped violently. "But Lester . . . *dumped* me!"

"And if you want to continue to think of it that way, then you can just wallow in your misery for the rest of your years and turn into a mean, resentful woman who's old before her time."

"Well, how else can I think about it?" Marietta buried her face in the tissues as new sobs erupted. "That's what happened, plain and simple."

"No, what happened . . . plain and simple . . ." Gran said, snatching Marietta's hands away from her face, ". . . is that the man came to his senses and decided to remain in his marriage. He decided to be a husband to the wife he already had and to be a father to his children."

"But I lo-o-ove him!"

"So, next time, choose someone to love who ain't married. You know I think the world of you, Mari, but you created this mess yourself. How many times have I told you girls not to set your cap for no married man? That's just an invitation to heartache. And that's why you're sitting here now, your heart achin'."

Marietta's lower lip trembled as she looked up at her grandmother. "Are you saying this is my fault?"

"I'm saying the same thing I've always said to you, Marietta Reid—you reap what you sow in this life. And this time, you've got a bitter harvest. You made a mistake. Accept the consequences like a woman and learn from it. But, whatever you do, stop that caterwaulin', cause it's getting on my nerves, and it's unworthy of a Reid."

As Marietta gathered the remnants of her tattered pride around her, Savannah slipped around the perimeter of the room to the recliner, where Waycross sat, staring at the ceiling, a half grin on his face.

"Can I borrow your truck again?" she whispered to him.

"Only if you take me to the garage first. I gotta get some air."

"I hear ya. I'll drive and you can hang your head out the window like Beauregard, ears and jowls flapping in the wind."

Savannah had asked herself the question: Who in town knows Bonnie Patterson best . . . other than Alvin Barnes, who ain't talkin'?

Having answered that question the best she could, she was heading out to the Patterson estate. Elsie had lived with Bonnie for the past few years. And with a sense of curiosity as sharp as Elsie's, she had to know something.

Housekeepers always knew more than they let on. While sweeping behind the refrigerator and cleaning out lingerie drawers, they uncovered more than a few dust bunnies.

And with a little friendly encouragement, Savannah had found them willing to share the dirt.

When she arrived at the mansion, Savannah rang the front doorbell and knocked hard at the back door. But no one answered.

Considering she had already broken into one house that day, she was pleased to find the back door unlocked and the lockpick unnecessary.

"Mrs. Dingle?" she called as she walked through the kitchen of the silent house. "Elsie, are you here?"

Curiosity led her to the library. She opened the door halfway and looked inside.

Other than some extra residue from Tom lifting fingerprints from the desk, nothing was different.

Apparently, Elsie was still boycotting the library, and considering the creepy vibes that remained, Savannah didn't blame her. She shut the door firmly behind her, as though that would somehow keep any evil spirits contained, and walked on through the dining room, the parlor, and the remaining downstairs rooms.

"Elsie? You up there?" she yelled at the bottom of the graceful, curving staircase.

She didn't know whether to be disappointed or relieved when nobody answered. No one to interview, but a full house at her disposal. . . . Could be worse.

But at the top of the stairs, she saw that one of the bedroom doors was open, and she could hear someone rummaging inside.

Instinctively, she reached inside her purse. Her palm curled around the handle of the Beretta. Amazing, she thought, how safe a 9mm with a full clip could make you feel, when you knew how to use it.

"Hello?" she said as she carefully poked her head into the room. "Anybody here?"

"Savannah?"

Elsie's shining face appeared from behind some billowing chiffon curtains. Savannah caught a whiff of vinegar and realized she was cleaning windows.

"Yes, it's me," Savannah said. "I'm sorry. I rang the bell and knocked, but . . ."

"Oh, my hearing isn't as good as it used to be," Elsie said, hurrying to greet her. "I'm glad you came on in."

Savannah looked around the room at the delicate pink and yellow, daisy-spangled curtains and matching wallpaper. The canopied bed was draped in delicate laces and covered with embroidered, ruffled pillows.

"What a gorgeous room!" Savannah said, walking over to a dresser where an antique silver comb-and-brush set was laid out on the polished rose marble top. "It's fit for a princess."

She lifted the lid of a carved wooden box and the delicate, tinkling sound of the music box filled the air. A tiny ballerina spun on one toe to the lilting notes of the old-fashioned waltz.

"She was a princess, my little Katherine," Elsie said, suddenly looking sad and a decade older.

"The judge's daughter?" Savannah said.

"Yes. He divorced her mother and sent her away, but he kept Katherine here with him. I wound up raising her. She was like my very own. I miss her so much."

"Yes, I heard that you lost her. I'm so sorry."

Elsie walked over to the dresser and sat down, as though her legs were suddenly too weak to hold her. She reached out and lovingly touched the silver hairbrush with one finger. "The Lord took her so quick; none of us had time to get ready, you know."

Savannah closed the top of the music box and sat down on the edge of the bed. "Tom said she died of a 'woman thing.' Being a man, he didn't know what it was."

Elsie sniffed. "They called it a 'topical pregnancy.' A little baby growing in the wrong place."

A topical pregnancy? A baby in the wrong place? Savannah ran the term through her mental medical banks and came up with the interpretation. *An ectopic pregnancy.*

"Yes," Elsie continued, "something burst inside her and she just bled to death there on her kitchen floor. By the time little Caitlin got home from school, it was already too late. She was gone."

"Caitlin is her and Mack's daughter?"

Elsie smiled and nodded. "She's the spittin' image of her mama, that little darlin'. She's such a joy to have around."

"Did she come to see you often?"

"Not as much as the judge and me wanted. His honor would call every weekend and say, 'Don't you have something to do with yourself, Mack? Don't you need a baby-sitter? Bring that young'un over here right now and let her spend some time with her grandfather and Elsie.'"

"That must have been nice."

"It was. And the judge was happy, because he and Mack, they had a long talk about her staying here more. A *lot* more. His honor told Mack that he worked too hard and wasn't home enough. That she was being neglected and needed constant supervision. And Mr. Mack agreed to let her come and stay here."

Savannah thought of Mack Goodwin, forceful, proud. "And Mack was going to allow that?"

Elsie chuckled. "Well, he didn't have much choice. The judge was used to getting his way on stuff, you know."

"I see."

"Yeah, his honor told me to get this room all fixed up for Caitlin, that she'd be movin' over here pretty soon. She'd be changing schools and everything."

"Really. Hm-m-m." Savannah's brain whirred, processing this new information. "But now?"

"Oh, she's still coming. She and Mr. Mack will be moving in as soon as the will's read and the estate's settled."

"The will?"

"Yes, the judge left everything he had to that little girl. She was the apple of his eye, I tell you, just like his daughter was. He'd have done anything for her."

"Judge Patterson left everything to his granddaughter, huh? Are you sure about that, Elsie?"

"Well, there's a bit of a problem, since he died before the divorce became final."

"You mean, Bonnie might fight Mack for the estate?"

"She might, but then, she'd have to show up, wouldn't she? And I hear tell that she's on the lam. Nobody's seen hide nor bleached hair of her since yesterday afternoon."

Suddenly, Savannah remembered why she had come to the mansion in the first place. "I know. I'm helping look for her. I was wondering if maybe you'd have an idea where she might be. I mean, you were her housekeeper for a long time, and you probably knew her as well as anyone, better than most."

"Nope. I don't have a clue. Bonnie doesn't really have anyplace to go. The judge and Alvin, they're the only ones she had in the world. And now they're both gone. It's sad."

"Yes, ain't it though."

Elsie stood and carefully rearranged the silver combs and brush. "I'm sorry I couldn't help you much, finding Bonnie, that is."

Savannah rose from the bed and looked around the room once more. The room that had once belonged to a privileged young Southern belle. The room that had been intended for her little daughter.

And if Mack Goodwin had his way, it might still be hers.

"Oh, you helped me, Elsie. You may have helped me a lot."

As Savannah trudged up the steps to her grandmother's doorway, she hoped that, this once, no major drama would be unfolding inside these walls. She desperately needed a sanctuary. Some down time. A hot bath and a few hours of rest, maybe a cup of decaffeinated coffee laced with a big slug of Bailey's Irish Cream and . . .

Oh, yes, she reminded herself. This is Gran's house. No drinking spirits and no cussing. Not even when you spilled a gallon of milk all over the kitchen floor.

Beauregard lay stretched across the porch, his front paws crossed over his nose. He was snoring soundly. Gran had always said that those with a pure heart and a clean conscience slept the sleep of the blessed.

Judging from the volume of his log-sawing, the colonel had no burdens of guilt to disturb his sleep. She noticed with satisfaction that the kitty scratches on his face and ears were healing nicely.

When she opened the screen door, Cleopatra and Diamante came running to greet her, their tails curled over their backs like big black question marks. They rubbed against her ankles and purred, telling her in basic cat language that they hadn't eaten in days and it was pretty much her fault.

"Okay, okay," she said. "You could have told Gran. She would have thrown you a fried catfish or something."

Savannah walked through her sisters' bedroom, then her grandmother's, to the kitchen, where Jesup, Alma, Cordele, and Gran sat around the table, sharing a banana nut cake.

"You're just in time," Gran said. "Pull up a chair and have a slice. It's still warm from the oven."

"I think I'm too tired to eat," Savannah said, lumbering over to the cats' dishes. She lifted the bag of cat food off the top of the refrigerator and bent to fill them.

"I already fed those two panthers of yours," Gran said. "They ate a big ol' bowlful of that stuff an hour ago."

"And I fed them earlier . . . around four," Alma added. "They looked hungry."

Savannah looked down at the cats, who were practically prancing on their tiptoes with anticipation. "Forget it, you gluttonous little liars. Now that I think of it, your stomachs are both pooching out somethin' fierce. Shame on you."

She returned the cat food to the top of the refrigerator, then walked back to the table. "And speaking of gluttons, I think I *will* have a slice of that cake. It smells heavenly."

"Okay," Gran said, reaching for a plate and the cake, "but before you get too comfortable . . . you should know that you got a couple of phone calls."

"Oh? From whom?"

"From *whom?*" Cordele said, twitching her nostrils distastefully. "My, aren't we hoity-toity now that we live up North."

"For your information, she lives out West," Alma retorted. "And just because a body talks right doesn't make them hoity-toity."

"Hush," Gran said. "Ain't nobody high and mighty in this household. Just regular folks tryin' to make it through. Kind words make the path easier, girls—for the person who says them as much as for the person who hears them. Don't be forgettin' that." She gave Cordele a pointed look.

"So, how did you get Marietta settled down?" Savannah asked. "Or did you have to check her into a mental-health clinic?"

"Gran talked her off the bridge . . . so to speak," Jesup said. "I thought *I* was depressed, but . . ."

"She'll be all right," Gran added. "Mari's always been a strong-minded girl. She'll pull it together somehow."

"Any progress on Macon?" Alma said, sliding a tall, cold glass of milk in front of Savannah.

"Maybe. Hard to tell yet. Have y'all heard anything?"

"Just that he's sick of sitting there in that cell," Alma said. "I took some of his comic books over there this afternoon and gave them to Tom. He said he'd let him have them. Said he'd have to check them first for files or machine guns."

Savannah laughed. "That sounds like Tom."

"I think he's still sweet on you. He asked about you, and I could tell by the way he said your name."

"You've been reading too many romance novels," Cordele said, "and watching too many soap operas. You think *everybody's* in love with somebody. It's disgusting how much you think about that stuff."

"Well, I think it's a little weird that you *don't* think about it, so there, Miss Prissy Pants," Alma replied.

"Anyway," Gran interjected, "as I was telling Savannah: Dirk called, wanted to tell you that he chased down Deputy Stafford and found out that Alvin didn't have water in his lungs, so Herb Jameson figures he was dead before he hit the pool."

Savannah nodded, self-satisfied. "That's what we thought. Anything else?"

"Not from Dirk. But that gorgeous fella, Ryan Stone, called from California. He said that Tammy told him and his friend John all about Macon's problems, and he wanted to know if there was anything they could do to help out. I told him you'd call him back."

Savannah felt a new surge of energy, no matter how faint, shoot through her bloodstream. It was hope.

"That's a good idea," she said, thoughtfully chewing.

"What is?" Gran wanted to know.

"Calling Ryan and John. Those guys aren't just gorgeous . . . they're fantastic snoops, thorough and discreet. And right now, that's exactly what I need."

"Savannah, love, how are you? We've been so terribly worried about you, dear girl."

Even the sound of John Gibson's deliciously smooth British accent was enough to calm her jangled nerves. Although they were nearly three thousand miles apart, he still radiated strength along with concern and compassion.

She settled back in Gran's recliner, clutching the phone as though it were his hand. "Oh, John . . ." It was all she could do not to start sobbing. "Things are a little rough around here."

"So we heard. How perfectly dreadful for you, darling. Tell me how we can help."

"Bless you, John. Ordinarily, I wouldn't ask, but . . . since you offered . . ."

Chapter
21

"Mack Goodwin, county prosecutor, is a cold-blooded killer. Two first-degree homicides, no less." Dirk shook his head as he turned his rental car down Main Street and headed for the sheriff's station. "That's going to be a tough sale, Van. You'd do better hawking ice cubes to Alaskans."

Beside him, Savannah fidgeted in her seat. She didn't need to hear her doubts spoken aloud by somebody who was supposed to be an ally. She, too, had to admit that by the light of a bright Sunday morning, the idea seemed far less plausible than when she was lying in bed in the moonlight, mulling it over.

"I guess it *is* going to be rough, if even *you* don't buy it," she said.

"I didn't say I didn't buy it. I said, I don't think Tom's gonna buy it. Personally, I think it's absolutely, positively . . . well, a possibility."

"Gee, a ringing endorsement if ever I heard one."

He pulled the car into a spot directly in front of the station, as the street was practically empty. Most of McGill was attending church services, and the few who weren't were home in bed, sleeping off Saturday night's booze.

"Well, I'm sorry, Van," he said, cutting the key, "but some things don't track."

"Like what?"

"Like if Mack was going to knock off the judge so that his little girl could get her inheritance, why would he do it a few days before the judge and Bonnie's divorce was final? It would make more sense to sit tight a little longer, so that Bonnie couldn't contest it."

Savannah sighed. "Okay, I thought of that . . . about two o'clock this morning."

"And?"

"And . . . nothing. I don't know. Maybe there was some reason why he couldn't wait. Or maybe he arrived at the mansion right after Macon and Kenny Jr. ran off and saw the perfect opportunity to kill the judge and blame it on them."

"Okay. That's . . . well . . . sorta possible."

"Wow, and the crowd goes wild again!"

He sent her an irritated sidewise look. "I'm trying, okay? I'm listening. I'm workin' with ya, but—"

"I know. We don't have enough."

"We don't have *anything.* Savannah, you want to accuse a prosecuting attorney, a highly successful, dearly beloved pillar of the community, of murdering two people, and you don't have jack shit."

"We'll get something. I'll talk to Tom, and he'll help us. You wait and see."

"You're nuts, Savannah. You've always been on the bright side of whacky, but you've crossed all the way over." Tom rushed over to the door to look outside, leaving the two of them sitting on folding chairs next to his desk.

He hurried back. "Sheriff Mahoney's late this morning, and you'd better thank your lucky stars, because if he heard you saying a blame-fool thing like that, he'd . . . Oh, Lord, I don't even know what he'd do."

"Tom, I—" Savannah ventured.

"And what's worse . . . he'd do it to me, too, just for talking to you. He found out that I took you out to the Patterson place, and

I'm still hearing about that. If he found out you were spreading crap like this all over . . . cheez."

Savannah stood and walked over to him. She stepped close, deliberately invading his space, and fixed him with her blue lasers. "I am *not* spreading anything anywhere, Tommy Stafford. I'm interested in solving some murders, not being a gossip-monger. And if you'd just stick your fear in your back pocket and listen to me, you might find the killer, too."

"Fear?"

"Yes, fear. You're scared spitless of Mahoney and Goodwin."

"I sure am, and you would be, too, if you had the sense God gave a cockroach."

"Hey, watch it." Dirk left his chair and strolled over to them in what Savannah could only describe as a John Wayne swagger. She could practically hear his spurs and pistols jangling. "You don't go callin' anybody a bug, hear?"

"It's all right, Dirk. It's just a quaint Southern term. He didn't mean any disrespect."

"I most certainly did. You're an idiot if you think I'm going to investigate Mack Goodwin, the best prosecutor this county has ever had, the finest—"

"Oh, stop already!" Savannah held up both hands in surren-der. "I can see now you're ready to canonize the guy, and nothing I say is going to change your mind."

She turned and grabbed Dirk's arm. "Let's get out of here. We've got a case to solve and boy, some people are sure gonna feel dumb when we wrap it up without any help from them!"

In a quiet, sane part of her brain, Savannah knew she had re-verted to the emotional quotient of a ten-year-old. She knew be-cause it was all she could do not to stick out her tongue and give Stupid Head Tommy a major raspberry.

She also didn't care.

Okay, she cared a little.

At the door she paused and, summoning her last vestige of ma-turity, said, in what she hoped was a very adult voice, "Of course, you could quietly check Goodwin's phone and bank records, compare them with the judge's and Alvin's. Goodwin would never know. No one would ever have to know. Hell, you wouldn't even have to tell *me* if you'd done it or not."

She sailed out the door, Dirk in tow.

When they were back in the car, Dirk turned to her, a wide smile splitting his face. "You're an evil woman, Savannah Reid."

She grinned back. "I am. And you love me anyway."

"Anyway? Baby, I love you *because!*"

Savannah stood in her grandmother's kitchen and looked out on the vast ocean of food that constituted Sunday dinner. For as long as she could remember, the ritual had been the same: Sunday school and church, then home for the best that Gran could afford. During lean times, it had been only one piece of fried chicken apiece; they had taken turns having to eat the wings. And during better times, a roast or maybe even a ham had been proudly displayed on the big blue platter in the center of the table.

It might have been bologna sandwiches during the week, but Sunday dinner was always an event.

"Don't you ever get tired of cooking?" Savannah asked, as her grandmother dumped an enormous bowl of milk into the browned flour and bacon drippings mixture that bubbled in a giant skillet.

"I like cooking," Gran said with a big smile to prove it. "I've gotta admit, now that my rheumatism's worse, I don't like doin' it as much as I do. But Sunday dinner's fine. It's family time."

"Are they all coming?" Savannah looked down the endless streams of plates lining both sides of the table and the counter.

"Sure. What else would they do with themselves?"

Savannah grabbed the panful of mashed potatoes and began spooning them into a bowl. "How do you afford to pay for all this food, Gran?" she asked. "Do they chip in at all?"

"Sure they do. Well, Alma and Waycross do. Alma's a darlin'. When she gets her check from Donut Heaven, she just signs it right over to me for food and the like. I have to make her take back some of it for the things she needs. Alma's got ways a lot like yours, Savannah. She's a real comfort to me. And Waycross, when he gets a big job there in the garage, like a motor overhaul, he slips me fifty dollars. Sometimes even a hundred."

"And Vidalia and Butch? Marietta? Cordele or Jesup?"

"Vi and Butch have a hard time making ends meet."

"They drive a brand-new car."

Gran shrugged. "And Jesup can't seem to keep a job."

"I hear she lost the last one because she showed up late five days in a row and insulted the boss."

"Jesup's got a bit of a temper. It gets the best of her sometimes. And Cordele, she's going to school. . . ."

"One class per semester. She's been going to college for ages, and you've been paying for it. She could work part-time, too."

Gran poured in the milk and stirred vigorously. "You don't understand, Savannah. Kids are different these days. They've got so many pressures on them that we didn't have."

"Like saying 'no' to sex and drugs?" Savannah cleared her throat. "Yes, I guess that's harder than working in the cotton fields and taking in laundry from the country club and cleaning people's houses in town. We just had to worry about how we were going to feed and clothe the younger ones, and how we were going to come up with the money for medicine when they got sick. They have to worry about getting AIDS and whether or not their tennis shoes light up when they walk. I don't know how they stand all that pressure."

Savannah put the bowl of mashed potatoes on the table and turned to see her grandmother staring at her, a startled and infinitely sad look on her face.

"I'm sorry, Gran." She rushed over to put her arms around her. "I shouldn't have said all that."

She hugged her grandmother to her and was surprised at how frail she felt, how drained.

"That's all right, Savannah girl," she said. "You can speak your mind to me anytime. You know that."

She pulled back and looked up at Savannah, tears in her eyes. "Seems you had something you needed to say."

"Seems so."

"And maybe I needed to hear it."

"Maybe," Savannah said softly. "I reckon you'd be the best judge of that."

Outside, the sound of a car pulling into the driveway and the shouts and laughter of Vidalia's energetic children broke the moment.

"Hail, hail, the gang's all here," Gran said. "And that gravy's getting lumpy. You know I can't abide lumpy gravy."

Like a giant twister sweeping across a plain, leaving destruction in its path, the Reid clan descended on the tiny kitchen. And after a flurry of forks and spoons, plates and glasses, jokes and insults, laughter and a few tears—shed by the recently jilted bride-to-be—they left.

They took the bags of clean laundry from the porch and left mountains of dirty dishes, pots, and pans in the sink.

Even Cordele and Jesup found places they simply had to be and silently slipped away.

"How convenient," Savannah said, standing in the kitchen, her hands on her hips. "Do they do this every week?"

"What?" Alma said as she began to scrape and stack the dishes on the table. "Oh, yeah. Usually. They all have busy social lives."

"In McGill? What's to do? Cruise up and down Main Street? That takes twenty seconds."

Alma laughed. "That's about all. But somehow they can make an afternoon of it."

Savannah placed the stopper in the sink, squeezed in a generous portion of liquid soap, and turned on the hot water. "How about you, Alma? What do you do for fun?"

"Oh, I had a boyfriend last winter for a while. But we broke up. And since then, I pretty much just work at the donut shop and help Gran. I teach Sunday school, too. The four- to ten-year-olds. I like that a lot."

"I'll bet they like having you for a teacher."

"I wish you'd gone to church with us this morning, but I know you were out helping Macon."

"Yes. I know we're not supposed to work on Sunday, but there's a scripture somewhere that says something like: If your ox is in the ditch, you can pull him out."

Alma carried a stack of the plates over and set them in the sudsy sink. "I guess having your jackass brother in jail is pretty much the same thing, huh? It's a bit of an emergency either way."

Savannah laughed, then leaned over and kissed her sister on the forehead. "You're a sweet girl, Alma. I'd like to take you and Gran home with me."

"Don't say that twice. You'll have one of us stuffed into each of your suitcases on that plane."

The phone rang, and Alma hurried over to the phone on the wall. "Hello. Sure, just a minute." She put her hand over the mouthpiece. "It's for you, Van. Somebody named Ryan. He sounds really cute."

Savannah dried her hands on a towel. "Oh, darlin', you have no idea how cute."

She took the phone, pulled up a chair, and sat down. "Hey, sugar, what's shakin'?"

"We miss you," Ryan said, his voice dark and silky.

"I miss the two of you, too. Tammy's going through hunk withdrawal."

"John's got something for you on your county prosecutor."

Savannah felt her heart leap. "Already? I just called him last night."

"Yes, but it was for *you*. He was on the phone most of the night."

"And?"

"I'm going to tell you something, but you're going to have to substantiate it with other means."

She nodded. "I'm hearing what I'm hearing, but I didn't hear it from you."

"Something like that."

"Okay, shoot."

"Mack Goodwin comes from the poor side of the tracks, but he's smart."

"Yeah, that's the consensus around town. A bit of a self-made man."

"Well, not completely. He had a lot of help along the way from your Judge Patterson. Even when he was a kid in law school."

"Okay, I think I heard something about the judge helping with his tuition. The judge's daughter, Katherine, and Mack were dating even back then, so the judge was probably just making sure he'd be a worthy son-in-law."

"From what John heard, that's exactly right. And Mack did well by the judge, good grades, kept his nose clean. Except . . ."

"Except?"

"Except for one rather nasty event that occurred during Mack's last year of school."

"Do tell!"

"I can't give you all the details, because John could only find out so much. But, you see, John is close friends with Lt. Governor Hastings. And . . . well, this tragedy involved both Mack Goodwin and the lieutenant governor's son. Some sort of awful accident with one of the boys in their frat club. A kid was killed in some kind of hazing ritual, though it was never proven that the club members were involved."

"Were Mack and the Hastings boy suspected?"

"Only for about two seconds . . . thanks to old man Hastings, who was a senator at the time, and Judge Patterson. They got it squelched before any harm was done to either young man's promising future."

"And the victim?"

"In the end, his death was ruled a suicide."

"Suicide? What method did he use?"

"Hanging. He was found dangling from one of the giant oaks on the Hastings estate in Athens, just down the street from the capitol building. His neck wasn't broken. They figure he strangled."

"Yuck."

"Yeah. A big old yuck."

Savannah gazed up at the cat clock, its green eyes switching back and forth with each twitch of its tail. But her mind was far away, beneath a moss-draped oak tree in the shadow of the state's capitol. And with a boy's family, who would have been told that he hated his own life enough to end it.

And if that weren't true, the lie was a terrible tragedy in itself.

"Savannah, you all right?" Ryan asked, drawing her back to the kitchen and the moment at hand.

"Yes. Just . . . thinking. Tell John I love him dearly, and I owe him a pecan pie."

"Only if I get half."

"Don't you always?"

When Savannah hung up the phone, she walked over to the screen door and gazed outside at the serenity of her grandmother's garden. Gran was walking among the tomato plants, her straw bonnet guarding her porcelain complexion—her only vanity—and a basket over her arm.

"Van?"

She jumped and turned to see Alma watching her. She had actually forgotten her sister was there.

"I couldn't help overhearing your phone conversation," she said. "Both this one and the one you made last night in the living room." She shrugged. "Sorry, but it's a small house."

"Of course it is. No problem. But it's important that you keep everything you heard to yourself. Really important. It could make all the difference for Macon."

"I understand. I'm good about keeping my mouth shut when I need to."

Savannah reached out and tucked one of her sister's glossy dark curls behind her ear. "Thanks, hon. I appreciate that."

"If you're trying to find out stuff about Mr. Goodwin . . ." Alma said, tentatively.

"Yes?"

"I heard something this morning in Sunday school. And normally, I wouldn't repeat gossip, but . . ."

"What did you hear, sweetie?"

"Little Caitlin, Mr. Goodwin's girl—she's in my class. And she was really sad about her grandpa dying. We talked a long time about how he was in heaven and she would get to see him again."

"I'm sure you were a comfort to her."

"Yes, but she's also really disappointed, because she says her grandpa told her that she could come and live with him. He promised he'd buy her a pony of her own. She said her daddy got really mad and said she couldn't, but that Grandpa told her not to worry about it. He was going to *make* her daddy agree."

"He did, huh?"

"That's what she said, and I believed her. Little kids, they don't lie about important stuff like that."

"No, they don't," Savannah said thoughtfully. "They leave the lying about important stuff to adults. Grownups are a lot better at it; they've had more practice."

Chapter
22

"Why do I feel like I'm never going to see my little house trailer in California again?" Dirk said as he held the flashlight for Savannah, while she picked the lock on Mack Goodwin's office building.

"Sh-h-h. Hold that light steady," she said. "I can't see a thing I'm doing with you bobbing it all over the place like that."

"It's because I'm shaking. In my whole stinkin' career, I've never broken into an officer of the court's place. We're going to wind up in a rotten little jail cell for the next fifty years with some of those snaggle-toothed yahoos from *Deliverance*, tellin' me to squeal like a pig."

She stopped what she was doing long enough to shoot him a dirty look. "As a Southerner, I find that comment highly offensive, just like that disgusting movie. Besides, you old fart, what makes you think you're gonna live another fifty years? You're already older than dirt."

"Just get the damned door open, would you? This place gives me the willies, big time. I wanna get in and outta here in record time."

"Then hold still and stop yapping for a minute and let me . . . there . . . got it."

"We're getting good at this," Dirk said as they slipped inside the building that housed the prosecutor's office, as well as those of other county officials.

"Don't you *dare* say something like that. Those sound like famous last words if I ever heard any."

They made their way down a short hallway until they found a door with Goodwin's name on it. Savannah had better luck with that lock and had them inside within seconds.

"Do you suppose there's a watchman for this building?" Dirk asked as they hurried in, guided by the beam of his flashlight.

"Naw. But Mahoney probably drives by once or twice a night, so keep that light away from the windows."

Savannah took her own penlight from her pocket and began her search. With such minimal light, she was only vaguely aware of a well-organized office with contemporary furniture and modern art on the walls.

"It would help if we knew what we were looking for," Dirk said as he opened first one drawer, then another.

"But how much fun would that be?"

"You call this *fun?*"

She stopped her search long enough to look up and give him a mischievous smile. "Yeah, don't you?"

He chuckled. "Yeah. We gotta get lives, Van."

"Really. We'll work on that when we get home. You can take me to Disneyland, and we'll ride Splash Mountain."

"This is the secretary's desk," he said, opening the last drawer. "Nothing hidden here but a box of chocolate-covered donuts."

"My kind of woman. Don't touch them! We don't want anybody to know we were here."

"What? You figure she counts her donuts?"

"Sure. Don't you?"

"Well, yeah, but . . ."

"Check *his* desk. The big one over there."

"How do you know it's his?"

"It's got his name on it." She pointed her light at the brass plaque on the front of the desk.

"Oh, yeah."

While he searched those drawers, she shuffled through several folders on top of the desk. She didn't have to look long before she found her brother's.

Opening it, she glanced over the various forms that had been filled out about his case.

"Damn," she said softly. "Goodwin's ready to go on Macon. He's dotting all the i's and crossing the t's. And I have to admit, if I wasn't Macon's big sister, I'd say he had an airtight case."

"All the more reason to nail the bastard, if he did it himself."

"Anything in those drawers?"

"Nothing good. Not even any donuts."

Carefully, she replaced the folders, then looked around the rest of the room. "I don't know how much more we're going to find in here," she said. "Maybe we should've broken into his house."

Dirk came to full attention. "No. Don't even think about it. This is as far as I go."

"Pansy."

She walked over to a large trash can that sat beneath a table next to the computer. Beside a laser printer was a shredder. The can had been placed directly beneath to catch the narrow paper strips.

On an impulse she pointed her light into the can and saw that it had been recently emptied. Only a few pages' worth of shreddings were lying in the bottom.

She had walked away when something rang a buzzer in the back of her brain. Returning to the can, she knelt beside it and looked again.

"Oh, howdy!" she said. "Dirk, get yourself over here, boy."

He came at a fast trot. "Whatcha got?"

"Shredded paper strips."

"Well, if it's shredded, it's worthless. You can't read that stuff. I know, I've tried."

"Look." She held up a couple of strands that were dark green. "I've seen this paper before. The judge had folders made out of this in his desk. Very classy looking."

"Oh, yeah?" Suddenly, Dirk was interested, too. "You figure this junk was the folder that somebody took outta there?"

"I sure do."

"A lot of good it'll do us. Like I said, you can't read that stuff once it's been through a shredder. No matter how hard you try, you can't figure out how to put it back together again."

"Maybe *you* can't. Maybe *I* can't. But I'll bet I know somebody who can. . . ."

"Okay, but if I can't even sneak a donut, you can't take that trash either. He might notice it missing."

"No way. He's a man. He'll just figure his secretary—a woman—cleaned up after him."

"Do you think you can do it?" Savannah asked Alma after she had dumped the pile of shreddings in the middle of Gran's kitchen table.

"Sure, I can. It's just another puzzle," Alma said, running a few of the strips through her fingers.

"I don't think anybody can do it." Dirk stood behind them, radiating gloom. "It's impossible."

"You, Mr. Sunshine, can just keep your negativity to yourself." Savannah gouged him with her elbow. "Alma is the all-time puzzle-putter-together champion. She did one that had two thousand pieces and was nothing but M&M's. I'm going to help her and we'll do it, no matter how long it takes or how cross-eyed we get."

"Speaking of M&M's . . ." Alma grinned. "I could work a lot better if I had a plateful of your M&M cookies, Savannah."

"M&M cookies?" Dirk's ears perked up.

Savannah chuckled. "They're like chocolate chip cookies only with M&M's."

"Sound great. I mean, I'd be willing to try too, if—"

"Okay, okay. Go get Tammy out of that burger joint and bring her over here, too. Alma might as well have a full crew to help her out here. And I'll start baking right now." She turned to Gran, who had just come in from the living room to see what all the fuss was about. "Gran, how about a pot of strong coffee? I figure four pots and about six dozen cookies should get us through the night."

"I told you it was impossible. What do you think people shred stuff for? It works. You can't read it once it's been shredded."

"Oh, shut up, Dirk, before I slap you with a frying pan." Savannah pushed away from the table and ran her fingers through her hair. Since she had been doing that most of the night, her dark curls were practically standing on end. Along with her nerves.

"It's not that bad," Alma said, though her voice sounded as tired as Savannah felt. "It's only four," she added, looking at the cat clock, "and we've already got a few sections together."

"Yeah," said Tammy, who had actually broken one of her personal standards and consumed caffeine and sugar to stay awake, "but they don't really say anything."

"They say a lot," Savannah said, bending over the few winning combinations they had found and cellophane-taped to a large piece of cardboard. "We just don't know what it means yet."

"Something about an expunged record," Alma said. "And we've decided that might be part of a coroner's report with all the medical terms there."

"This is promising," Savannah said. "Really. It's just a bitch to do."

"Watch your language in there," came a voice from the bedroom.

"Sorry, Gran. Are we keeping you awake?"

"Only when you cuss."

Savannah sighed, stood, and stretched her knotted shoulder muscles. "More coffee, that's what I need. And in a couple of hours, it'll be officially breakfast time. We can switch from cookies to donuts."

* * *

Six hours, two dozen donuts, and a full Gran breakfast later, the gang was still at it, although they had taken turns slipping away and catching a few winks on the living room sofa.

Every time someone suggested putting it away for a while and living life normally for a few hours, another section would come together and the accompanying adrenaline boost would keep them going.

And they were so absorbed that they didn't know they had company until Deputy Tom Stafford knocked on the back door.

"Hey, y'all," he said through the screen. "What are you up to there?"

They all jumped, and for half a second entertained the idea of sweeping the ill-gotten evidence under the table, but it was too late.

"Nothing much," Savannah said, standing and hurrying over to the door. "How 'bout you?"

She looked down at Beauregard, who was coercing a pet from Tom by nudging his hand with his muzzle. So much for the vigilant watchdog routine. Savannah silently promised to withhold the mashed-potato leftovers from his supper dish.

Shifting first right, then left, she tried to block his line of vision. Behind her, she heard the flurry of shuffling papers and scooting chairs.

He stood on tiptoe and craned his neck to see over her shoulder. "Oh, just came out to shoot the breeze with you for a while. How about some coffee?"

"Sure!" She bombed out the door, moving faster than she thought she could after a night with no sleep. "Donut Heaven? The Burger Igloo? Anywhere you like! How sweet of you to buy me a cup of coffee, Tom."

She grabbed his arm and hauled him off the porch. "Let's take your car, okay?" she babbled on. "Gee, what a nice surprise. You've always been such a great guy with your . . ."

* * *

"When are you going to tell me what was on the kitchen table?" Tom asked her, once they had their coffee and were settled into a booth at Donut Heaven.

"When we get . . . uh . . . done with it," she replied, locking eyes with him across the table.

"I see."

"You do?"

"No, but I will, eventually."

She smiled, thanking him for not pushing the issue. "You'll be the first person we show it to."

He stirred several tablespoons of sugar into his coffee and shook his head. "Why does that send a chill up my spine instead of warm the cockles of my heart?"

"Why did you come by the house, really?"

He looked around, but other than the clerk behind the glass cases filled with pastries, the shop was empty.

Pulling some papers from his pocket, he said, "I wanted to show you these. I mean . . . it's not like I could show them to anybody else."

"Anybody, like Sheriff Mahoney?"

"Yeah. Exactly like Mahoney."

The first paper he showed her was a phone record. She didn't recognize the number at the top.

"Alvin's or Mack's?" she said.

"That one's Mack's." He gave her a second one. "This one's Alvin's."

Her eye skimmed the columns. "Seems they've had quite a bit to say to each other."

"Yeah. Considering that they didn't call each other even once before the evening the judge died."

"Tragedy's a bonding thing," she said with a grin.

"So's collusion."

Her mood rose several notches. Tom was coming around, and just in time.

"They've talked to each other several times a day," she noted.

"Until Friday night."

"When Alvin croaked."

"Exactly."

He pulled a third paper from his shirt pocket. "This is the judge's record. The last call he made was to Mack. And if I'm to believe your brother's version of what happened that night, the call would have been made right after the judge threw them out of his house."

"So, after he killed the judge, Mack picked up the phone and punched in those nonsense numbers to throw y'all off if you checked the redial."

"Yeah. It's kind of insulting that he didn't think we'd check the actual phone records."

"Don't take it personally. Even the smartest criminals don't think of everything. That's how we get 'em."

Savannah curled her fingers around the coffee cup, enjoying its warmth and the small victory of the moment. They had an important ally. And he had crossed the line just when they needed him most.

"Then there's these. . . ." He produced still more papers.

"Bank statements, too. You've been busy," she said.

"The judge was killed last Monday night." He leaned back in the booth and rubbed his fingers across his eyes as though he had a headache. "On Wednesday morning, Mack withdrew $35,000 from his accounts. On Thursday afternoon, Alvin deposited $28,000. I don't know what he and Bonnie did with the other $7,000. Probably pissed it away. Friday night, Alvin's dead."

"So, was the money a payoff for a hit, or was Alvin blackmailing him?"

"I figured you could tell me. You guys seem to be about a million miles farther down that road than I am."

"No, we're not, Tom. Just a few steps. But they're pretty big steps. Come back to the house with me, and we'll get you up to speed."

Chapter
23

When Savannah returned with Tom to Gran's house, she was greeted at the door by an excited Alma, who practically pulled her into the kitchen.

"We've got something, Savannah," she said. "We've got more of that autopsy report thing and another couple of pages, too. Dirk says it's good stuff. He said it was nails in Goodwin's coffin."

Savannah glanced back at Tom, who was following close behind, and saw the mixture of excitement and apprehension on his face.

In the kitchen, none of the gang appeared to have moved from their chairs. Dirk sat, as he had been, at the head of the table, with Tammy on one side and Gran on the other. The cardboard sheet in front of them held several blocks of paper strips, taped together to form pages.

Dirk gave Tom only the briefest look, tinged with something resembling petulant jealousy, then turned to Savannah. "You were right, Van. It's the coroner's report on a young guy who died by strangling."

"And it says he had ropes around his armpits, too," Gran said. "Why do you suppose somebody would do something like that? I mean, if you're hanging a guy, why put ropes there?"

Savannah sat down at the table and looked at the fruits of their long night's labor. One of the pages they had reconstructed bore a diagram of the ropes' ligature marks around the victim's neck and upper arms.

"It was supposed to be a joke," she said, suddenly overcome with a deep sense of sadness. "A stupid, cruel joke. The ropes around his arms were probably intended to support his weight and keep him from actually strangling. But, as we can see, they didn't."

Dirk pointed to another of the partial pages they had reassembled and said to Tom, "Take a look at that, Stafford, and tell me what a fine, upstanding citizen your Mack Goodwin is. How would the voters in this county feel about their handsome, charming prosecutor if they read that?"

Tom leaned over Savannah's shoulder and read aloud, "Victim's face has been smeared with an unidentified black substance with white around the mouth in a crude imitation of minstrel makeup."

Dirk leaned back in his chair and crossed his arms over his chest. "Those rich frat boys took one of their own, and in part of a hazing ritual, they made him up in black face and then strung him up, lynch-style, from an oak tree there on the family plantation. Nice, huh?"

Tom buried his hands deep in his slacks pockets and closed his eyes for a long moment. "They were stupid kids. It was years ago."

"It was a horrible crime," Savannah said. "And this autopsy report was suppressed. In spite of all this, the coroner ruled the death a suicide. All this time, they've let that poor kid's family think he'd killed himself."

Gran stood, walked over to the refrigerator, and got herself a glass of water. "I can't imagine Mr. Goodwin doing something so awful as that. I don't imagine his political career in these parts would be worth a plugged nickel if folks knew what was in those papers."

"Do you suppose," Tom said, "that's why he killed the judge . . . or had Alvin do it? Patterson was going to let this out?"

"I think so," Savannah told him.

"But why? After all these years, why would the judge want to expose Mack now?"

"Because Patterson's daughter was dead; she couldn't be embarrassed by the scandal, like she would have been if it had come out before. And because the judge wanted to get his hands on his granddaughter. He saw her as some sort of substitute for Katherine. He wanted her to come live with him so that he could raise her, mold her as his own. And Mack wouldn't have it."

"Okay." Tom nodded thoughtfully. "But where do Alvin and Bonnie fit into all this?"

"I think we're going to have to find Bonnie before we'll know that." Savannah sighed. "I guess I could go talk to Elsie again. She's been pretty helpful so far."

"Oh, I wouldn't bother her," Gran said. "She's kinda under the weather."

"What's wrong with her?"

"I saw her at church last night, and she said she was feelin' poorly on account of worryin' about his honor."

"The judge?" Dirk asked. "He's the last person we have to worry about now. He's layin' dead out in the cemetery."

"That's just the problem," Gran replied solemnly. "He's not restin' easy. Elsie says he's been causin' her a heap o' grief, hauntin' the mansion there. Especially at night. She's thinking of having Pastor Greene come out and pray over the house, see if they can put him to rest."

"A restless haunt, huh?" Savannah raised one eyebrow and looked across the table at Dirk. "Yeah . . . an exorcism might be exactly what the Patterson mansion needs."

After an extremely vigorous argument, Tom and Dirk had decided to allow Savannah to "ghostbust" the Patterson mansion alone. Not because they had been eager to acquiesce to her wishes, but because she had yelled the loudest and the longest, and had threatened physical violence if they didn't see things her way.

Too much human activity in the form of heavy-stepping males would be enough to scare off any self-respecting haunt. And she was determined to catch this one.

Armed with her Beretta, Dirk's large flashlight, and a detailed map of the interior of the mansion—courtesy of Tom and the local library's historical section—she entered the back door of the house at just past midnight.

Thanks to a full moon, there was enough light coming through the windows that she could see well enough to move about without bumping into walls and furniture.

It sure looks different in the moonlight, she thought as she crept through the kitchen and into the hallway. *Feels different, too.* She had to admit, she regretted her decision to have the guys stay behind and let her do this alone.

You don't believe in haunts, do you, Savannah girl? she asked herself.

Of course not. Don't be silly.

Then why don't you want to check the library?

Oh, shut up and check it yourself.

Okay, I will, chickenshit. You just watch.

She was grateful no one could hear the multiple personalities warring inside her brain. And she was equally glad that Dirk and Tom weren't around to hear her teeth chattering on this hot summer night.

Every ghost story that she had heard as a child at her grandmother's knee, every tale of Civil War atrocities . . . some happening within these very walls . . . came back to her with unsettling clarity as she walked up to the library door and quietly pushed it open.

Perhaps Elsie was right. Maybe the judge was a restless presence inside this house. She had to admit that the room didn't feel empty, as it should have. The air seemed charged, rather than still and peaceful, as it should.

But Savannah wasn't searching for the judge's ghost. She was looking for the reasons behind his murder.

As she walked on down the hallway and into the dining room,

she thought of the deaths that had occurred in this room, a temporary surgical ward for wounded Confederate soldiers. There, on that very table, amputations had been carried out, some without anesthetics, and boys had died before they had become men. *They can have their mansion*, Savannah thought. *They can keep their antique silver and their gilt-framed mirrors.*

She would be glad to be back at Gran's humble house again, snuggled safe beneath the handmade quilt.

But for now, she had work to do.

She hadn't expected to find anything on the ground floor of the house. And, likewise, nothing seemed out of order on the second. One by one, she checked the bedrooms and the baths. Other than some dampness in one of the tubs, everything appeared undisturbed.

She had memorized the map, which was now tucked into her pants pocket. And she knew where the servants' staircases were—the one that led from the ground floor to the second story, and the other one that went from the sewing room at the far end of the hall up to the attic.

"Nobody ever uses those stairs no more," Elsie had told her an hour earlier when they had talked to her. "And nobody's been in that dusty old attic for years. I told the judge, he couldn't get me to go up there for love nor money. There's rats up there, ones the size of cats. And you know I can't *bear* rats!"

Savannah wasn't fond of cat-sized rodents, either, but that was where she was headed. The unused attic.

What better place to find a restless spirit . . . or a fugitive wife, who had her own reasons for not wanting to be found?

And Savannah was more interested in those reasons than she was in the woman herself.

The stairs *were* dusty, Savannah decided as she crept up them, shining her light only one step above her. And someone was, indeed, stirring in the attic.

Someone too big and too heavy to be a rat, even an oversized one.

Someone walking on two feet.

And if that someone was a ghost, he was a particularly fastidious one, because he was using something that sounded suspiciously like a hairdryer.

Savannah smiled. "I got you, Miss Bonnie Prissy Pants," she whispered as she hurried up the steps. "I got you cold."

She managed to get to the top of the stairs before the dryer stopped. Thank goodness Bonnie Patterson had a lot of hair.

Slowly, her hand on her pistol's grip, Savannah opened the door and stepped into the dimly lit, cavernous attic.

A jumble of household artifacts were scattered around the room and hung from the open-beamed ceiling. Chests, shelves of books, cardboard boxes, tables and chairs, an ancient sewing machine, a child's sled and rocking horse all collected the dust of years gone by.

At the far end of the room, Bonnie Patterson stood before a cracked mirror that was propped against the wall and dried her hair. She had plugged the appliance into an electrical socket that dangled from the ceiling.

The dim light was coming from a small Tiffany-style lamp suspended over a makeshift cot. On an old dressing table, Bonnie had set out her makeup, along with some potato chips and sodas, pilfered from the kitchen downstairs.

In spite of the mythical rats, Bonnie had made herself a snug little nest up here.

She was still drying her hair when Savannah approached her and tapped her on the shoulder.

She screamed and jumped away.

"Oh, my God! You scared me to death!" She turned off the hair dryer and dropped it to the floor. "When did you . . . ? How did you . . . ?"

"Just now. And it wasn't all that hard after Elsie told me she'd heard ghosts running around the house after dark. You should have been quiet."

Bonnie plopped down on the cot, looking disgusted and exhausted. She was wearing a tank top and shorts, and her feet were bare. Her mascara and liner were smeared under her eyes, and she looked as though she hadn't eaten a meal in several days. Since Friday night, Savannah figured.

"When you touched me just now," she said with a shudder, "I thought you were . . ."

Savannah sat on a crate across from her. "The cops? Or Mack?"

She shrugged. "Take your pick. It's trouble, either way. I'm telling you, I'm screwed."

"Why don't you tell me?" Savannah pasted on her most sympathetic face, the one that sometimes worked, even with hardened criminals. "Maybe I can help."

"I need some help. I've been hiding out up here, trying to figure out what to do. But I'm dead," she said, tucking her bare feet under her. "No matter what I do, I'm dead meat. He killed Alvin, and as soon as he finds me, he'll kill me, too."

"Mack?"

Bonnie hesitated, then nodded. "Yeah, Mack."

"What did Alvin do, ask for more money?"

A flicker of surprise passed over Bonnie's face; then she sighed, her shoulders sagging. "I told him not to ask for more. The $35,000 was enough, but he had to get greedy."

"That's not a lot of money—I mean, for committing murder for hire."

Savannah knew her dart had missed its mark when Bonnie looked confused. Then angry.

"What are you talking about? Alvin didn't kill anybody! He wouldn't do a thing like that. Al was a sweetheart." Tears welled up in her eyes, and she sniffed loudly.

"So why was Mack paying him? Just because of what he knew?"

Bonnie nodded. "Alvin lucked out. He was in the right place at the right time. He overheard my husband and Mack arguing about Caitlin coming here to live. He threatened to expose Mack—that thing that happened when he was in college—if he didn't give her up. Then he showed up dead. Alvin went to Mack and told him he'd keep quiet if the price was right."

"And Mack paid him?"

"Not until Alvin broke in here and got some stupid file out of the library desk. Alvin figured that should be worth something, too. But Mack just told him to do that so that he couldn't go to the cops. He'd done something illegal, too, see? He was like an accessory or something."

"Did Alvin plant those medals under my brother's bed?" Savannah held her breath, hoping for the right answer.

"No, Mack did that." She laughed, a nasty, bitter laugh. "That dog of your grandma's, the old hound . . . he bit Mack. Bit a plug outta his ankle. Mack said he tried to kick him in the head, but the hound bit him again. Mack was really pissed about that! Alvin and me laughed our butts off about it later."

"Did you see Mack kill Alvin?"

"No. But when I came home late Friday night, to Alvin's place, I saw Mack driving out of our alley. I recognized that big black car of his. And I'm pretty sure he saw me, too. Then Alvin turned up dead the next day and . . . "

She started to sob. Pulling the end of her tank top up to her face, she wiped her nose.

"And that's when you hid out up here?"

"Yeah. I called my mom in Tennessee, but she said she didn't want me to come back there. So I didn't really have a choice."

"Why didn't you go to the sheriff or to Tom, tell them what happened?"

"Mack had told me I was an accomplice, too, 'cause I was with Alvin when he took the money. And besides, who's going to believe me against somebody like Mack Goodwin? Everybody thinks I'm just a bimbo gold-digger."

Savannah couldn't resist that one. "Didn't you marry the judge for his money?"

She shrugged. "Well, yeah . . . but I kinda liked him, too. He wasn't so bad. He gave me really nice presents on my birthday. Alvin usually forgot."

Hm-m-m, a lady with her priorities in order, Savannah thought. "Bonnie, I think you're underestimating the law," she told her. "Okay, so you knew about Alvin's blackmailing. You may have even put some money down on a car for yourself with part of it. But you're in a very good position to bargain with the powers that be. They're a lot more interested in nailing somebody for two premeditated murders than a small fry like you."

"You think so?" Her face lit up with hope.

Savannah was almost touched, in spite of herself. "I know so."

"But I'm afraid if I leave here, if I come out of hiding, Mack will kill me. I know he must be looking for me. He even came by here yesterday and poked around. I saw him out that window. I was scared to death that he'd think to come up here. But he didn't."

"I promise we'll keep you safe from Mack."

"We?"

"Yes. Me and my friend, who's a cop, and Tom Stafford. They're waiting right now at the end of the driveway in Tom's cruiser, and they've heard everything we've said."

She opened her blouse to show the microphone clipped to her bra. "They've heard it and recorded it. Anybody who listens to this tape will want to work with you, I promise."

Bonnie's mouth hung open, her eyes huge. "Well, I'll be damned."

"No, you'll be helped. Cross my heart and hope to die." Then, speaking into the vicinity of her left breast, she added, "Come and get us, boys. We ladies will meet you on the front verandah."

Savannah crouched in the bushes at the edge of the picnic area and surveyed the riverside park for the umpteenth time in the past few minutes. Feeling chiggers, ticks, fleas, and probably a copperhead snake crawling up her legs, she cursed Dirk and Tom. Only under her breath, but enough for the sensitive microphone on her walkie-talkie to pick it up.

"I heard that," Tom said, his voice crackling in the air waves.

"Up yours. I don't care if you did or not," she replied. "This sucks. And I'll tell you again, if anything happens to her—after me promising her we'd keep her safe—I'll get you."

"She agreed to do it," the walkie-talkie replied in Dirk's voice. She could see the bush on the ridge above them where he was positioned. From there he could watch the road leading into the park and let them know who was arriving when.

"Like she had a lot of choice," Savannah said. "Sheriff Mahoney telling her that if she didn't he'd—"

"Heads up. She's coming in," Dirk said. "The old Dodge is turning off the highway right now. And here she is."

The Charger rumbled down the dirt road, raising the dust in its wake. Savannah didn't know whether to be relieved or not. For a moment there, she had entertained the thought that Bonnie Patterson might get behind the wheel and not stop until she had crossed a foreign border.

But she had decided to go for it. And Savannah had to admit that her estimation of the woman had crept up a few notches. For a frosted blond bimbo-head with big boobs, she wasn't so bad.

The Charger came to a stop near Savannah's position.

Good, she thought. *Miss Bonnie can follow directions, even when she's nervous.*

"That's fine," she heard Dirk say. "Just sit right there and wait. I'll tell you when I see him."

"Okay." The word was hardly more than a squeak, but at least Bonnie's microphone was working.

After a frantic call to John and Ryan in California, a batch of top-notch surveillance equipment had been couriered to McGill from Atlanta within hours. Savannah intended to kiss them both soundly the next time she laid eyes on them.

Bonnie had made her phone call to Mack, suggesting their meeting . . . also taped, of course . . . and they were in business.

He had agreed to show up at noon, here beside the river, for a little business chat, as Bonnie had phrased it.

Savannah wondered if he was already making plans to dump the remains in the river once he had finished his "business" with Bonnie.

"Okay, I see him now," Dirk said. "He's in his Mercedes, and he's entering the park. Hold tight, Bonnie. Everything's cool. I'm on my way down right now, and Savannah and Tom have got you covered from the left and right."

"Pull your car up closer to the bushes there by the side of the road," Savannah told her. "Get really close."

Bonnie drove the Charger so near to Savannah that she could see the terrified look and the sheen of sweat on her face.

"That's good. Right there. I'm only a few feet from you, kiddo," Savannah said in her best big-sister voice.

"I . . . can't see you," Bonnie replied.

"That's the whole idea. Neither will he."

"But I'm so nervous. He'll know something's up."

"No, he won't," Tom said. "He'd expect you to be nervous under the circumstances. Are your doors locked?"

"Yeah."

"Good. Wait till he comes over to the car and just roll your window down an inch or so to talk to him. Do you remember what we told you to say?"

"Yeah. I think so."

"Okay, everybody stop talking now. It's show time," Dirk said.

Out of the corner of her eye, Savannah saw him slipping through the brush coming up behind her. Tom was out of sight, but she knew he was only twenty feet away.

As the Mercedes made its way slowly down the dusty road, she ducked deeper into the brush. No matter how many times she did this, she was convinced some part of her anatomy—her elbow, her butt—would stick out, giving her position away.

As the car pulled closer, Savannah could see Mack Goodwin behind the wheel. He was looking right and left, scanning the bushes. Mack might be a murderer, but he was no dummy. Like a brown bear in an apple orchard, he smelled a trap.

Dirk crawled up behind her and touched her lightly on the back. She nodded ever so slightly, not taking her eyes off the car.

Finally, Goodwin cut the engine and got out. He strolled up to the Charger and looked through the back window, checking the rear seat and floorboard before speaking.

"Okay, I'm here," he said. "Now what?"

"I . . . I figured you were looking for me," Bonnie said. "I saw you pull out of our alley Friday night and . . ."

"And?"

"And I thought we should talk."

He hardly looked at Bonnie at all. His eyes constantly scanned the surrounding brush, the road, and the path leading down to the lake.

Savannah looked him over as best she could from her limited position. He was wearing a polo shirt and slacks. No obvious bulges that indicated a weapon. But he could have something in his rear waistband or on his ankle.

"So, talk," he said. "And roll that fuckin' window down."

"No," Bonnie replied, her voice shaking but definite. "I don't want you to grab me. I don't want you to kill me like you did Alvin."

"Look, you stupid broad. You asked me to come out here and talk to you, so tell me what you want."

"I want to leave town. That's all. I want to go home to Tennessee. I'll let you have the mansion and all the money. I don't care about it anymore. I just need enough for a plane ticket. About four hundred would do it."

Savannah watched his face, watched his eyes.

She had seen killers' eyes. They went cold, vacant, just before . . .

"How do I know you won't come back for more, like your boyfriend did?"

"He was stupid. I told him not to do that. I warned him you'd hurt him. I won't. I promise. I know you'd kill me."

"And how do I know you haven't told anyone else anything?"

"I haven't. I swear! I'm too scared of you to do anything like that."

His eyes glittered, then went empty. "What makes you think I won't kill you right here and now?" His voice was strangely flat, as though he was giving a weather report.

He stepped closer to the car.

Savannah knew she couldn't wait any longer. She crawled to the back of the Charger. Dirk moved to the front.

Mack reached behind him and pulled a pistol from the waist-band of his slacks. He stuck the barrel through the gap at the top of Bonnie's window and pointed it at her face.

"Open the door, you miserable bitch," he said. "You and I are going for a walk down by the river."

"No!" Bonnie started crying hysterically.

"Open it or I'll blow your fuckin' head off right now!"

"No, you won't," Savannah said calmly, rising from the back of the car, holding her Beretta in both hands, combat-style. "You're going to lay your weapon there on the top of the car, real nice and slow. Otherwise . . . you're dead."

She watched the shock in his eyes turn to fury and indecision. For half a heartbeat, she thought he was going to turn his gun on her. But he didn't. He just stood there, staring at her.

"I'm an excellent shot," she said. "Are you? I mean . . . you took down the judge, but he probably wasn't expecting it. And he wasn't armed with a 9mm that would rip a hole in you like a cannon ball."

"I'm pretty good, too," Dirk said, leaning over the hood of the Charger. "Not as good as her, but I can hit a stationary target. Drop it."

Tom stepped up behind Mack and cocked his own pistol, shoving the barrel against the back of his neck. "Lay it on the top of the car, now, Mr. Goodwin. I don't know about them, but *I* can't possibly miss from here."

Mack Goodwin let out a long breath, like a balloon deflating, and placed his gun on the car.

Dirk grabbed the pistol, and Tom wasted no time cuffing the prosecutor and reading him his rights.

Inside the car, Bonnie Patterson collapsed across the steering wheel, sobbing hysterically.

Savannah ran up to Goodwin and knelt beside his feet in the dirt.

"Now," she said, "the moment of truth!"

"What?" Mack looked confused. He looked upset. Savannah simply loved the way he looked at that moment.

She reached over and yanked his pants leg up to his knee, then pulled down his sock. "Damn. Nothing."

She did the same to the other leg.

There, on Mack Goodwin's ankle, were four rows of deep puncture wounds. One set looked seriously infected.

"Ah-ha! Beauregard, you're the best hound in Georgia!" she shouted. "I love you, you flop-eared beast!"

She looked at Dirk and Tom, who were beaming with the glory of the capture.

"And you two mutts aren't bad either."

"What is that stuff?" Gran eyed the tall, narrow green bottles sitting on the kitchen table with a skeptical eye.

"Non-alcoholic sparkling apple juice," Savannah assured her, as she peeled the foil off the first bottle and began to pour the bubbly gold liquid into tea glasses.

She handed the first glass to Tom Stafford, then proceeded to fill over a dozen more, passing them to her friends and family who had gathered, en masse, to share this moment of victory.

With everybody present at once, the kitchen was fairly bursting at the seams.

When everyone, even the children and Gran, had a glass in hand, Savannah raised hers. "First . . . to Deputy Thomas Stafford and Detective Sergeant Dirk Coulter, the scourges of the criminal world, the defenders of justice and the American way."

"I thought that was Superman," little Jack piped up.

"Hush," Vidalia told her son. "Aunt Savannah's making a toast. And don't drink it, Jillian, till we all do."

"Here, here," Tammy said. "To the deadly duo!"

Everyone raised their glasses in salute.

"And . . ." Tammy added, "to the third member of the trio, super sleuth Savannah Reid!"

"I think that's Nancy Drew that you're thinkin' of," Waycross muttered. "Savannah's just good at her job because she's nosy."

"And to the rest of the team," Savannah said, hefting her apple juice again. "Tammy, Gran, Alma, and everybody who sacrificed their vision to put those pages together. And to Beauregard, who was kind enough to give the vet a plaster cast of his teeth."

Savannah looked through the screen door at the hound, who was contentedly munching on a giant bone, courtesy of Tom Stafford and the local butcher.

"He had to be sedated before he complied," Dirk mumbled.

"Doesn't matter. He did what he had to do for the cause of justice. And," she continued, "here's to Bonnie Patterson, who can't be with us today because she's in bed, heavily tranquilized and highly distraught because she was informed that Caitlin Goodwin is going to inherit the bulk of her grandfather's estate."

"Hip, hip, hooray!" Alma cheered. "I never did like Bonnie, and Caitlin's a cute kid. I hear Elsie's going to raise her."

"Here's to Elsie, too," Gran said, getting into the spirit of this suspicious act of toasting. "She's gonna need good luck, raising another child at her age."

When they had all drained their glasses, Gran cleared her throat. "I don't mean to break up a good party," she said, "and I don't want to be disrespectful to these fine friends who helped us so much during our time of need. But I need to say some words and I need to say them to family alone. If y'all don't mind excusing us, just for a few minutes."

"No, of course not," Dirk said, rising from his chair and nudging Tammy. "We'll all go out on the front porch and finish off this sparkling crap." He picked up the remaining bottle of apple juice and walked out the back door with Tammy and Tom.

Savannah sat down in the chair he had vacated next to Gran. "What is it?" she said. "What have you got to say?"

Gran folded her hands demurely on the table and stared down

at them for a long time before speaking. "I have to ask forgiveness from my family," she began. "I've done you a terrible injustice, and it took this terrible tragedy with Macon for me to come to my senses."

Savannah looked around the table at her sisters. Marietta and Vidalia looked shocked, apparently clueless as to what their grandmother was talking about. So did Alma, Jesup, Cordele, and Waycross.

"You don't have a thing to apologize for," Waycross said. "You've never done a wrong thing to us in your life."

"That's not true," Gran said. "I've stood in the way of you growing up and becoming independent adults. You see..." Tears filled her eyes and spilled down her cheeks. "... I just enjoyed it so much, taking care of you all, tending to your needs, helping any way I could, that I wanted to keep doing it forever. And that's not right."

Alma reached over and patted her hand.

"I tried to justify it to myself," Gran continued, "telling myself that you needed my help. But you're adults, every one of you. And by letting you live here for free, by cooking for you day and night, by doing your laundry and paying your bills when you asked me to, and minding your children more than I should have..." She gave Marietta and Vidalia pointed looks that caused them both to cringe. "... I crippled you. You needed to be doing those things for yourselves long ago. By doing it for you, I robbed you of the self-respect you would have gotten by caring for yourselves."

Savannah realized she wasn't breathing. Nobody at the table seemed to be breathing. Even the children were silent.

"So, I prayed about it and here's what we're going to do around here from now on. Anybody who lives here is going to chip in money the first day of every month. Thanks to your grandpa's hard work, the property's been paid off for years, but there's taxes and utilities and upkeep and food to buy.

"And speaking of food. I'm going to cook a nice, big dinner every Sunday, but other than that... if you intend to eat supper here, you'd better be bringin' along a bucket of chicken or a pizza pie—enough to feed you and me, too. And before you leave, every dish had better be washed and put away, the garbage taken out and the floor swept.

"This coming Saturday, I want you all here at one o'clock sharp, 'cause we're going to have a little laundry lesson, right out there on the back porch. I'm going to show everybody, once and for all, how to sort lights from the darks and how to hang clothes on the line. And after that, I don't want to see another bag of dirty laundry dumped on my porch. The only underdrawers I'm ever gonna wash again are my own."

Savannah felt a surge of pride as she watched her grandmother, this quintessential steel magnolia, drawing her lines in the sand. No wonder she loved this woman, this lady who never stopped learning, growing, and showing them how by example.

"One more thing," Gran said. "When the time comes for Macon to go on trial for stealing that stuff, we'll all go on the stand and say how much we love him and how good he's been to us. But other than that, no one is to lift a finger to try to get him out of this mess he's gotten himself into. If I'd let him take his lumps long ago, it never would have come to this. He's gotta learn, even if it hurts." She sighed. "Learnin' always seems to hurt, no matter how old we get."

She looked around the table, loving each one with her eyes. "You mean the world to me, you kids. And that's why I'm going to stand by everything I said here today. Those are the new rules of the house. Abide by them."

There were silent nods all around the table and murmured assents.

The law had been laid down.

Granny Reid had spoken.

Savannah and Tom walked side by side down the dirt road that led from Gran's house to the highway. With each step their shoes stirred small clouds of dust. And every step gave rise to another swirl of memories.

In the beginning of the walk, Tom had reached for her hand. But after briefly squeezing his fingers, she had released him. Now they strolled along with no physical contact except the occasional bumping of their shoulders.

Briefly Savannah wondered whether she had refused to touch her old beau because she feared that Dirk might be watching from the house. But she decided that her reasons were much better than Dirk's jealousy. Her reasons were all her own, born of self-protection.

To their left and right, acres of cotton shimmered blinding white in the afternoon sun. Picking would soon begin, and Savannah wasn't at all sorry that she would be home in California and miss the event.

Heat waves rippled in the air above the road, distorting the view of the black-topped highway in the distance. And she decided she wouldn't miss the sweltering humidity either.

They hadn't spoken, and the only sounds were the occasional rumble of a vehicle on the main road, crickets chirping in the weeds, and the plop of startled frogs leaping into the rain-filled ditch on either side of the road as they passed.

Crawdads—poor man's lobster—wriggled through the thick red mud, and somewhere in the distance a cicada rattled furiously like a tiny maraca, serenading a prospective mate.

"Remember when we used to walk along this road?" Tom said. "Until I got my car it was the only way to get away from your brothers and sisters, who were always pointing their fingers and giggling at us."

Of course I do, she thought. *I was a kid head over heels in love. I lived for those walks . . . for those stolen moments with you.*

"Yeah, I guess so," she murmured.

"And remember how we'd duck into those bushes there at the end of the road and make out?"

Kisses . . . quick, slow, gentle, rough. I'd never been kissed like that before. Never since.

"We're not walking to the end this time," she told him. "We're only going halfway, then turning back."

"Okay."

They continued on for a few more yards, then Tom asked, "You leaving tomorrow?"

"Yes. I'm going home."

"Has *he* got anything to do with that?" Tom nodded back toward the house.

"With what? Me going home?"

"Yeah."

"I live in California now, Tom. Have for years. I don't belong here anymore."

"I thought that maybe you'd miss . . . being here. That you'd wanna stay."

"I'll miss some things about here."

He grinned, and the self-satisfied smirk grated against her nerves. Damn men and their egos, always thinking that everything was about them.

And, of course, it usually was.

"I'll miss Gran and Southern cooking," she added with what she hoped was just enough cool detachment in her voice. "I'll miss the moss hanging from the trees. That's about all."

His smile sagged, and she mentally patted herself on the back.

"You really *are* mad at me, huh?" he said, stopping abruptly in the middle of the road and facing her, his burly arms crossed over his chest. "After all these years, you're still pissed off at me for breaking up with you."

Pissed off? No, just being pissed doesn't make your heart ache.

"For breaking up with me?" she said. "If you'll remember, you didn't bother to break up with me, at least not officially, before you took Lisa Mooney up to Lookout Point, or Jeanette Parker out to *our* peach orchard, or—"

"Okay, okay." He held up both hands in surrender. "So, I wasn't a monk back then."

She felt the sting of tears beneath her eyelids and cursed herself for feeling . . . feeling anything, after so long. "Hell, Tommy," she said softly, "I never asked you to act like a monk. I would have settled for you acting like a gentleman."

When his own eyes grew moist and red around the rims, she was surprised that it didn't bring her any pleasure, perverse or otherwise. Mostly, she just felt sad for two young people who had grown older and wiser and would never be able to love so completely again. Only the innocent, the naïve, could love completely.

"I gotta know," he said. "I've worried about it for years. Did you leave Georgia because of me? I mean, was it all my fault?"

Ninety-five percent, she thought. *Maybe ninety-eight.*

"No, it was mostly other stuff."

He looked so relieved that she wanted to reach out and embrace him. But decided not to.

Again for reasons all her own.

"I'm glad," he said. "I'd hate to be responsible for that. A lot of people miss you around here."

She turned and started back toward the house. So much for strolls down memory lane. Some roads were best untraveled.

"You were special to me, Savannah," he said, catching her by the arm and turning her to face him. "You still are." He hesitated, gulped. "And I'm going to prove it to you. I'm going to tell you something that I never told you before."

Savannah tensed, not knowing what to expect. She had seen the same look on hardened criminals seconds before they confessed to first-degree homicide. "Okay. I'm listening. What is it?"

He choked as though his chest was tightening, squeezing out his breath. "I know I was your first . . . that is . . . when we made it there in my car in the peach orchard that night. You know . . . on your birthday."

Her own throat clenched. "Yes. And . . . ?"

"I never told you, but . . . well . . . you were my first, too. That night I was a vir . . . I mean, I hadn't . . . you know. Until you. That night."

Her mind flew back to that moonlit orchard, fragrant with the rich sweet smell of the ripened fruit, and her legs went weak.

"I'm telling you this now," he said, "because I want you to know that you're special to me. Really special. Always will be."

She remembered. The back seat of his '56 Chevy, slipping on the plastic seat covers, his shaking sweaty hands, his awkward fumbles that passed for caresses, the act that was over nearly as soon as it began.

"So, that was your first time, huh?" she said, giving him an affectionate smile, mixed with what she hoped was a convincing hint of surprise. "Gee . . . I never would've guessed."

She slipped her arm through his, not caring who might be watching from the house. For the first time in years, not caring about Jeanette Parker or Lisa Mooney.

"You're special to me, too, Tommy," she said. "You always will be."

"Really?" He looked so grateful; she was glad she had decided to be kind.

"Absolutely," she said. "Every time I smell ripe peaches, I think of you."

They walked along in silence until they were nearly back to the house. Then he cleared his throat. Staring down at the dusty road, he said, "There's not a lot of peaches in California."

She chuckled and nudged him in the ribs with her elbow. "Oh . . . more than you think, Deputy Stafford. Far more than you think."

"We're going to have to go in soon or the 'skeeters are gonna eat us alive," Gran said.

Savannah sat in the swing beside her on the front porch. They were watching the sun set in the cotton field across the road. Its crimson light stained the white puffs a pale pink, and behind the field the sky was turning steel blue.

"I think we're gonna get some rain," Savannah said, sniffing the moist, fresh smell in the air.

"Maybe some lightning and thunder."

"My cats will be up on the pillows with us tonight. They hate the thunder."

"That's okay. I like 'em."

Savannah put her arm across the back of the swing and pulled her grandmother closer to her. "I'm going to miss you when I go back tomorrow."

"You, too, Savannah girl."

"You've got to come see me soon."

"Only if you take me to Disneyland again."

"You've got it."

They swung a few minutes without speaking, watching the cotton change from pink to dark gold, listening to the crickets and the creak of the swing's chains.

"What am I going to do with all this free time I'm gonna have now?" Gran asked.

Savannah could hear the fear, the uncertainty, beneath her words.

"If I'm not y'all's grandma, who am I?"

"Oh, you'll always be our grandmother. But instead of mashing all those potatoes and folding all those towels, you'll be doing things that feed your soul."

Gran thought for a moment, then nodded, a smile spreading across her face. "I'll spend less time raising vegetables and tend my flower garden, maybe put in some more rosebushes."

"There ya go."

"And I'll embroider and crochet more and read my Bible more. Maybe I'll bake a bunch of cakes for the church auction."

"Yours have always brought the highest prices."

They swung a while longer, soaking in the silence and the sacred gift of each other's company.

"Is there anything you always wanted to do?" Savannah asked. "Something special that you didn't have time or money to do?"

Gran blushed like a little girl about to divulge a deep heart secret. "I always wanted to paint pictures, but I never could draw worth anything."

"How about taking some lessons?"

Her face lit up. "There's a lady over at the library, Rose Harkins, who teaches that sort of thing. Do you suppose I could do that?"

Savannah leaned over and placed a kiss on her grandmother's

cheek. "After what I saw you do today there in that kitchen, changing your whole life and your grandchildren's for their own good . . . I know you could do absolutely anything."

Granny Reid returned the kiss to her granddaughter's cheek. "Thank you, Savannah girl. I love you, darlin'."

"I love you, too, Gran."

They continued to swing until the cotton turned indigo blue.